THE DAME
WAS TROUBLE

COFFIN HOP PRESS

THE DAME
WAS TROUBLE

A COLLECTION OF THE BEST FEMALE
CANADIAN CRIME WRITERS

Edited by Sarah L. Johnson
Halli Lilburne and Cat McDonald

COFFIN HOP PRESS

Coffin Hop Press
200 Rivervalley Crescent SE
Calgary, Alberta CANADA T2C 3K8
www.coffinhop.com
mailto:info@coffinhop.com

A Proudly Canadian Publisher

Cover Design ©2018 Coffin Hop Press
Cover element: Clash_Gene - Shutterstock ID: 420761533
Book Layout ©2018 Coffin Hop Press

The Dame Was Trouble/Various —1st ed. Paperback
ISBN: 978-1-988987-10-1

For all the Dames of Crime Fiction,
past, present, and future,
Canadian and otherwise.

Thanks.

CONTENTS

Introduction

Dames. They've been around since the dawn of time. From the biblical templates of Lilith, Eve, Jezebel and Mother Mary, to the relatively modern character tropes of the *femme fatale* and the girl-next-door, literary conventions have long cast a wary eye on the female of the species. Let's not mince words here. The ladies have historically gotten a bum rap, nowhere more distinctly than on the page. Most female characters have fallen on one side or the other of that same ol' ancient Madonna/Whore dichotomy and been little more than window dressing for the tales of manly men. Female crime and mystery authors have barely fared better: for every few hundred Chandlers and Hammets and Mickey Spillanes there's one female crime writer of vintage reknown like Agatha Christie, and there are dozens upon dozens of lesser known, but equally talented authors like Dorothy B. Hughes and Canada's own Margaret Millar, that were equally worthy of praise, but have long been overshadowed by the men of their era. Which is not even mentioning the untold numbers who could have been, but never saw the opportunity to try because they happened to be women.

Even as recently as the 1990's, you'd be hard pressed to find a popular female author in the genre that wasn't Patricia Cornwell or Elizabeth George. If you did, they were hiding in plain sight, under pseudonyms and initials, like J.A. Jance.

Thankfully, times are changing. Writers-who-happen-to-be-women are now dominating the genre. For every James Patterson or Lee Childs, there are fifteen female authors holding their own on the sales charts and reshaping the viewpoints, motivations and personalities of their own female characters. We're no longer stuck with two flat options of *Good* vs *Easy,* or a shelf full of two-fisted heroes and the women who love 'em. I daresay we're the better for it.

Storytelling is how a society explains who it is, and what it believes in. It only speaks truth when all of the people have a voice. It's how we find empathy and respect for each other, and how we share our experiences. The dames who are included in this book, are some of the best that Canada has to offer today, and we're damned proud to put their voices out there.

Axel Howerton
Coffin Hop Press

"When you're counting alibis and not apples,
one plus one equals none."

— Margaret Millar, "The Weak-Eyed Bat" (1942)

Indispensable
Kelley Armstrong

Working for Dougall Lake, private eye, meant following three basic rules, as Ivy had discovered on her first day. One, the water tumbler on his desk should be permanently half-full and contain a single ice cube. Two, the main office door was to be kept locked unless they were expecting a client, and then only opened exactly ten minutes before the appointment time. Three, the "water" in Lake's tumbler should be eighty proof.

Vodka was Lake's drink of choice, and he prided himself on that. Scotch was for common gumshoes. He took his vodka straight, too, not watered down in one of those

Moscow Mules they served at every gin joint in Chicago. One week after being hired, Ivy presented him with a bottle of the good stuff bought at a fraction of the price. She got it from an old friend who worked at the docks and knew how to filch a crate as he carried them to the warehouse. When she told Lake the price—and promised she could get one bottle a week—he declared her "indispensable" for the first time. It only took a few more days of working at the agency for Ivy to discover rule number one for *continued* employment with Lake: *be* indispensable. Two years later, she was still there, which meant she must be doing something right.

She checked her watch. Eleven minutes to ten. Lake had his first appointment of the day at ten, which meant he'd roll in around five past. By ten to the hour, she was at the door, undoing the deadbolt. In a neighborhood like this, leaving that open all day would not be wise.

Lake could afford a better neighborhood, and he could certainly attract a higher level of clientele if they didn't need to park their cars under broken streetlights and climb over drunks in the stairwell. As Lake explained, though, in this business, "higher level" didn't mean "higher paying." His best clients were comfortable here. They lived in the neighborhood or at least did their business here, and that was fine by Ivy, born and raised here herself.

After undoing the bolt, she returned to her desk. When the knob turned, her right hand slid under her desk to her handgun. With her left hand, she left kept riffling papers, her gaze on them, as if unconcerned about who might walk through that door. It opened, and she counted to three before glancing up with a beaming smile, her fingers grazing the stock of her gun. When she saw who it was, she reluctantly released the gun and rose, smile firmly fixed in place.

"Mr. Hudson," she said. She didn't express any surprise at the fact that this was not Joe Smith, the name in the appointment book. She did wish, however, that Lake had warned her who "Mr. Smith" was.

Teddy Hudson. The man who owned the barges that her friend pilfered vodka from. The man who owned that entire corner of the wharf. Owned the ships and the docks and the girls who teased the sailors and the boys who sold them cheap hooch and dope and favors, too, if that was more their style.

Closing in on fifty, Hudson had the gray pallor of a man who'd already passed it. In his youth, he'd been an enforcer. Six foot three and wide as an icebox, they said, with the muscles of a sideshow strongman. Now, it looked as if those muscles had been pricked and deflated, leaving a man with a gaunt frame, drooping eyes and bulldog jowls. Even his smile sagged.

Hudson didn't recognize Ivy, of course. It'd been years since she'd been a wharf rat, running errands for Hudson's girls, trading insults with his boys, picking the pockets of the sailors when they'd had too much of whatever Hudson's employees sold. Another time. Another girl. Mostly.

"Please come in, sir," she said. "Mr. Lake is out on an emergency case." *Kittens, trapped in a tree.* That's what she always thought of saying. She didn't, of course, but it made her smile to think it, and clients liked it when she smiled. Hudson perked up, giving her a fresh once-over.

"I have to spend a little more time with you?" he said. "There's a hardship."

As she passed—out of reach, she thought—he moved with rattlesnake speed to cup one hand against her buttocks.

"Mr. Hudson!" she said, tittering. She waggled a finger at him. "None of that, sir. Now, can I fix you a coffee? Tea? It's a little early for whiskey but…" She winked. "I won't tell if you won't."

"There's a good girl," he said. "Whiskey in a teacup will do just fine. I'll take that and your name."

"Ivy," she said.

He sidled closer as she poured the whiskey. "Are you poison, Ivy?"

She laughed, throatier than she intended. "Not at all, sir. Just young. Barely more than a seedling."

"*How* young?"

"Nineteen," said Lake's voice from the doorway. "Too young for you, old man."

Ivy passed over the "tea" as Hudson said, "Still legal."

"I'm the one you're hiring, Teddy. Not my girl."

The two clasped hands in the way of men who pretend to be friends. As they talked, Ivy poured coffee for her boss and gave it to him with a smile of thanks for his intervention. She was not nineteen; she'd turn twenty-one next month. Still, she appreciated the fiction, even if she suspected Lake had simply forgotten her age.

Lake was a decade younger than Hudson. Trim and fit, with a full head of dark hair staunchly resisting gray...with the help of shoe polish, she suspected. A handsome man who knew he was handsome and intended to cling to that for as long as he could.

Lake ushered Hudson into his office, and Ivy followed with her steno pad.

"You don't mind if Ivy here takes notes, do you? Lake asked.

"Mind a pretty girl in the room? May I never be so old. I don't see another chair, though. Guess she'll just have to sit on my knee."

"That'll cost extra," Lake said.

Hudson met Lake's gaze, his lips parting in a shark's smile. "Add it to my bill."

Lake only laughed and motioned for Ivy to take her seat on the edge of his desk. She perched there while Lake leaned back in his chair, his hands steepled, eyes closed as if deep in thought. Napping, actually, while Ivy took notes and asked questions, her legs crossed enough to show off a bit of skin...and keep Hudson from realizing that Lake had drifted off.

Lake's local clientele might pay very well, but the cases were as dull as ones they'd get uptown. Hudson's was no exception. In summary: "I think my significantly younger wife—who married me for my money—is catting around." The only part that would be shocking is if she *wasn't*.

Five years ago, Hudson had married a twenty-year-old girl who danced in one of his bars. Only danced, he insisted—he'd never marry a girl who sold herself. Prettiest dancer in town, he bragged, and Ivy vaguely recognized the name: Missy.

The way Hudson saw it, he'd rescued Missy, putting a ring on her finger before her looks faded. He'd whisked her out of that seedy life and locked her up in a gilded cage. Now, he thought she was cheating on him. He gave names. A former boyfriend who worked in an illegal casino. A down-on-his-luck soldier who came around for odd jobs. Or possibly Hudson's own right-hand man, a handsome thirty-year-old who took far too much interest in his boss's young bride. One of them was trespassing on Hudson's private property, and he needed proof.

When Ivy had all the details, she said, "Is there anything more you'd like to ask, Mr. Lake?" and that was his cue to rise from his drowsing.

"Sounds like you got it all, Ivy. You're a good girl." He patted her leg. "Indispensable. Now, go fix us another coffee, and the menfolk will discuss the crude subject of money."

She left, feeling Hudson's gaze glued to her hips. Not just his, of course, but her boss was more discreet about it.

As she closed the door behind her, Hudson whistled, as if the thin wooden barrier would stifle his loud appreciation. Ivy headed for the coffee pot, listening as they talked, their voices as clear as if she were still in the room with them.

"Now that is a secretary," Hudson said.

"She is, indeed."

"You better tell me you're getting some of that."

Lake only chuckled. "Girl makes me feel old. She tells me I remind her of her daddy."

"Nothing wrong with that. Most girls are looking for, whaddya call it? A father figure. Someone to look after them, just like Daddy did. I'd say it's a compliment."

"She seems to think it is."

"Then it is. Wish I had a little piece like that in my office. My gal's pushing forty. Built like a steamship. Keeps *my* office shipshape, though, so I let her stick around. Young girls are pretty to look at, but they spend more time filing their nails than filing my papers. Yours seems competent, though."

"I've trained her well."

Ivy added exactly the right amount of sugar to Lake's coffee, then took it to him along with his water tumbler, filled with vodka, of course. She delivered the drinks and then retreated to her desk to make herself indispensable.

When Hudson left, Ivy took over his chair in Lake's office and summarized the notes for her boss.

"I'll type them up and put them into the file," she said.

Lake said nothing, just leaned back in his seat, his feet crossed on his desk as he sipped from his tumbler.

"Seems like an easy case," he said. "Waste of my time, really."

"Not a waste of your money," she said, pointing at the retainer Hudson had left.

He snorted a laugh. "Clever girl."

"You trained me well."

"Just like your daddy?"

She smiled. "Exactly like my daddy."

Lake deflated a little. Then he set the tumbler down and got to his feet. "I need to go down to the wharf, see a man about some new business."

That business being putting money on horses, which was certainly not new.

"How about you get this case started for me, Ivy," he said. "Stretch your legs and see what you can find. Get the Brownie and grab a few bucks from the kitty for cab fare." He pursed his lips. "Nah, take a fin and buy yourself a nice lunch uptown."

He waited for her to thank him, which she did, dutifully and with a smile. Then he took his hat and coat from the rack and left.

Three days later, Ivy was riding the elevator up to Hudson's office. It wasn't on the Loop. He could afford that, but such an address might make the IRS take a closer look at his tax returns, and everyone in this town knew better than that.

That's how they got Al, people whispered. The mighty Al Capone, brought down for tax evasion, left to rot from the clap in Alcatraz.

Hudson's office was a perfectly respectable place up-town, justified by his legitimate business interests, which were helpfully listed on the door. Ivy paused beside the sign to straighten her dress. As she did, she caught sight of two girls about her age heading toward the elevator. Seeing her, they slowed and assessed, sparrow quick, their eyes darting over her. That was all they needed before they tittered and whispered and resumed walking.

Ivy's hands slid over her dress again. No amount of ironing or washing would bring it up to their standards. Indeed, an overabundance of both was part of the problem. Thrift store goods, a couple of years out of fashion, the hem too low, the fit not quite right.

Ivy watched the girls sashay down the hall. Then she squared her shoulders before pausing to relax them and add a touch of little-girl-lost to her eyes as she pushed open the door to Hudson's office. She looked around the reception area as if she couldn't see the secretary's desk right there. Then she hurried over to it.

"Is Mr. Hudson in?" she asked, her voice rising to a near squeak.

The older secretary took Ivy's measure. Declared her pretty enough to catch the boss's eye but not bold enough to claim it. Her gaze then dropped to Ivy's midriff, and Ivy almost laughed at that. Apparently, she looked like the sort of girl Hudson might dally with on a slow day, returning with a swollen belly and tear-filled eyes.

"Would you tell him it's Ivy, here to discuss Joe Smith—" Ivy began, and Hudson poked his head around the corner, nose lifted as if following the waft of Ivy's perfume. Which would make more sense if she were wearing any. Scent cost money. Good scent, that is, and Ivy wouldn't wear anything cheap. She had no choice with her clothes. Perfume and jewels would wait until she could afford those that would not make uptown office-pool girls snicker.

"Ivy," Hudson said. "Come on back, girl. Your boss said you'd swing by with an update."

She followed him into his office and, with reluctance, let him close the door. Given the sensitive nature of their conversation, there wasn't much chance she could wedge herself into the gap and keep it ajar. She did, however, possess some talent for ducking and weaving, having cajoled boxing lessons from her dockside childhood friends. Of all the skills she'd learned, this proved the most useful for a young woman her age, and it kept her just out of Hudson's reach as she gave him the update.

When she finished, he stopped sidling closer and frowned. "And he's sure of that?"

"No, sir, Mr. Lake cannot guarantee that your wife isn't stepping out on you. Right now, he can only say that his surveillance efforts have failed to turn up anything untoward. What he needs from you is more information. He's looking for times when Mrs. Hudson isn't home. Regular, scheduled activities that take her away from the house. Perhaps a weekly book club?"

Hudson laughed so hard a clerk poked his head in, eyes round with alarm before a snap from his boss sent him scurrying.

"Believe me, honey, my wife ain't going to no *book* club."

"She might *say* she is, while secretly meeting her lover. Perhaps not a book club but an activity you're less likely to question. A standing appointment at a beauty parlor? A weekly manicure? Any time when she is out of the house for an hour or more with a seemingly valid excuse."

"I don't keep my wife's schedule."

"Perhaps I could speak to someone on your household staff."

He thought for a minute and then nodded. "We have a housekeeper who doesn't much like Missy. She'll know when the lady of the house goes out." He wrote his address on a scrap of paper. "I'll ring and tell her you're coming."

"Thank you." Ivy reached for the paper and then paused. "Oh, I'm so sorry, sir. I completely forgot. Mr. Lake told me I needed to mention that your original contract only covered basic surveillance. If you'd like him to dig deeper . . ."

Hudson gave a humorless laugh. "It'll cost me. All right. Wait right here, and I'll go freshen up that retainer."

Ivy finished the job. Lake's sole contribution was placing that call to Hudson, letting him know she'd come by his office with an update, so it wouldn't seem odd when the secretary stopped by instead of the investigator. Lake was a busy man, and what was the point of having an office girl if you couldn't send her out on errands?

When Ivy completed her work, she developed the photographs and typed up the notes, each page listing dates and times and hours spent on surveillance, to justify the billing. Of course, those hours were inflated. Ivy knew what her boss expected, and she delivered, as always.

Two weeks after Hudson hired her boss, she handed Lake the file folder and relayed a summary as he thumbed through it. Then he set it aside and told her to call Hudson in for a meeting.

"I already have," she said. "Ten AM, tomorrow."

He beamed and leaned back in his chair. "You know what you are, Ivy?"

"Indispensable?"

He lifted his glass in a toast. "You got it, doll. Now, go take a couple bucks out of the kitty and buy yourself a new scarf."

"I was thinking of a hat. Maybe a nice fedora, so I look like a proper private eye."

He choked on a laugh and shook his head as he lifted his glass again, this time showing her that it was below the halfway mark, that single cube of ice nearly melted. She took the bottle from its hiding place, refilled it to exactly the right spot and then brought over one cube in the tongs and dropped it in.

"You'll make some man very happy one day, Ivy," he said, a little wistfully.

She leaned to kiss his temple. "That's what my daddy always says."

The next morning, Ivy perched on Lake's desk corner, in exactly the same pose she had two weeks ago. Same dress, too. Not surprising, since she only owned three. This one had a spot just above the knee. A smear of...well, she didn't want to know what, considering she got it squeezing in behind an alley dumpster to take surveillance photos of Missy Hudson. She mentally calculated the cost of a new dress as her boss gave Hudson "their" findings.

"I've seen absolutely no evidence that your wife has been unfaithful," Lake said.

Hudson's facial sags rearranged themselves, wrinkles bunching. "You sure?'

"Your housekeeper gave Ivy a complete rundown of Mrs. Hudson's activities. Beauty parlor, two PM, Tuesdays. Bridge, ten AM, Wednesdays. Visiting a friend every Thursday for lunch...The list goes on. Your housekeeper was very, very thorough. I followed Mrs. Hudson for a week, waiting outside the house each time she had an engagement. What I found..."

Lake slid a photo on his desk. "Your wife at the beauty parlor Tuesday." Another one. "Your wife at her bridge game Wednesday." He continued with photograph after photograph, showing Missy Hudson exactly where she was supposed to be.

Lake handed the stack of photos to Hudson. "For one week, your wife didn't leave the house unless she had an engagement, and I verified all of those. That's in addition to the general surveillance I performed the week before."

Lake leaned against the desk, his shoulder brushing Ivy's. "Now, if you think you might have tipped her off about our surveillance…"

"Nah, I never said nothing."

"I can assure you that Ivy here was very circumspect speaking to your housekeeper. It's still possible *she* suspected what was afoot and warned your wife…"

Hudson snorted. "The old bat hates Missy. She's always trying to get her in trouble."

"All right. Well, if you have any doubts about my work, we are more than happy to continue for another week."

"Yeah, and charge me for it."

Lake stiffened. "I believe my work speaks for itself—"

"Get your back down, Lake." Hudson shook the handful of photos. "I got no questions about your work. It's what I wanted and more. You ever need a reference, you've got it. Hell, I have a few other jobs I might put you on."

The older man rose, photos still in hand. "I'm just taking it all in. I was so sure Missy was stepping out on me.

You've seen her. What's a piece like that doing with an old guy like me?"

"I'm sure she's very fond—" Lake began.

"Fond of my billfold," Hudson said. "I ain't fooling myself on that. But..." He shrugged. "Maybe I was a little paranoid. Didn't have any reason to suspect her. It's just what I expected, being an old man with a young wife."

"You're not that old, Mr. Hudson," Ivy said.

He perked up at that and looked over to see whether she was flirting. From his expression, he could tell she was only being kind, but he took that and tipped his head in thanks.

"Ivy?" Lake said. "Go draw up Mr. Hudson's final bill. We're going to have a drink to celebrate the good news."

Ivy cast a pointed look at the clock, not yet ten thirty.

"We'll have coffee," he said and then winked. "Just make it extra strong."

Ivy waited in the café, smoothing the crisp linen of her new dress. New to her, at least. Still, it was consignment shop rather than thrift, and it looked as if the original owner hadn't worn it more than a few times. No spots. No fraying. It was even a fashionable style, she realized as she surveyed the young women coming and going.

Ivy sipped her tea and eyed the chalkboard menu. She would splurge on cake when her guest arrived. It was the sort of shop that demanded cake eating—doll-house pretty

27

with cloth napkins and bone china. A café catering to women and filled with them, the tinkle of feminine laughter underscored by the clink of silver against china.

When her guest entered, a few patrons looked over. Quick surveys, followed by approving nods as they took in her dress, her hat, her shoes. No flashes of recognition at the young woman's face, though. They weren't in a neighborhood where Missy Hudson would be recognized.

Missy spotted Ivy and flashed a smile showing perfect white teeth between lips painted with the kind of precision Ivy envied. Missy applied makeup with an expert and light hand, subtle paint to an already flawless face.

Missy glided over and lowered herself into the chair, and before Ivy could say a word, she leaned forward and whispered, "Thank you." Ivy started to respond, but Missy lifted a hand to stop her and passed over what looked like a silk makeup case. "Thank you," she said again, with emphasis this time.

Ivy opened the case to see a wad of bills.

Missy smiled. "Better than mere thanks?"

"I appreciate both."

Missy laughed. "So tactful. You should give lessons in that. I know I could use them."

Ivy lifted the case. "Did you have any trouble getting…?"

"Not at all. As I said, I had it. And I've been repaid in full already."

She flashed a diamond bracelet that Ivy hadn't seen the last time they met. A gift from a relieved husband. Ivy had to laugh at that.

Ivy liked Missy. That was not, naturally, required in this situation. There'd be very little profit in a business where you only worked with people you liked. Ivy's childhood had taught her that. People like Missy needed to be measured in profitability alone. Missy had proved quite profitable, and the fact she was also likable was only a bonus.

Had Missy been the stereotype of a gold digger—avaricious, narcissistic—that would have been fine with Ivy. Teddy Hudson knew what he was getting when he married her. A pretty bauble for his arm, nothing more. He'd be expected to pay for that, and if she stepped out on him, well, that was to be expected, too. He wasn't keeping his vows, so why should Missy?

Yes, Missy had a lover. It'd taken barely a day of surveillance for Ivy to ascertain that, though she'd followed the young wife for two days more before approaching her. Two days to fully understand the situation. Then Ivy had made her move.

Missy's lover was none of the three men Hudson had suspected. In fact, he could probably have caught Missy naked with her lover and still bought whatever explanations she sold him. Peter Carr was a schoolteacher. Widowed. No children. Thirty-five years old and nothing much to look at. He tutored on the side, and that's how Missy had met him, wanting lessons in diction and elocution to scrub the streets from her voice.

Carr didn't win Missy by telling her she was pretty. She'd heard that all her life, and she knew it to be true. No, he won her by telling her she was smart. Sometimes, that was all it took when you'd been raised to believe otherwise. He told her she was smart, and he meant it, and he proved it, too, giving her more varied and more difficult lessons, improving her education.

The two of them traded classical books the way other lovers traded risqué poems, and watching them, Ivy had been so charmed she'd nearly offered to protect their affair for free. *Nearly*. The impulse had passed quickly, driven back by common sense. Missy *was* clever, and she had money, and therefore she did not need pity or charity.

They'd devised the plan, and Ivy had taken all the appropriate photographs in the appropriate settings. For that week, Missy had been chaste as a nun. Now, freed from her husband's suspicions, she happily paid Ivy's fee, and they ate cake and chatted like school chums.

This did not, however, mean that Missy was truly free. Ivy knew from their conversations that Missy wanted that. She had, as Hudson himself suspected, seen him as a life raft, carrying her from the squalor of the streets before age and fading beauty sent her into dark alleys with her skirt hiked up to her hips.

Missy had gambled, and as with all such gambles, it only partly paid off. Freed from the streets, yes, but tied to a man who treated her like a servant, cuffed her when she displeased him, flaunted his own lovers, and did not require her consent for marital relations. Missy told Ivy she'd leave him in an instant if she dared. Her husband terrified her, and she knew he'd never let her go. Of course, she said no such thing to Carr—it would imply she wanted her lover to rescue her…by ridding her of the problem. She cared for Carr too much to ask that.

As Missy and Ivy nibbled their cake and sipped their tea and discussed the delights of Dante, Ivy said, casually, "What if you could buy your way free of him?"

Missy stopped, fork halfway to her mouth. She set it down carefully. "If you mean hiring a widow-maker…" She shook her head. "I won't do it that way. He's a brute, not a monster."

"No, I didn't mean that," Ivy said with a quiet laugh. "I wouldn't know where to find such a person." A lie. She could list a half-dozen names, one of whom she'd grown up with, still had a drink with, on occasion.

Ivy sliced icing from her cake and licked it off her fork as Missy waited. Then she said, "There isn't a clean way to do it, though. You'd need to get your hands dirty."

"Dirty, yes. Bloody, no."

"No blood on anyone's hands if it's done right." Ivy took a portfolio from her bag. It was white, covered in tea roses, the sort of thing that might contain a young woman's amateur sketches or mawkish poetry. She took out a sheet and passed it to Missy. As the young woman read it, her eyes rounded.

"There's more," Ivy said. "Enough blackmail material to win your freedom and a decent settlement. The trick will be knowing how much to ask for. Enough to be comfortable, but not so much that he'll balk."

Missy kept reading the page. "Where did you get this?"

"He made the mistake of leaving me alone in his office." Ivy finished the icing. "And giving me an excuse to be in your house."

"But he keeps his papers locked up."

"I have a way with locks," Ivy murmured.

Missy grinned. "I bet you do. I could hug you, you know. Throw myself across the table and hug you." At Ivy's reaction, Missy let out a laugh loud enough to startle neighboring diners. "Now there, I've found something that *does* frighten you. Don't worry. No hugs. Just cashier's checks. I presume there's a price on that folder."

"There is."

Missy settled in, still smiling. "Then let us do business."

Ivy arrived home that evening, at seven as always. She was supposed to finish at five, but Lake always had "just a few more things" for her to do. Things he could have easily done himself, but that would require *him* staying late.

When she opened the apartment door, a querulous voice called, "Ivy? Is that you?"

"Yes, Daddy."

"Have you seen my glasses? I can't read the newspaper without my glasses."

"That's why I leave them right beside the paper," Ivy said with a trill, good-natured because there wasn't any other way to be with her father. She walked in and picked up both paper and glasses, and then she delivered them to him.

Her father sat in his armchair. Gray-haired and thin, he had a blanket pulled up over his legs like an invalid, fire blazing to "warm his old bones" as he said. His bones were exactly forty-six years old, not ancient by any means. They'd be strong enough, too, if he'd use them.

Her father used to be a dockworker. Hale and hearty. Then, when Ivy was three, the owner's son had fumbled a crate. It dropped twenty feet and hit her father square in the back as he'd been bent over. The owner paid him handsomely, and her father lunged at the excuse to retire, due to his disability. The fact he'd recovered a few months later hardly mattered.

The payoff money hadn't lasted, and soon her mother had been working two jobs to keep them in their dark, tiny apartment. She'd died five years ago. Escaped, really. Ivy had been at her bedside, and in the final moments, she'd seen the relief in her mother's eyes, spotting release from endless demands and backbreaking work. Her last words to Ivy had been "I'm sorry." It'd been a half-hearted apology at best, but Ivy didn't hold it against her. Hers had been a heavy life, and Ivy's young shoulders were better able to bear the burden.

Ivy stoked the fire for her father without waiting for him to ask. Sweat dripped down her brow, but she didn't complain about the heat, just shed her cardigan. Then she topped up her father's drink as he raised his tumbler.

"That boss treating you right, Ivy girl?" Daddy said. "He's not chasing you around the desk, is he?"

She laughed. "No, Daddy. Not at all. Like I've said, he reminds me of you."

Which was true. Five years of taking care of her father had prepared her for Dougall Lake. The more work Lake shirked, the more experience she got, and the more her bank account grew. Plenty of opportunities in the world for a girl who knew how to use them. She figured her father had another five years before his liver gave out. Dougall Lake had about the same—if the drink didn't kill him, the gambling would ruin him, and whichever way it went, she'd be there, ready to take over the business.

She adjusted the table light so her father could see his newspaper. As she did, he clasped her hand.

"I don't know what I'd do without you, Ivy girl," he said. "You're one of a kind."

"I believe the word you want, Daddy"—she smiled and kissed his forehead— "is indispensable."

Playing Dead
Elle Wild

Sachiko Satō strains against her sun-red *yukata* to move faster, the heavy cotton fabric swishing hotly against her ankles. The year is 1941, and the warm breeze carries the scent of cherry blossoms. Sachiko is fifteen and her heart thrums like a *chū-daiko* drum, her wooden *geta* keeping the shuffling, urgent beat. She glimpses the soldier again as she rounds the corner, the flash of his aviator jacket as he weaves through the crowd. Sachiko steps forward to follow, and in a sudden blur of motion is struck.

The boy on the bicycle had been balancing a long bamboo pole across his narrow shoulders, freshly boiled pots of noodles hung precariously at each end, until boy and girl and noodles come crashing down in a singular disaster.

The Dame Was Trouble

Sachiko lies on her back, twisted in folds of rich cloth. She thinks of the soldier she has just lost, pictures his face turned upwards, toward the clouds. The young man with the sky in his eyes. Pain flows from Sachiko's shoulder and right leg, spiraling larger like ink in water. Somewhere an *inu* barks, the sound echoing in her head like a temple gong. Blood or broth is running down her forehead. Broth, she realizes with relief, as a stray *akita inu* licks the sticky soup from her face. The creature is more monkey than dog, but the expression on the *inu*'s small, pointed face makes it difficult to be cross with him and she is suddenly thankful for his presence. She knows already that she will keep him.

People gather around, but their words are muffled. Several are shaking their fists, chanting something. A tsunami of light crashes through her thoughts. Sachiko blinks against sunlight streaming in through a window as she awakens. She attempts to lift her head, but the full weight of her ninety-some-odd years settles back into her bones. Even the slightest motion causes tiny ripples of pain, like wind on water. Instead she lies still for the moment, allowing herself more time.

The sun illuminates the grime coating her window. "*Soji*", she thinks; cleaning time. But it's difficult to keep any window clean in this city, let alone a window so high up. Although the window is open, the sweltering air barely stirs. There is the sound of a protest below. So many people are angry nowadays, though she can't quite remember why.

She recognizes this room. Sachiko searches her memory for a clue to where she is, but finds only a sound: a familiar, high-pitched bark. She turns her face toward the noise, drowning for a moment as the tide of pain rushes in. She closes her eyes and remembers a childhood pet, the *inu* she adopted after her accident. Good, she thinks, I'm going backwards again. Backwards is so much easier than forwards. But when the *inu* yaps a second time, the sound is clear and present, not softly edged the way her memories are. There is something else not quite right about this sound.

Sachiko opens her eyes. A toy-sized robotic dog is rolling toward her across the *tatami* floor. Inubot. She smiles. He is rust-coloured, like a proper *akita inu*, but his ears flop forward and his fur is extra woolly, more like a pup. His bright eyes blink. The only indication of his true nature is a small blue light on his dog collar – a facial recognition camera that Sachiko barely notices.

Inubot wags his tail. "His" tail. She remembers that he is male and that she loves him. That is all. Inubot wheels in a circle, chasing his tail, apparently. When she calls to him, the robot dog spurts over and licks her face enthusiastically. Sachiko gives a wheezy old cough of a laugh.

Inubot carries a pill dispenser around his neck. He makes an exuberant sound as a light flashes on the device. Sachiko pushes the blinking button.

"*Ohaiyogozaimasu!*" says a *genki* female voice. "Two blue, one pink, with a full glass of water, before breakfast. Once you have received your medicine, please return the dispenser to its original position around your inubot's throat. Then give him the "fetch" command."

Sachiko follows the instructions. Secretly, she is happy that Inubot cannot talk. This way, he never asks anything of her, he seeks only to be of quiet, cheerful assistance. Sachiko closes her eyes and listens to the pleasant whirring sound of the robot in her kitchen, punctuated occasionally by the shouts of the crowd below her window as she falls asleep.

She is awakened by an aggressive ringing sound: Inubot is holding a phone in his mouth, very close to her head. He offers an apologetic little "yip". When Sachiko answers she is still caught between her dreaming and waking world and feels irritated by the interruption. She doesn't recognize the voice on the other end, but someone is coming to tea. Possibly it's a birthday party, or some kind of celebration. She can't quite remember. *Hai.* Must be a birthday party. But whose? She sits up stiffly as Inubot wheels in *asagohan* – morning rice. Well, she can't very well greet her visitors like this. She pulls on a bathrobe and instructs Inubot to fetch her hat.

Sachiko is whisking matcha tea when the door buzzer sounds. Inubot pretends to sniff the red bean cakes on the kotatsu table. Sachiko chuckles, warming up her vocal chords.

Sachiko sits on a faded silk cushion across the table from two strangers, who are sipping tea. Not as easy as it once was to maintain a formal kneeling posture, but Sachiko isn't quite sure how well she knows the strangers, and she'd hate to appear disrespectful by sitting informally if they're not on intimate terms. She eyes them up. The taller woman has a bony face with cheekbones so sharp that she has an alien look about her. The smaller one has a milky complexion, tea-coloured teeth, and a dreamy de-meanour. This one catches Sachiko looking and clears her throat. Sachiko smiles at her and nods in encouragement.

"*Satō-san*...."

Aha, thinks Sachiko. The woman has used her surname, so they must be on formal terms. It's a good thing Sachiko has remained kneeling. "*Hai*," Sachiko responds agreeably, wondering who the stranger might be.

"Do you remember what day it is?"

Sachiko thinks. Really, she has no idea. How could this stranger possibly expect her to remember something so... precise? "*Hai hai*," Sachiko answers. Yes yes.

The woman seems to be appraising her. Inubot inter-rupts with a snuffling noise and lies down, pretending to sleep. Sachiko wishes she could do the same, but instead she picks up a bean cake and takes a delicate bite, taking her time to chew it carefully. The creamy sweetness of the *anko* fills her mouth. The smaller stranger still wears a quizzical expression, as though waiting for an answer.

Sachiko swallows. "I made *anko* to celebrate the occa-sion," she says. Ha! Sachiko thinks. A clever response.

"Yes, very tasty. Thank you very much for your hard work," says the taller woman. The milky-faced woman says nothing. Sachiko thinks she has successfully dodged the question, but then the strangers exchange a look.

"Would you like to see Inubot do a trick?" Sachiko asks. Mostly because she doesn't like the way the conversation is headed. She has no idea whose birthday it is. Honestly, it surprises her that these strangers would expect her to remember their birthday. Obviously, they are not even well acquainted. Perhaps Sachiko should just guess. She has a fifty-fifty chance of guessing correctly. Sachiko wonders if there will be repercussions for guessing incorrectly. But then, at her age, what could really be so terrible?

"What occasion are we celebrating, *Satō-san*?" the angular woman prompts her. Clearly, this woman is suspicious. Not very polite of her, but that's the younger generation for you. No respect. The thing to do, Sachiko decides, is to answer with confidence.

"Your birthday," says Sachiko, firmly.

"Eh?" says the small woman. Her mouth drops open. "*Tanjobi*?"

"My birthday?" echoes the sharp woman.

Sachiko knows that there is something wrong with her answer. Well. Can't be helped. What's needed now is a pleasant distraction. She calls Inubot over to her and motions to him. "Play dead," Sachiko commands. Inubot "runs" in circles, then makes a low whimpering sound and falls over in a disconcerting mechanical clatter. The ladies

40

are silent. "Good boy!" Sachiko calls out a little too loudly. She claps her hands in delight, and the ladies reluctantly murmur, "*Sugoi*" in false tones.

Then Skinny Face asks, "Please pardon the question, *Satō-san*, but how is your hearing these days?" The two women exchange a sidelong glance.

Impossible to please these strangers. Who do they think they are, anyway? Sachiko's cramped legs are throbbing and she feels a sudden flash of impatience. She leans heavily on the *kotatsu* table to lift herself to a standing position but falters. The larger woman swiftly catches her elbow and helps her to her feet. Humiliating, Sachiko thinks, but apologizes for inconveniencing the woman. "More tea?" Sachiko asks, hoping they will leave.

Sachiko's hands shake noticeably as she pours, her veins the knobby texture of ginger root. The women lower their gaze and nod politely. "*Arigatou gozaimasu*."

"*Satō-san*," says the larger woman. The room feels oppressively warm. Sachiko wonders if there is a fan somewhere she can turn on. "*Satō-san*," the woman repeats, gently this time. Now Sachiko senses a stormy electricity about the room, the feeling that some bad news is about to be announced. Who are these people?

But Sachiko answers politely, "*Hai hai!*" Thinking, Get on with it.

"There's a matter we must discuss with you, as I mentioned on the phone," the skinny woman persists, the tension apparent in the muscles of her long neck. But the rest of what she says is lost in the din of the protest outside.

"*Gomenasai*," Sachiko says, "but I didn't catch that. Perhaps you could tell me what all the noise is about?" She smiles a little.

"You don't know?" The smaller stranger, the one with the milk-pudding face, asks in surprise. A stupid question, really. Sachiko decides not to honour the question with a response.

The larger stranger shoots Pudding Face a look. The smaller one bows her head. "The protest is about the ibos, like your inubot." Inubot cocks his head at the mention of his name. "Your apartment is across from A.T.R.I.I."

"Eh?" says Sachiko. "A-T-R...?"

"Hai. It stands for Advanced Telecommunications Research Institute International. The institute that did the research for the ibos, funded by KyōTec, and now also does the production."

"I see," says Sachiko, though she does not. Sachiko feels duped. She was sure there was supposed to be a birthday party. She wonders if anyone would notice if she ate another cake.

"*Satō-san*," the woman continues, "recently there have been some... unfortunate incidents... involving the ibos who look after elderly patients. Sometimes, for example, a patient's hearing might erode, and they might not hear the ibo's instructions clearly. That's why we're here."

Sachiko straightens up a little. Had Inubot made a mistake? Was he in trouble? Something inside her tightened like a fist. "My hearing is fine." A sharp edge to her tone.

"Some people are protesting the care of our elders by robots, you understand. Other people, some families, are upset that the ibos are being retired."

Sachiko is alarmed now. She listens to the surge of voices below. "Inubot…" she says. Inubot responds with a gleeful yip.

"*Hai*. You've had your inubot for one year today."

For a fleeting moment, Sachiko feels relief. "It's his first birthday," she says. She knew all along there was a birthday. She did get it right after all.

"It's time for his review," the stranger says, her expression softening. For some reason, Sachiko feels the most frightened by this sign of sympathy. She scans the woman's face, then Sachiko's gaze falls on the smart navy scarf tied around the stranger's throat, which bears a little pin with a corporate logo. KyōTec.

"No."

"The company cannot afford a lawsuit, *Satō-san*. Your family is concerned for your well-being, you see."

"Inubot," Sachiko calls, and the dog comes to her immediately with a whispered hum. She wraps her arms protectively around his warm, plush body, listens to Inubot's hushed panting, and tries to imagine what he must be feeling. She struggles to remember a single day before Inubot but finds only her childhood and the stray dog with the fox face who comforted her after an accident. He'd stayed with her after the war. When all the others were gone.

As the sunlight falls on his face, Inubot closes his eyes against the brightness, making the reassuring noises that he has been programmed to make during human contact.

It comes to Sachiko then. A kind of half memory. Someone in her family perhaps? A young man (her grandson?) concerned about her safety. He'd insisted on making adjustments to Inubot. Sachiko had been upset, but the young man had soothed her, saying that it wouldn't hurt Inubot. "Just a security upgrade," he'd said. Not that she would ever need it, he'd hastened to add.

Now Sachiko is glad that it's been done. She knows just what to do. "Inubot," she says in a dry voice, like a snake rustling leaves. "Attack." And she picks up another cake.

A Cure for the Common Girl

Hermine Robinson

Tony would be home soon. Mandy felt it in the tickle across her shoulders, in the itch at the base of her skull, and in the cold sweat running down her cleavage. With the heat turned down to save money, the dreaded trickle between her breasts meant only one thing; Tony was close, a few hours away, half a day at most. Time to leave, but not before she set out his supper. She placed a can opener on the laminate countertop beside an expired tin of Hearty Chicken something-or-other she'd found in the pantry. Tony hated soup.

Mandy surveyed her handiwork, adjusted the position of the soup can closer to the empty pot sitting on the stove and tossed the can opener into her purse. The weight of it in her bag felt reassuring as she gave a final 'fuck you, Tony' salute to the soup can.

"Hey, babe, going somewhere?"

Mandy froze. How the hell had Tony made it back to Calgary so soon? She whirled around, wide-eyed, and hoped her terror came across as elation when she enveloped him in a hug, heart pounding against his chest. He felt wooden in her embrace.

"Oh my God, Tony, you're here." Mandy could tell he'd lost weight as she clung a little tighter, ignoring the stubble and the stink of him to buy herself a few extra moments to think.

Tony pushed her away. "Glad to see me?" he asked, running his finger beneath the strap of the bag on her shoulder. "Because it looks to me like you're all packed up to leave."

Mandy had no way of knowing how long he'd been watching her. "Just for a couple of days," she said. "I got scared, Tony. I couldn't stay here by myself anymore."

Tony grabbed her roughly, his fingers digging into her upper arm as he looked her in the eye. "Why not, Mandy? I told you I was coming home, didn't I?"

Tony called three days earlier and told Mandy to wire him some money so he could fly home from Las Vegas on the next available flight. Las Vegas. Huh. Mandy hadn't guessed that one. Tony wasn't a gambler. At least she thought he'd resisted that particular vice until now. She'd stared at the receiver, wondering how a girl could get so lucky. The only thing worse than a no-good-cheat, was a dead-broke-no-good-cheat. As for sending him money for a flight home from Las Vegas? It wasn't going to happen.

"You've been gone a month, Tony. You didn't leave a note. You didn't call. Nothing. How's that supposed to make me feel?"

"I'm calling now, ain't I?"

"Only because you need money," Mandy replied. "Well, guess what, there is no money. You took it all when you left me behind in this dump, remember?"

"How come the phone is still connected if there's no money?"

"I sold your grandmother's fancy china with the gold trim. I know you told me not to touch the stuff stored in the basement, but I didn't have a choice. It was enough to keep the heat and the lights on." And to pay the overdue phone bill, because deep down, Mandy had expected Tony to call.

"Are you saying you paid all the bills?" Tony sounded impressed instead of angry, which was only appropriate considering the slew of final notices Mandy found stuffed in the bottom of a waste basket right about the same time she discovered that Tony had stolen her tip money from working at Denny's. "Wow, that's good, Mandy. You've done good while I was gone."

"Didn't I always say your grandmother's china was worth something?"

"Sure you did, babe, and I'm sorry I doubted you." Tony paused. "Is there more stuff you could sell quick-like and wire me the money so I can grab a flight home?"

Mandy contemplated the diamond ring on her finger. She turned the solitaire inward and closed her fist around it. "I don't think so, Tony. Airplanes are expensive. It would take a week to put together that kind of money."

"A week? No way," he said. "I gotta get out of this hellhole tonight. Can you send me enough for a bus or a train?"

"How much do they cost?"

"How the hell should I know? Jeez, Mandy, just send me what you've got. I'll figure it out."

"That's what I'm trying to tell you, Tony. There's no money to send. Everything I made from selling the china went to pay the bills."

"Fuck."

"It's your stupid house I'm keeping afloat here."

"Yeah, yeah, I know. Shut up for a second, I'm trying to figure things out." There was a pause at Tony's end of the line. Mandy guessed he was doing the mental arithmetic of calculating how long it would take to hitch-hike from Nevada back to Alberta. "Okay, I should be able to make it home in four days, five tops," said Tony. "That'll give me a week to sell more crap from the basement and scrape up the money I need before the end of the month."

"Eleven days."

"What?"

"March has thirty-one days. If you get back in five days, that will make it the twentieth, and you'll have eleven days before the bills come due at the end of the month."

"What the hell, Mandy. I'm not asking for a fucking math lesson. What I'm saying is that you've got five days to sort through more of the junk in the basement. As soon as I'm back we're going to start selling it off."

"What if it isn't worth anything? I mean, now that the china and the silver is gone."

"Silver? You found silver?"

"Forks and spoons — silverware or whatever you call it — the guy said it was sterling."

"Okay, see, that just proves my point. I've been sitting on a gold mine all this time and didn't even know it."

"I guess." Mandy didn't have to guess; she'd been rooting around in the basement for a month already. Of course Tony didn't know that, and she wasn't going to tell him. Stupid Vegas. Gambling was the surest way to blow an inheritance, even a decent one like he'd gotten from his grandmother. How much had he lost? All of it, thought Mandy. Maybe more than all of it considering his sudden urgency to pillage what was left of his grandmother's estate. It meant there was a lot more at stake than just paying utilities.

"Hey, Mandy, what do you want to bet that the old bat's jewelry is hidden somewhere in all that junk? Keep an eye out for it."

"I will," said Mandy. She twisted the diamond ring on her finger. "I'll see you in a few days."

49

When they first met, Tony talked a lot about finding his grandmother's jewelry hidden somewhere in the house. He never got further than knocking a series of ragged holes in the walls while searching for a non-existent lock box. Mandy did a bit of poking around after she moved in and thought chances were good that something valuable was tucked in amongst the piles of furniture, rolled up carpets, and wooden chests stacked in the basement. Tony balked at her suggestion to sort through it. "There's nothing down there but a load of old lady crap."

"That's not true," Mandy replied. "I've been checking it out. Your grandmother had some fancy looking china and there's nice antique furniture down there. If you sell it, that would clear up space for a rec room and you could use the money to buy one of those new projection televisions."

"I don't need the money and I don't want a basement rec room."

Mandy chewed her lip. "Well, can you at least bring up the dining room set so that we have a place for proper sit-down suppers?"

"Sure, we'll invite the neighbour lady over on Sundays."

"That'd be so—"

Tony's fist on the Formica top of the kitchen table made her jump. "Fuck no, Mandy. What the hell are you thinking? Get it in your head; I don't want you snooping around downstairs and finding make-work projects or ways to rearrange my life. And we sure as hell aren't going to invite that old hag, Edna Morrisey, over for supper." Tony grabbed his jacket. "Fuck this shit, I'm going to the Duke."

Mandy chewed her fingernails to the quick wondering what had gone wrong. It was bad timing mostly. Tony had been tetchy lately and she'd approached him from the wrong angle. He didn't have her vision of how nice the house would look if they did a bit of redecorating to drag it out of the sixties and into the nineties. She should have done the work herself while he was out. Maybe she still would. Not today, not when Tony was in a foul mood and drinking, but some day when he was out with his buddies from the Napa store. That way he'd come home to see the dining room all set up with supper served on fine china and he'd have to admit she'd been right all along.

The next day, Mandy returned from her morning shift at Denny's to find a brand-new padlock on the basement door. Tony sat at the kitchen table looking smug as he twirled a silver key around his index finger.

"Why do you have to be like that?" Mandy asked. "How the heck am I supposed to do laundry if you lock me out of the basement?"

"It's called a laundromat," said Tony. He pocketed the key and headed out to his car.

"I'm not lugging your skivvies to some laundromat when there's a perfectly good washer and dryer down-stairs," Mandy yelled from the front step. A flicker of the

51

window blinds next door caught her eye, and she waved at Mrs. Morrisey before heading back inside.

Mandy was sure that Tony would give up the game soon enough. It was winter for goodness sake; he couldn't really expect her to hump baskets of laundry back and forth through the snow. A month later, the only concession he had made was to give her a roll of quarters and a ride to the nearest laundromat just as long as she did his laundry too. Mandy took it because the middle of a bitter cold spell was no time to throw out unreasonable ultimatums.

Sitting on a plastic chair at the laundromat, watching the spin cycle, Mandy remembered her mother's mantra, 'this too shall pass', and Mom was right. It did. On Valentine's Day, Tony ran off with a slutty waitress named Vickie.

The first place Mandy checked when Tony didn't come home for a couple of days was Duke's Pub. The line-up of afternoon regulars assembled along the bar simply shrugged at Mandy's inquires and went back to lamenting the fact that Vickie, their favourite eye-candy, had recently quit.

Ben, the bartender wasn't much help either. "Dunno where Tony is," he said. "I just know he ran up a big tab the last time he was here and then took off with my best girl." Ben eyed Mandy up and down. "You need a job, sweetheart? I've got an opening for a new waitress. We can go to my office and discuss the particulars."

Mandy cringed and pulled her jacket tight despite the warmth of the bar. The money she made at Denny's was crap, but at least her manager didn't expect a back-room blowjob as part of the interview process. "No thanks," she said. "I'm just looking for Tony."

"You could check with the guys at the Napa store. If they don't know where he is, no one will," said Ben. "By the way, if you find him, tell Tony I'll cut him some slack on his tab if he brings Vickie back. That girl was good for business."

At the auto parts store, a guy with 'Lionel' stitched on his shirt was no more helpful than Ben the bartender. "Nope, I haven't seen Tony in a week or more," said Lionel. "Who's asking?"

"I'm Mandy," she said. "Tony's girlfriend."

"Oh, hey, are you the one with the sweet red 300 SL convertible?" he asked.

"Red convertible?" said Mandy. "No, I don't drive."

Lionel shrugged. "Sorry, I must be thinking of someone else."

"Vickie?"

"Yeah, that's it." Lionel leaned casually on the counter. "So, you're the girlfriend, eh?"

"Yes, we've been living together for a few months."

"Well, I wouldn't worry too much about Tony. He has a way of turning up."

Mandy left the Napa store feeling stupid and willing herself not to cry. She'd actually seen Vickie one day at the mall. The woman's ass-cheeks were showing as she loaded

53

a half dozen shopping bags from high-end stores into a cherry-red Mercedes Benz convertible. Tony stopped to admire the car and chatted to her about discount auto parts. Vickie had laughed a little too loudly at Tony's jokes, but Mandy convinced herself it was nothing to worry about. High maintenance wasn't Tony's style and the woman leaning against her Mercedes probably had better prospects.

The easy familiarity Tony had with everyone he met was part of his charm. Mandy had experienced it herself the first time she served him at Denny's. She'd pegged him as a 'skillet scramble' kind of guy, but Tony had looked her over and ordered a short stack with two eggs over easy with a side of sausage, instead. Tony made a point of sitting in her section again the next day, and the day after. He was generous with chit-chat and lingered over free refills long enough for them to exchange some pleasantries beyond the weather. By the end of the week, Mandy knew Tony was rattling around in his grandmother's house all alone, and he knew she was living in a flop house with five roommates who seldom appreciated her cooking and cleaning skills. It had made sense to move in with Tony even before undercurrents of sexual tension drew Mandy to his bed.

Back at the house, Mandy jimmied the padlock on the basement door. The china was more beautiful than she remembered. Gold trim and a band of cobalt blue set off a colourful pattern of pansies unlike any she'd ever seen. Displayed on the kitchen table it looked like the perfect tea party with delicate cups and saucers waiting for a pour of Earl Grey from the matching teapot. The only thing better would be seeing it on a real dining room table. Mandy's musings about how to get the furniture upstairs to the main floor were interrupted by hammering on the front door.

"What am I supposed to do with this?" She asked the man who handed her a final notice courtesy of the gas company.

"The best advice I can give you is to pay it in full within forty-eight hours," he said. "Otherwise you'll have reconnection fees and frozen pipes to go with the late-payment penalties."

Mandy stared at the notice in disbelief. Tony hadn't paid the gas bill in three months. What other messes had he left behind? Her search uncovered more trouble than she expected. The gas, electric and phone bills were all overdue, and the household account was overdrawn.

The lump in Mandy's throat grew tight with the memory of her mother begging collection agencies for more time. The new microwave oven and dishwasher disappeared when burly men came to the door demanding payment for items her father had bought on credit. Her mother called it 'reassessing priorities' when she sold her wedding ring and a set of silver candlesticks brought from the old country.

Looking at Tony's grandmother's china, Mandy decided she had a few priorities of her own to reassess. She wrapped a single place setting and a few serving pieces in tea towels and nestled them in a laundry basket. The nearest antique shop was two bus rides away. The dealer examined the marks on the bottom of the sugar bowl and listened to Mandy's description of the rest of the set. The price he quoted was bullshit.

"You know they're worth more than that."

"They're worth whatever someone is willing to pay, Lady, and this kind of stuff doesn't exactly fly off the shelves," he replied. "I've got overhead to consider."

Mandy weighed her options and realized she didn't have many – no car, no money and no time – in the end she sold him the entire set of china for cash and paid off the most urgent bills first. Mandy returned to the basement and began her search in earnest. A box of silverware looked promising but sifting through boxes of dusty Christmas ornaments and ragged books was disappointing. Dear Lord, how many bibles did one old lady need? Tony had been right, most of it was junk.

Mandy decided to sell the dining room set. She phoned around looking for a free appraisal without much luck but cajoled her least favourite antique dealer into coming by to take a look.

"Teak," he said, running a finger over the back of a chair. "How much are looking to sell it for?"

"Fifteen hundred for the whole set including the cabinets," said Mandy. The guy owed her after ripping her off with the china.

"I can give you eight hundred."

"I'll take twelve if you arrange to pick it up."

"You're killing me, Lady," he replied. "Pick-up costs extra and my guys are going to have a bugger of a time getting the larger pieces up those stairs."

"One thousand."

The warm winds of a chinook blew in overnight and the next day a couple of movers came with a truck and carried the dining set away. Mandy sat on the front step after they left and listened to the sound of snow melt trickling from downspouts. One thousand dollars sounded like a lot of money until she considered what it really took to keep a house going. Even if she picked up extra shifts at Denny's there was no way she could afford to live here on her own for long. What if Tony didn't come back?

Mandy hugged her knees and felt sorry for herself for exactly as long as it took to decide it didn't matter. This was the only home she had, and she'd find a way to make it work. She got up and gave a little 'hello neighbour' wave toward Mrs. Morrisey's house before heading inside.

Edna Morrisey left the security chain in place as she peered through the gap of her front door. "What do you want?"

"I'm Mandy. I live next door and since we're neighbours I thought it might be nice to get to know each other better. I've put on some coffee, so if you're free, pop on over for a visit."

"You think that's a good idea?" Edna looked like a hesitant turtle, maneuvering for a better look at Mandy on her doorstep. "Last time I heard, I wasn't welcome in that house ever again. Tony told me so to my face."

"Well Tony's out of town on business, so what he doesn't know won't hurt him."

"It isn't him I'm worried about getting hurt."

Mandy shrugged. "It's your choice. I'm home all afternoon."

A few minutes later Edna sat in Mandy's kitchen nibbling on cookies and warming her hands on a stoneware mug. She took a break from chatting about the weather and her grandchildren to look around at Mandy's attempts at redecorating. "You've been busy."

"I'm doing as much as I can while Tony's away," said Mandy. "He isn't much of a handyman and he really isn't interested in décor. This way it will be a nice surprise to have it all done when he gets home."

"I saw the movers hauling stuff away the other day," said Edna. "Will Tony be okay with you getting rid of Doreen's furniture while he is gone?"

"Who's Doreen?"

"Tony's grandmother, of course." Edna tilted her head and looked at Mandy sideways. "Are you saying that boy hasn't told you about her?"

"Not much," Mandy replied. "I think he lived with her for a bit when he was a kid, but they weren't all that close after he moved away. He did say that she was old and crippled, and I know for sure she died from a fall because Tony talked about suing some agency that left her living on her own when she shouldn't have been."

"Well isn't that rich. He was going to sue them, was he?" Edna said. "The best thing that could happen to Tony was having her death being ruled accidental. It doubled the insurance pay out and no one looked too close at his part in it."

"Are you saying her death wasn't accidental?"

"I'm saying that Doreen was doing fine. She couldn't climb the stairs on account of her knees, but a senior's service converted her dining room into a bedroom and set her up nicely to live on the main floor. She hired a house-keeper to do laundry and keep things tidy, and the home care people checked on her three times a week. They're the ones who found her dead at the bottom of the base-ment stairs." Edna shivered. "That's what pains my heart. She could have been laying there dead the whole week-end, no one knows for sure."

"That's horrible. No wonder Tony doesn't want to talk about it."

"Don't be feeling too sorry for Tony. He played the grieving grandson just fine, but I've got my suspicions. I think the police might have had suspicions too, because they came around asking if I'd seen Tony at the house that weekend."

"Did you?"

"No, Frank and I were away visiting the kids," Edna replied. "Which doesn't mean Tony wasn't around."

Mandy sat a moment, processing Edna's implication. "Tony's lazy and a cheat, but a murderer?"

"How long have you known Tony? Six months maybe?" Edna leaned forward and grabbed Mandy's hands, her grip surprisingly strong. "I've known Tony since before his Momma died, and I saw him grow up wrong even though Doreen tried her best to raise him right. Trust me, he's got a temper and a mean streak. Maybe you haven't got a taste of it yet because he's been sitting pretty with Doreen's money and her house. Or, maybe he's staying on good behaviour on account of the police checking him out, but trust me, it's there."

"You're wrong," said Mandy, but a niggling doubt crept down her spine. There had been a disorganized rage behind Tony's search for his grandmother's jewelry; not so much methodical demolition as a venting of suppressed frustration on innocent walls. Then, when Mandy suggested searching the basement, Tony's glare had shut down the discussion, but what if she had persisted? "I don't know," she admitted.

"I'm betting you do know," said Edna. "Otherwise, you wouldn't be playing house while Tony's gone and pretending everything will be fine if you just work a little harder to scrub away the filth and cover up the holes with pretty pictures before he gets back."

Mandy didn't like the direction of this conversation. She pulled free of Edna's grip and leaned back, arms wrapped across her chest. "It's not like that."

"Isn't it?" said Edna. "I've lived my life and no one knows better than me that pretending everything is perfect won't make it true. So, what's your excuse for putting up with a guy like Tony? Were you bullied? Did your daddy beat your momma?"

Now Mandy really didn't like the direction of this conversation. "Why would you even ask a thing like that?"

"Sorry, my mistake," Edna replied. It was less an apology than an admission that she had merely guessed wrong. "Frank always called me a Nosey-Parker, but I prefer to think of myself as a student of human nature. I get to wondering how nice girls end up with selfish jerks like Tony."

"It sounds to me like you already know the answer," said Mandy.

"Of course I do. It's because we're so busy taking care of everyone else that we forget to take care of ourselves," Edna replied. "The next thing you know, you're thirty-eight years into a marriage and wondering what happened."

Mandy nodded, fairly sure Edna would tell her exactly what had happened. The woman did not disappoint.

"The thing is, my father was a man of his times. He was strict, authoritarian, never sparing the rod, and I got out of there as quick as I could by marrying the first man who asked me. Frank was safe and stable – a decent husband and father – everything I thought I wanted. For the next

61

thirty-eight years I was so good at pretending to be happy that I even convinced myself."

"It must have been hard, losing your husband after all those years."

"It was hard losing myself for all those years we were married," said Edna. "When Frank passed away, I didn't have a clue how to be happy just for myself. It took me two years of staring at him sitting on the mantel before I figured it out."

Mandy smiled awkwardly as she pictured Edna's husband stuffed and mounted precariously above the fireplace. "On the mantel? Is he still there?"

"No, no. A few years ago I decided to have his ashes pressed into one of those memorial diamonds. Now I take him along on trips, and we go to the movies together, bingo, bridge, all those things he never wanted to do before." Edna sat back looking quite pleased with herself. "Frank really was a boring old grump when he was alive, but now he's as fun as can be."

"I suppose that made him a diamond in the rough," said Mandy.

"Doreen used to make that joke," Edna replied. She leaned forward and her tone got serious. "Listen Girlie, I don't know what you're playing at by setting up house here with Tony but be careful. Frank may have been set in his ways, but he was never mean or cruel."

"Tony's not—"

"Oh sure he is," Edna interrupted. "I've seen you heading off to the laundromat week after week. Why are you doing that when Doreen had a perfectly nice washer and dryer in the house? Are they broken?" Edna didn't wait for a reply. "Tony can afford to get them fixed and if he won't do that for you, it tells you something about his nature. My Frank may have been a lump of coal, but Tony is dynamite. If you press him too hard, he'll explode. Remember what happened to Doreen. Not that I expect you to listen. But at least I've said my piece."

"I appreciate your concern," said Mandy. It was time to derail this particular topic of conversation. "Before I forget, would you like to take a look at some of Doreen's collectibles and choose something for yourself as a memory of her? She had a lot of bibles and Madonna figurines if you're into that kind of thing."

"No thank you, Girlie. I've got plenty of dust collectors of my own," said Edna. She checked her watch and stood up. "I better get going. Frank and I have a movie date tonight."

"Well, if you're sure," said Mandy, seeing Edna to the door. "I just thought I'd offer, before it all goes to Goodwill."

Edna stopped short. "Don't give away any bibles before you check them first," she said. "Doreen was the kind who trusted in the Lord more than the bank." She hurried away without explaining what she meant.

Mandy thought about Edna's advice as she cleared the table and nearly dropped a mug when it dawned on her what the old kook was talking about. She hauled out a box of bibles and flipped through the pages quickly, then again more slowly as she found five and ten dollar bills tucked in every one. Chapter and verse, Doreen's trust in the Lord added up to almost five hundred dollars. Thank you Jesus.

Mandy dragged an upholstered chair across the concrete floor. The stupid thing was heavier than it looked. It was one of a pair, and they were perfect for her plans to convert the empty dining room into a parlor. Tony wasn't exactly the 'front parlor' type, but she hadn't heard from him in over three weeks and every day he was gone, Mandy felt a little bolder with her plans.

The thick upholstered back of the chair made it difficult to get a proper grip as Mandy hauled it up the stairs one step at a time. Two steps short of the landing, her hand got wedged against the handrail and she tipped the chair sideways to adjust her hold. Something she couldn't see from her angle broke free and it tumbled down the steep wooden stairs with a resounding crash. Mandy maneuvered the remainder of the chair into the kitchen to examine the damage. The chair was missing a carved panel on one side. Hopefully it wasn't splintered too badly and she could glue it back in place.

Halfway downstairs, Mandy stopped and blinked. She sat on the steps with a thump and slid down them one by one, not trusting herself to walk. Smashed on the concrete floor was a wooden drawer. Strewn all around it were gold chains and assorted bangles. Tony was right, his grandmother did have a stash of jewelry and it glowed like pirate treasure in the light of a naked incandescent bulb.

The sparkle of a diamond ring caught Mandy's eye and she slipped it on her finger with a satisfied smile before gathering up the rest of her booty into the remnants of the drawer. She spread it out on the kitchen table and saw that much of it was simply costume jewelry, but not all. With a start, Mandy remembered there was a second chair still in the basement. She found the latch to release its secret drawer and revealed a trove of silver dollars. A coin dealer on Centre Street counted and weighed out a value of $3,000 and Mandy had him make out the cheque in her name. A pawnbroker paid cash for the gold chains and gemstone pendants.

Things looked good until Tony's call from Las Vegas burst Mandy's bubble. A phone message left on the answering machine a day later proved once and for all that it was time to forge a new path without him.

Tony? Answer the fucking phone, Tony. It's me, Vickie. Please. I'm stuck in Vegas and those assholes took my car. They ain't messing around, Tony, and I don't know what to do. You gotta get back here and sort this out. Tony? Tony? Shit.

Mandy's first inclination was to erase the message, but she hit 'save' instead. Vickie's plight was a good reminder of why she intended to be gone before Tony returned, but greed compelled her to squeeze a few more dollars out of the remaining jewelry before she left. The thing with the

65

tin of soup and the can opener was just plain petty and stupid.

"Ow, you're hurting me, Tony."

Tony's fingers dug a little deeper into Mandy's arm. "You'll be hurting a whole lot more if you don't tell me what the hell is going on."

"Vickie called," said Mandy. "She left a message warning you about some guys looking for money."

"Oh her." Tony loosened his grip.

Mandy pulled away, rubbing the tender spots on her arms. "Yeah, her."

"Honestly, that whole thing in Las Vegas wasn't my fault. Vickie tricked me. She's bat shit crazy. I see it now, and you don't have to worry. I'm done with her and all that shit."

Mandy folded her arms protectively across her chest and purse as she sidled closer to the door. Forget the suitcase sitting in the front hall. If she walked out with her ID, cash, and debit card it would be enough. "It's not Vickie I'm worried about." Mandy tilted her chin toward the answering machine. "Listen to her message. Vickie didn't sound crazy; she sounded scared. There's guys looking for their money. Whatever happened down in Las Vegas, it isn't done with you."

Tony positioned himself between Mandy and the door. "I told you, it's nothing. I'm home now, and those assholes can't touch me. Canada's huge. They won't even know where to find me."

"Don't be stupid. They know exactly where to find you."

Mandy tried to push past Tony but he grabbed her by the wrist. "What are you talking about?"

"They got to Vickie and she called here looking for you. Here, to this house. Think about it." Mandy saw a flicker of doubt in Tony's eyes. She wrenched herself free and took a gamble. "That's not all. There was another call this morning. I heard heavy breathing, and then they hung up. What if it was them, Tony? What if they were checking who was home? I'm not going to be here when they come to break your kneecaps." Mandy retrieved her suitcase and strode toward the door.

"Where the hell do you think you're going?"

"Somewhere safe, a motel or something."

"Oh yeah?" Tony grabbed Mandy by the hair and yanked her back. She tried to twist free but Tony pinned her against the wall. "A motel? Where'd you get the money for that? Were you holding out on me when I called from Las Vegas?"

"No. It's not like that," Mandy cried. "You didn't give me a chance to tell you. After you called, I looked around downstairs like you said. I did it, Tony. I found your grandmother's jewelry. Look, this is one of her rings." She flashed the diamond solitaire on her finger as proof. "It was all hidden in a couple of secret drawers built into those ugly flowered chairs she had."

Tony grabbed Mandy by the neck and wrenched her close with a violence that negated the kiss he pressed against her lips. When he drew back to take a closer look at the ring, she said, "There's more. I found a whole collection of old silver dollars. I looked it up and they're worth a lot more than a dollar. It's closer to ten dollars. Each." Mandy played with her ring and wondered what the hell she would do when Tony discovered the only treasure left downstairs was cheap costume jewelry. She turned the stone inward. "That's good, isn't it?"

"Yeah, real good," said Tony, pulling her close again. "You done good, Babe."

"Can I keep the ring?" Mandy asked. "I mean, when you sell the other jewelry to pay off those goons, can I keep just the ring? I never had a diamond before."

"Sure, you keep it," Tony replied. "All I need for now is a couple thousand for seed money."

"Seed money?"

"Yeah, I gotta win back what I lost." Tony smiled. "Don't look so worried, I had an unlucky streak down in Vegas, that's all. It's crooked as shit down there, but I've got a system now, and we'll be sitting pretty in no time." He pulled her close and kissed her hair. "All thanks to you, Babe."

All thanks to me, thought Mandy. She gave Tony her best 'I done good' smile. "Do you want to see it?" she asked.

"Shit, yeah," said Tony, rubbing his hands in anticipation. "Where's it at?"

"Downstairs," Mandy replied. "I knew it would be safe if I left it in the secret drawers until you got home."

"Good thinking, Babe." Tony hesitated on the landing as if steeling himself for the descent into the basement.

"Tony?"

"What, Babe?" He turned back to Mandy.

"Don't call me Babe."

The weight of the old can opener added some heft to the arc of Mandy's handbag as it landed an upper cut to Tony's jaw.

Mandy stared at the odd angle of Tony's head. A dark pool seeped into the concrete from his skull and she convinced herself it had to be this way. If Tony saw the drawers were empty except for a few odds and ends of costume jewelry, he'd have killed her. If she gave him the money, it would be gone. If she ran away, he'd find her.

Tony dead was better than Tony alive, but his death did present some problems. Hiding a body was complicated. Calling the police to report it as an accident or self-defence was risky. If she left the house with her packed bags, Tony's body could lay down there for days or weeks before it was found. Vickie's urgent plea on the answering machine would muddy the waters if an investigation showed Tony's death wasn't an accident. Touch nothing. Leave. Mandy knew it could not be that simple; she was missing something crucial. She twisted the diamond solitaire and realized the problem. Edna Morrisey was always watching. Outside, a car door slammed and startled Mandy. She peeked out the window and saw a driver helping Edna out of a taxi cab. Perfect. She and Frank must have been away when Tony came home.

Mandy stepped out and called to Edna. "Ask the cabbie if he can wait a moment. I need a ride to the Greyhound depot." She ducked back into the house and emerged with her bags. "I was going to take transit, but this is easier."

"Where are you going?" Asked Edna.

"Away," said Mandy. "As far from here as possible."

"What happened?" Edna looked at the house. "Is Tony back?"

"Not yet. He called from Las Vegas a couple of days ago looking for money to get home."

"Las Vegas? You said he was away on business."

"And you probably guessed that I was lying," said Mandy. "So, if it's any consolation, you were right."

Edna hugged Mandy. "Do you have money? Will you be okay?"

Mandy smiled. "I'll be fine. I took your advice and trusted in the Lord."

"Good for you, Girlie," said Edna. "Good for you." She hugged Mandy again and drew back. "I feel like an old fool. I've been calling you 'Girlie' all this time because even though you told me your name, for the life of me I couldn't remember it."

"Girlie was fine, that's kind of who I used to be. My real name is Amanda, but people call me Mandy for short."

"I like Amanda better," said Edna.

"Me too." Amanda shifted her purse to the opposite shoulder and remembered why it was so heavy. She looked at Edna and had an idea. "I want to thank you for your help, Mrs. Morrisey. I know you didn't want anything from Doreen's collection, but could you use a can opener? It's a good one, a real life saver." Amanda handed it to Edna and slid into the cab before the woman could protest. "If you happen to see Tony, tell him a woman named Vickie called. Apparently there's some people in Vegas looking for the money he owes."

"I'm not telling Tony a damn thing," Edna replied. "He deserves whatever's coming to him."

"You're probably right," said Amanda. She glanced back at the house one last time before tapping the cab driver on the shoulder to indicate she was ready to leave Mandy behind.

A Premium on Murder
Pat Flewwelling

Gar was toying with her handheld Comm-Patriot when someone knocked on the frosted glass of her office door. Normal people touched the "Ring" icon on the pad beside the door frame. Gar grumbled as she got up to answer the door the old-fashioned way. She hated meeting new people. She hated being seen. And there was always, *always* the chance of a set-up.

Standing in the hall was a chin-high woman dressed in a steaming raincoat and broad-brimmed hat, a filtration scarf, fashionable goggles, and some kind of ankle-length robe. She was looking down and shaking mud from her hem.

"Can I help you?" Gar asked, scratching her bulbous, deformed forehead.

Without looking up, the woman said through her scarf, "I...I'm looking for some confidential advice, please."

"For?" Gar snapped.

The woman glanced up, jarred, and clapped her hand to her chest. "Oh!" She looked Gar up and down, while studiously avoiding eye contact. "Oh, I...I'm sorry. I don't mean to stare."

Gar sighed. "Confidential?" She blocked the doorframe. She could lose her work permit if the Citizens' Police suspected her of accepting payment, and this woman smelled like money. A BMW keychain hung from her clutched keys. "You know where you are, right?"

"Miss Grove's Cultural Consultancy for Young Hegemonic Girls," the woman said.

"Then what do you need *my* advice for?"

The woman's sequined goggles were tinted for additional UV protection, so it was hard to read her expression, but Gar sensed offended pride in the woman's stare.

"Legal advice?" Gar asked.

"Well – "

"George Winter, down the hall, third on the left." Gar began to close her door.

"No, not legal," the woman said in a rush. "Not yet."

Gar leaned closer, rubbing her swollen mouth. "What, are you in some kind of criminal trouble?"

The woman replied after a long, telling pause. "Not yet."

"George Winter, down the hall –"

The woman put her foot and elbow into the closing crack of Gar's door. "Please," she said, her voice thick and trembling. "I don't know who else to turn to. I heard…"

"You heard what?"

"That you could help me."

"I'm a consultant for rude little Hegemonic girls," Gar said. "There's nothing I can do to help the likes of *you*."

"He said you're the last recourse in a callous world."

Recourse, and callous. Two of three code words required to secure Gar's interest. This was a woman who knew people, and it meant she was involved in some next-level shit.

"I'm no port in the storm," was Gar's counter-sign.

"Better to scuttle the ship than answer the siren's call."

Son of a bitch, Gar thought. They stood a while longer, Gar glaring down at the stranger, who stared at her own black boots. "Who sent you?" Gar asked.

The woman shook her head quickly. "Not in the hall."

Sensible, Gar thought.

"Please," the woman whispered.

Gar let the woman in. She peered into the hall, then closed the door. At a touch, her reinforced smart glass window changed from frosted to opaque, adorned with the words "Miss Grove's Cultural Consultancy for Young Hegemonic Girls – Counselling | Training | Fashion Advice – Office Currently Closed." Contact information and hours would be displayed at the touch of an inquiring finger, but neither the ringer nor intercom would work. "Have a seat." She went to the rain-soaked picture windows, sweeping her hand in an arc. Clear glass became a real-time view of the swirling, flickering North Pacific Microbead Typhoon. "Before we get started, I need to know who sent you," Gar said as she turned to sit at her dented, steel desk.

The woman had removed her goggles, filtration scarf, and hat.

"What the *hell*," Gar snapped.

The woman's hands trembled as she began to take off her gloves. She was careful to keep her cuffs past the bones of her wrists, even as she lifted her hands to adjust her shiny, purple *hijab*.

"Are you *insane*?" Gar blurted. "Are you trying to get us both killed?"

The woman's lips were narrow and pale, as if she was fighting back angry tears. She tucked a stray black hair under her head-scarf and sat down, knees pressed together, ankles touching but resting to one side. She opened her purse and put on a pair of purple-rimmed glasses over dusky, puffy eyes, threading the arms carefully under the tight purple material of her *hijab*. She appeared much older than her voice let on, but she wore money and class consciousness in every bangle, necklace, and ring.

Gar's license and good standing with the Citizens' Police demanded she call the hotline immediately. Just being in the same room with a *hijabi* was an indictable offense under the New American Patriot Act.

"Stripe *me*," Gar whispered. "Is this a joke?"

"No," the woman answered softly.

"A set up? Is that it? You're with the Citizens' Police –"

"No," the woman said, more sternly.

Gar ran her big hand over her puffy mouth. "Do you have *any* idea what kind of a position you're putting me in right now?"

The woman's lips trembled and her eyes reddened, but she didn't seem inclined to leave. "I remember a time when modesty wasn't a crime."

"History doesn't mean jack shit!" Gar replied.

"There are more important things at stake, Miss Grove."

"Who sent you?"

"A friend of my husband," the stranger said. "He told me to tell you, 'The Pool-boy in Panama.' He said you would understand."

"Good God..." *Clayton. That bastard is still alive and operational!* She sat down hard. "When did you see him?"

"Three days ago," the woman answered. "I meant to come earlier, but this was my first chance to get away. The weather..."

Hurricane Yolanda-Najjemba had been hanging around Northton District for days. It had been the deadliest hurricane in Manitoba in the last six years.

"He's still underground?"

"I think he has a job at the Anatolian Consulate."

Gar grinned. "Crafty old fox..."

"I'm so sorry," the woman said. "I need to ask an impertinent question. I hate making assumptions."

Gar lost her smile. "The face?"

"Was it the rains? Or were you in one of the mines...?"

"Acromegaly. Makes bones grow in my hands, feet, and face. That's why the long face," Gar said with a grunting, humourless laugh. She had a protruding chin, whopping underbite, bulging forehead, thick lips, a potato nose, and cheeks so large they turned her face into a perfect diamond. Every two years or so, she was required to update her facial recognition profile, because her face never stopped growing. "Tumour on the pituitary gland. Might have been environmental, could be congenital. Who knows?"

"Oh," the woman said. "No insurance..."

"No, no insurance, God," Gar growled. "You need a taxable income for that." If she had insurance, she could have had the tumour removed, and with some additional treatment, her face and soft tissues would return to normal. But those few doctors who operated on the uninsured often took more than authorized, like kidneys, once the patient was under sedation.

"Not even your husband can...?" She seemed to regret the words as soon as she said them.

Gar rolled her eyes. "This face has won me so many marriage proposals that I *still* can't decide which lucky bastard to marry first. How much do you pay in Liberty Premiums?"

The woman blanched. "Enough."

"Failed the Canadian Values test, too?"

"Among other things, I refused to renounce my faith or my husband," she answered. "Even though he's an attaché with the Anatolian ambassador."

Gar pointed at her *hijab*. "You a convert? Naturalized, pre-war?"

"I'm sixth generation Canadian," she said, "and I have always been Muslim, as was my father, and his family before him. My mother was Métis. I don't see how —"

Gar raised her hand. "I don't like to make assumptions, either."

The woman blushed, smiled a little, and lowered her eyes again.

"Listen, we've done this introduction ass-backwards," Gar said. She put out her knobby, oversized hand.

"Qadira Demir," she said, shaking Gar's hand. Gar felt like she was shaking the hand of a mannequin. This was a woman who was too demure to demonstrate her strength, but she had her limits, and a secret, iron will. "And you are Garland Grove."

"Or, as I'm sure our mutual friend called me, 'Gar-*Goyle*.'"

"...I thought he was exaggerating."

Gar raised her eyebrows. "And now you *don't* think he was exaggerating."

Qadira flushed. "I thought he meant you liked to sneak onto rooftops and brood over the city."

Gar smothered a smile. "You need a fix with the Citizens' Police? Is that why you're here?" The woman looked up, curious and confused. "You pay Liberty

Premiums so you can at least wear your *hijab* around your own property, but you can't stop assholes from looking over the fence and reporting you for seditious behaviour, is that it? If that's the case, the simple solution is stay inside."

"I thought we were past making assumptions."

"People could shoot you and claim Standing Ground."

"People are going to shoot me for walking while being a *brown woman*. For all that, why *not* declare my devotion to Allah? Should I fear an early return to Paradise?"

Gar shut her mouth. This time, she was the one who couldn't make eye contact. They were silent for a long moment, while the hurricane thundered outside.

Then, softly, Qadira said, "But now that you mention it, he might be with the Citizens' Police. Undercover."

"Who?"

"Bill Addison, the man giving me trouble. He does have that kind of..." Her lips pursed.

"Attitude?" Gar asked.

"Arrogance."

Gar grunted. "Great. Harassment or blackmail?"

"...Blackmail."

"Listen, Qadira...Did uh...your husband's friend ever tell you what kind of 'consultation' I do?"

She shook her head. "Only that I should exhaust all other avenues before visiting you."

"And you exhausted them in three days?"

The woman shook her head. "Our mutual friend underestimates the...urgency of my trouble." She shifted uncomfortably in the military surplus – Second Civil War era – metal chair. "You're well-known among certain circles," the woman answered. "Among...sympathizers."

"Damn," Gar sighed. "And here I thought I was subtle."

"You are. At least, enough to fool the lower echelons of the Citizens' Police."

Gar snorted. "You have no idea." Qadira, clearly, had contacts in the Resistance, which led Gar to recognize signs of a kindred spirit. The woman probably wasn't a spy, per se – she couldn't be, if she stuck out so stubbornly – but she was secret intelligence of some kind. Gar began to wonder if "my husband's friend" was a euphemism for "my own informant."

"You asked me if I was in criminal trouble," the woman said.

"I did."

"No, not me, and not yet," she said. She was gaining confidence, but clearly, she was carefully choosing her words. "I believe a damning political document is about to be stolen."

"By who?"

Qadira's hands fidgeted in her lap. "By you."

Qadira Demir married her husband three years after the end of the Second Civil War, and five years before the American Invasion. Once Canada surrendered and became a protectorate of the New American Hegemony, Qadira –

like all people of colour – was forced to take the Patriotic Values exam. She failed it by "incorrectly" answering the questions about homosexuality, offending both the law and the Holy Quran. She had to surrender everything, including her house, car, liquid assets, her right to vote, and the right to seek gainful employment. She nearly lost custody of her daughter, too, what with cultural rehabilitation residential schools being mandatory, again. If not for the intervention of the New Anatolian government, now a nuclear power, she and her infant daughter might have been incarcerated in one of the SWX corporate internment camps in the Arid States. But, because her husband was a citizen of the Anatolian Emirites, a diplomat, and independently wealthy, she was able to afford the ever-rising Liberty Premiums, entitling her to wear a *hijab* in private. She had the kind of life – and the courage – that Gar envied with a passion bordering on hate.

If Gar wanted an extra thousand bucks, all she had to do was pick up the phone and swear a false accusation. It wasn't like *Gar* was rolling in dough. Gar also lost the right to seek gainful employment, even though she was unmarried and had undergone state-enforced sterilization. (Even though the Hegemony had outlawed all forms of birth control, they were rabidly keen on eugenics, especially when the potential mother was as unsightly as Gar.) Since she also failed the Patriotic Values exam – too soft on homosexuality and deportation – she lost the bid for special employment exemption. She could work – was encouraged to work – but wasn't allowed to draw a wage. Technically, she could live off whatever the Resistance slipped her way. She didn't really *need* any more bounties from the Barbaric Cultural Practices Hotline, though they helped.

Still, she *needed* to work. Employment was thinly disguised insurgency, wrapped in a crusty layer of vigilantism. And this case was right up her alley.

Gar thought this over as she pushed her way upwind through the lashing, steaming, smelly rain. She didn't mind. Everyone wore a filtration scarf in weather like this, so she didn't stand out. Traffic was insane, though. She was on the corner of Victory and Crow when a black and chrome Heavy-Chevy drove through the intersection and t-boned a diesel Lightweight against a smog-stained office building. Both drivers got out. Then came the shoving, the screaming bystanders, and the gun battle. Gar kept on walking. Statistically speaking, she was just as safe on the road as she was indoors during a battle like that, but when a bullet ricocheted off the reinforced shop front window beside her, she picked up the pace and rushed homeward down Crow Street toward the municipal border between Patriot Plaza and Brownville.

Earlier that week, Qadira's husband had received a memorandum marked Top Secret. Usually, he trusted his wife enough to hint at the contents of such missives, but this time, he refused to answer any question. Instead, he locked himself in his office for hours, yelling on the telephone about history repeating itself. A few days later,

Bill Addison of the Citizens' Police had called up Qadira, reciting the contents of that same document. (To Gar, that meant Qadira must have had unauthorized access to that memo, otherwise she couldn't vouch for the authenticity of Addison's stolen copy; this reinforced Gar's suspicion that Qadira was a spy.) During that call, Addison then demanded two million in New American Corporate Funds, or he'd release the memo to members of the Hegemonic Security Council, outing her husband as a Fifth Columnist and threat to the Empire. Pretty standard blackmail, and yet something just didn't ring true. Qadira was swimming in greenbacks. Two million was *nothing*. If she needed more, why not just ask her husband? Why the secrecy between man and wife?

Once inside her apartment block, Gar pressed her thumb to the biometrics scanner beside the elevator, and the car opened. The elevator video screen turned on, and the AI concierge smiled at her. "Ascending to Floor…fifty-five. Private mode." The elevator doors closed, and the car begin to lift. "How can Tay-Care Corporate Housing help you today —" The feed glitched as the server fetched Gar's profile. "Miss Grove?"

"Any messages?" Gar asked as she loosened her filtration scarf.

Thunder boomed throughout the building, and the power faded briefly.

"You have eight new messages," the concierge said, once the lights were restored.

"Playback subject line and sender."

"Subject: You have one new candidate. Healthy and open-minded. Apply today!"

"Skip," Gar said.

"Subject: You have one new candidate. Seeking long-term relationship with –"

"Skip," Gar snapped.

"Subject: You have one new –"

"Are they all from the same sender?"

"Checking," the concierge said. "Confirmed."

"Skip all and delete."

"Warning," the concierge said. "Failure to seek marriage partners is an indictable –"

"Get striped," Gar said. She flinched and gritted her teeth, half-annoyed and half-amused at her own outburst.

"Warning. This use of aggressive language may be considered assault and/or subversive, and may be used against you in a court of the Citizens' Police. You may be issued a fine of up to…" Another glitch as the server searched legal precedent. "Four thousand eight hundred New American Corporate funds."

She stuffed her fist in her pants pocket and flipped the middle finger.

This isn't right, she thought. *None of this. The violence, the damned Protection of the Sanctity of Marriage laws…the weather…*

If she went online to compare that February's weather with, say, the winter of 2028, ten years earlier, she'd find that there was no significant meteorological difference. Hurricanes had always come this far inland, equipped with

85

first and last names. They'd always been named after enemies of the state, too, like Grace-Hopper, Viola-Desmond, and now, Yolanda-Najjemba. Always female, too. If she searched weather records as far as the year she was born, 1995, same thing. If she searched weather records all the way back to 1776, she'd find that the average February temperature in Manitoba had always been a balmy 14 degrees – or rather, 57 – and the growing season had always been ten months long. It didn't matter what she remembered. Nothing she recalled could be *proved*. And overtly questioning state science was punishable by imprisonment and/or execution. On the upside, one day people might rue the wrath of Hurricane Garland-Grove.

The elevator let her out at the 54th floor. The hallway was silent. She thumped toward her apartment. A neighbour flung open her apartment door to yell, saw who it was, swallowed her threats, and went back inside.

Gar's tiny apartment was spotless. The Rehabilimaid Service had returned her stiff furniture to right-angles, folded the Murphy bed against the wall, incinerated the trash, and left the TV tuned to some screaming zealot preaching on the state-sponsored station. Gar opened her refrigeroven and took out that day's delivery of Bachelorations™, the one and only thing she appreciated about the Hegemonic era. No matter what, as long as she paid her premiums, she'd have two hot, square meals a day, tailored to her personal nutritional needs. Sure, it was catered by the Barnocorp Incarceration Company –

literally prison and hospital food – but, left to her own devices, Gar would subsist on Coca-Cola and Ultra-Honey Lucky Charms. She unhitched the folding table and sat down to eat.

"Concierge," she said. "Mute."

The sound stopped, but the TV continued to feed bold red headlines, and the debate moderators wagged fingers at all the naughty viewers out there in TV Land.

She ate in relative silence, thinking over Qadira's words, testing their authenticity. The more she probed, the more she knew Qadira had been holding back. Gar never worked for liars. *And yet…*

Gar wasn't even sure what was the Bacheloration special that day, except to say that it had some hamburger-flavoured protein mash. One day, due to a clerical error, she'd been delivered soft tacos. (Hard tacos had been outlawed as a choking hazard in 2034.) Soft tacos, she decided, would be an adequate last meal, but not this shite. *Or maybe a nice steak, with corn on the cob, garden salad, and maybe some fresh baked bread. I would literally kill for corn on the cob right now.*

"Concierge," she said.

"Listening."

"Search contact Qadira Demir."

"One contact found. Place video call, direct message, or –"

"Voice call."

"Contacting," the disembodied voice said. "Contacting. Conta –"

"Hello?" It was a very young voice.

"Could I speak to Qadira Demir, please?" Gar asked between spoonfuls.

"Just a minute." Distanced from the speaker, the girl said, "Momma, it's a voice call, it's for you!"

Gar could hear footsteps. "How many times have I got to tell you not to answer Momma's message system – Yes, hello?"

"Mrs. Demir?"

"Is this Gar?"

"Yeah. Listen, I've been thinking…"

Gar heard the sound of material rustling, and Qadira's hushed voice was close to her microphone. "Tell me you'll help me…" Qadira pleaded.

"Have you told me the whole truth?" Gar asked. "Everything?"

Aside, Qadira said, "No, sweetie, go back to your homework. I'll help you in a second." To Gar, she said, "I'm sorry, what?"

"Tell me again," Gar said. "Everything."

"I can't," Qadira said. In a rushed whisper, she said, "My daughter is right here."

"I can't shake this feeling you lied to me, Qadira."

"How *dare* you –"

"Then take me off speaker and just answer yes or no."

Qadira followed instructions. "Why are you doing this to me?"

"You were approached by Bill Addison, correct?"

"Yes."

88

"Who may or may not be a member of the Citizens' Police."

"Yes."

"What's in the memo?"

Qadira didn't answer.

Gar sighed. "Mrs. Demir, there's a reason why I'm called the last recourse. It's because if I fail, one of us dies."

Silence.

"Frankly, I don't know you well enough to give a damn if you live or die, but if it means I can punch the Hegemony in the crotch, I'll usually give it a shot. But if I'm the one who has to die, I need to know I'm doing it for the right reason. Just tell me yes or no: is this about blackmail, or something bigger?"

She heard more shifting of material, and something brushed against the microphone of a privacy headset. "It's a memorandum, telling the staff of the Anatolian embassy to prepare to evacuate."

"Where is this memo now? He has it?"

"He says he does."

"And he hasn't released that copy to the authorities yet," Gar said.

"Correct."

"You're sure?"

"Believe me, you would know if it had been leaked. The world would know."

"And he's holding it for blackmail," Gar said.

"...Yes."

"For how much?"

"Two million, I told you," Qadira answered.

"Mrs. Demir…" Gar sighed. "You can afford a BMW on top of the Liberty Premiums you pay for you and your daughter." There was a short, angry exhalation, but Qadira said nothing. "Premiums run into the tens of thousands every month, per person, but they only extend to your personal property line. And yet, you walk around wearing your headdress in public, which means you don't give a damn about public insurrection fees. All of that tells me that two million is just a drop in your gem-encrusted bucket."

Another long pause.

"Fine, don't answer that. But if you don't answer this next question, I'm dropping your case. Understand?"

"I understand." There was a subtle growl under the soft response.

"Are you lying to me when you say he's asked for two million dollars?"

"…Yes."

"Good. No more lying to me from here on out, you got it?"

"Fine. I understand. But only yes or no —"

"Is he asking for something other than money?"

"…Yes," Qadira answered.

"Something you don't want your husband finding out?"

"Yes."

"And you don't want to give Bill what he's asking for?"

"No! I can't! It's not something either a mother or wife can give."

Gar began to see the light. It was glaring, and tinged red. "What happens if you don't give Bill what he wants?"

There was another long pause, followed by a quivering sound, as if Qadira was trying to cover up a sudden sob by clearing her throat.

"Could you answer that question if your daughter was out of the room?" Gar asked.

"Yes and no."

"If you answered that question out loud, would you be in danger with the Citizens' Police?"

"Yes."

"If you answered that question, would you be in danger with the Hegemony?"

"Yes."

"And with the Anatolian Emirites?"

"...We will *all* be in danger, Gar," Qadira said through clenched teeth. "From both."

Hairs rose on the back of Gar's neck.

In the beginning of the Hegemonic era, New America and The Anatolian Emirites got along like great pals. Then came Anatolia's successful nuclear self-armament. Then came the Çatalhöyük Accord and the Sino-Russo-Anatolian Alliance. Now, Anatolia was recalling its ambassadors from Ground Zero. If the memo was leaked, if the Hegemony found out that Anatolia was planning a pre-emptive strike, the Hegemony would retaliate before the war had even begun. Global, nuclear war.

"Well, stripe me," Gar whispered. "That bad?"

"Yes."

Gar rubbed her distended forehead. "Mrs. Demir, I'm going to ask you two more questions, and I need you to answer them both honestly."

Qadira replied tensely, "I will answer it if I can."

"Is this worth sending someone else to their death?"

The response was soft but immediate. "Yes."

"Even if it means running the risk of your own execution?"

"Yes."

"That's all I need to know," Gar said. *This life's never going to get any better anyhow.*

Qadira said, "I will pay you whatever you need."

"I don't need money. My expenses are already covered," Gar said. "But there is something I need you to do for me."

"Name it."

"I need you to tell everything to our mutual friend. Tell him what's in that memo. Then the two of you have got to put a stop to whatever's about to happen. Find a way."

"There's nothing I can —"

Gar snarled, "As one professional to the other, Mrs. Demir...Our mutual friend does not speak with diplomats, especially those from countries that routinely execute those of his sexual persuasion. He is not your husband's friend. He is *yours*. That puts you in a completely different, and very clever, class of individuals. You can and will find a way."

"But –"

Eavesdroppers be damned, Gar thought. "If you let Anatolia throw the first punch, what kind of world will you be leaving for your daughter?"

Qadira breathed into the microphone. "What do I do?"

"Tell somebody important that nothing good ever came from starting a fight. Ask them what happened after December 7, 1941, the last time somebody sucker punched America."

"...You don't think the Hegemony could lose against the Allies?"

"One bomb and we'll *all* lose. Listen, there's one more thing I need you to do."

"What?"

"Meet me at the Bull's Balls Bar, tonight, in Brownville. Leave the *hijab* at home."

"Brownville?" Qadira asked.

"You'll fit in better there." It was called 'Brownville' for a reason, just as Blackstown was named for a reason, as was Jewston. "Citizens' Police are notorious for being unable to tell people apart in Brownville. You'll be safe there. Sit at the counter. Do not leave until I arrive."

"But why there?"

"So I can give you his copy of the memo, idiot," Gar snapped. "Just go."

"Well...all right..."

"No matter what happens tonight," Gar said, "you have to trust me, even if they arrest you. Don't tell anyone we've talked. Don't tell anybody about our mutual friend.

Play dumb if they ever ask you about the embassy – it's your husband's job, and as the wife, your duty is in the home, out of men's business, right?"

"As one professional to another," Qadira said, "trust me to do my part of the job."

"Fine," Gar said.

"But...what if you get killed?"

"Wait until morning. Go home, grab your daughter, get the hell out of Northton. Our mutual friend will find you and get you out of the country. Now get going. And leave your daughter at home. Brownville is no place for a poor little rich girl."

"Gar?"

"What?"

"...Don't get killed."

"You go save the world, *hajibi.* I'll save you."

The call disconnected. Gar sat back, eyeing her unfinished Bacheloration and contemplating the meaning of life and death.

She could read between the lines. And what she didn't already guess, she could always confirm later that night, or, *insha'Allah,* hear it from Clayton himself.

"Concierge," Gar said. She stood and dumped the last of her Bacheloration into the under-counter incinerator. Leftovers erupted in a brief flash of flame and ash.

"Listening."

"Voice call, Citizens' Police."

"Contacting."

A man's bored voice joined the line. "Citizens' Police. State the nature of your complaint."

"This is Citizen Officer Garland Grove, badge number 14382. I'd like to report an overheard conversation between two suspected Muslim extremists."

Suddenly, the man sounded alert. "Go ahead."

"There's supposed to be some kind of secret meeting between the two of them tonight, at Bull's Balls Bar. A man and a woman." She proceeded to give Qadira's description in full detail, then described Clayton. "I don't know their names, though. The man's the real danger. She's just supposed to give him money or documents or something. Wait and watch her, and you can grab that stinking bastard, too."

"Good work, Citizen. Two thousand Corporate funds will be credited to your account upon successful capture and incarceration of both suspects."

"Oh, hey. Could you do me a favour?"

"That depends."

"I was supposed to meet a fellow Patriot tonight," Gar said. "Bill Addison, you know him?"

"The one out of Execuville?"

"Yeah, that's him. I was supposed to meet him near his place. Triumph block?"

There was a pause.

"Okay, I know I'm not supposed to comment on an open case," Gar said, "but I've been ordered to follow him. Suspected contraband – videographic, mainly. Pretty sick stuff."

"You know I'm not authorized to divulge –"

God help us all...this had better be worth it.

Gar said, "The orders came from Vice President Macdonald, authorization 148818-SH. Please follow your confidentiality protocol."

These were million dollar numbers. The Resistance had spent more than a year's worth of illicit income to secure that authorization code, and it could only be used once, maybe twice. And only God knew if it was still valid or not.

"Monument Corp, in Execuville," the dispatcher said. "One hundred twelfth floor, suite 11218."

"God bless the Hegemony," Gar said.

"God bless the CEO."

She disconnected the call, opened her closet, and unlocked the fireproof safe. She began to assemble her kit.

Security technology had improved greatly during the Hegemonic era, but the bulk of humanity was as dumb as ever. All Gar had to do was press a print-free glove on the exterior call board and talk with one resident after another until someone bought her story about missing keys and an abusive husband coming home right behind her. With Hurricane Yolanda-Najjemba throwing her last weak kicks at the city beneath her, Gar could keep her hat and filtration scarf on without anyone – including any concierges – from complaining about being unable to recognize her. She passed through the gleaming lobby in search of the elevators.

The key to success in this mission was speed, not subtlety.

In fact, a lack of subtlety was the whole point.

She rushed to an elevator marked "Coloured Personnel".

"Please state your authorized contractor ID," the automated service personnel asked.

Shit, she thought. *This is new. Think! Shit!*

"Uh...Djamila Haddad," Gar answered. It was her birth name. "Rehabilimaid Cleaning Services, Limited." It was the same company who kept her apartment stocked and geometrically aligned.

"Warning," the elevator said as it closed its doors.

Shit.

"This given name has been deemed un-American."

Oh God, she thought, limp with relief and laughter.

"Warning. This surname has been deemed un-American. For your convenience, please consider anglicizing your name in order to avoid fines, harassment, and other forms of employment discrimination."

"Thank you," Gar answered. Sweat rushed down from the brim of her slouch hat.

"Warning," the elevator said.

Shit! What now?

"Our language processors indicate trace accents of foreign origin. You are recommended to attend remedial speech therapy in order to avoid fines, harassment, and other forms of employment discrimination."

"Thank you," Gar answered impatiently. She stuffed her fists in her coat pockets and flipped both birds where the cameras couldn't see them.

"Which floor?"

"One hundred twelve."

"Which suite?"

"Eleven-two-eighteen."

"For which resident?"

"Bill Addison."

"Checking." A pause. "Unscheduled appointment."

"He said it was urgent," Gar answered. Fearing the worst, she scrabbled in her coat for her personal Comm-Patriot.

"Please stand by."

Stripe me...

The lights in the elevator turned from bluish-white to red and back again.

Ah, stripe me!

On her Comm-Patriot, Gar pressed the emergency call button with the logo for the Citizens' Police. "This is a Citizen Officer Garland Grove, badge number 14382, leaving a message for anyone in the area of Triumph and Wealth, Execuville," she said as fast as she could. The lights had begun to blink from red to white, red to white, while the elevator continued to say, *'standby.'* Into the Comm-Patriot, Gar said, "I've tracked a suspicious person of colour to the Monument Corp apartment block, and they just tripped the Suspicious Persons alarm. Will continue to pursue. Requesting back-up." She hung up just as the lights turned to a steady red.

"Warning," the elevator said. "Unscheduled appointment. Warning. Unauthorized contractor. Please standby. Citizens' Police have been dispatched."

"Damn it," Gar snarled. She fished out her wallet and Citizens' Police badge. The latter she pressed against the card reader. The alarm stopped. A control panel popped open. She quickly tethered her Comm-Patriot to the control panel access port, and ran a Resistance-designed program. The malware would overwrite the surveillance feed with false IDs and a copy of previously recorded video from the same elevator. Some other contractor might get embroiled in the inevitable investigation, but as soon as the police found the bug in the elevator data, the suspect would be released uncharged. Or lynched before trial – that was always fifty-fifty these days.

Once the fake data had been seeded, she relaunched the elevator's greeting program.

"Welcome, Citizen Officer," said the level-headed voice of the elevator. "For which fl –"

"One hundred twelfth floor, suite eleven-two-eighteen, resident Bill Addison, do not ring ahead. Urgent and undercover Citizen business, authorization code 14382-delta."

"Confirmed." She disconnected her tether, closed the panel, and dropped her Comm-Patriot into her pocket, as the elevator began to rise. Gar checked her watch. *Damn it, damn it, damn it!* Her Comm-Patriot buzzed. She took it out. It was a callout from Headquarters, requesting all Citizen Police in the area to respond to an unauthorized person-of-colour in that very apartment building, in that very elevator. *Stripe me bloody*, Gar thought. It wouldn't take long for them to arrive. Her only saving grace was the hurricane outside and the arduously slow elevators inside, but Execuville was chock-a-block with zealots and low-ranking members of Hegemony-approved corporations. That meant a horde of local Citizen Police only steps away.

The elevator opened, and Gar thumped, nearly ran, down the hall. A curious, grumpy, squat and balding, olive-skinned man flung open the door to 11218. "Whoever the hell is making all that racket is going to get *striped*."

Gar kicked him where his t-shirt and jogging pants failed to meet, knocking him to the floor.

"What the hell?" Bill Addison screamed as she slammed the door behind them.

Gar looked around for cameras, and found two small, black globes on the ceiling. "You people have taken away everything from me!" Gar said. She whipped off her hat, revealing a red *hijab* with designs in gold thread. She kept her filtration scarf on. Bill Addison's eyes widened. "And then you try to take my *daughter* away from me?"

Bill Addison smiled nervously as he tried to pull himself up off the floor. She rushed at him and kicked him in the belly and the groin.

"You've taken everything away from me! My mosque, my freedom, my safety, my life!" She stomped on him again. "And now you want to take my daughter? Like *that*?"

There was another buzz on her Comm-Patriot. That meant either a second call-out, or a confirmation from responding Citizen Police.

Bill Addison had the gall to laugh. "She's just a *girl*."

Gar stomped on him again.

"I only wanted her for a night!" Bill Addison groan-laughed. Another kick. "You're still young! You can always make more!"

It will never get better. Do it. "Bastard!" She broke his nose with her heel.

Gar stripped off her coat, revealing the silver-trimmed black *abaya* her mother had given her on her sixteenth birthday. It barely fit, and it smelled like the inside of a fireproof safe. "You will never have my daughter! I will kill you!" From under the draped hem of her *abaya*, she drew a holstered automatic. Bill's eyes bulged.

Gun laws were lax for people identified as Hegemonic, though weapons were nearly impossible for any visible minorities to lay hands on. This was why Gar never sought treatment for her acromegaly. People couldn't see past the surface distortions to the Saudi Arabian heritage beneath. Once she'd Anglicized her name, people assumed she was White and ugly. They let her live in Patriot Plaza. They let her buy a gun. And they even accepted her application into the Citizens' Police.

Gar shot out the two cameras first, making Bill Addison scream both times. When he got up to run, she shot him in the knee, and he stayed down, bellowing into the blood-dappled white carpet. She quickly scanned the room for any additional cameras. "Where's the memo?" Gar asked.

"I don't know what you're talking about –"

"I've got twelve bullets left, and none of them have to be fatal. Next shot takes out your balls."

"I – I –"

She shot him in the other knee. "I missed."

"God! Stop! Stop it! I don't have it here!"

She shot the floor beside his ear so he could get a good whiff of the powder and smoke.

"Refrigeroven," he screamed. "It's in the refrigeroven!"

She dashed into his kitchen, and in her haste, she tipped the machine off the counter, and it cracked. A good thing, too. He wasn't lying, but he hadn't been very specific. The fingernail-sized storage device had been wedged into a crack in the coolant casing, at the back of the refrigeroven. She picked up the device and slid it into her glove. "Do you know what's on this?" she asked Bill.

Bill nodded hurriedly. "Please – just take it and go. I'll leave the girl alone, God – I swear!" He lifted a bloodstained hand in a stop-sign fashion, as if to push her away.

"What's on this?" she demanded. She didn't have time for this filibuster, and she had yet to formulate an escape plan. "Tell me!"

"It's the order to evacuate the embassy," Bill cried. "In ten days."

"Why?"

"I don't know," Bill wept. "God, please just go!"

"*Why*?" Gar shouted. When he didn't reply, she dropped to his side and pressed the mouth of the barrel against his temple.

"I don't know!" he screamed. "It doesn't say in the memo!"

"Which ambassadors?"

"All of them, any of them in the Hegemonic states!" Bill answered. "They're planning an intercontinental airstrike."

"Stripe me," Gar growled.

"They're planning to liberate Canada."

Just like how the Americans liberated Iraq, Afghanistan, and Syria, Gar thought. "What did you do with the memo?"

He made more noises of pain and torment.

Out in the hall, an alarm went off. Residents were advised to remain in their apartments, for their own safety. The Citizens' Police had arrived.

"What did you do with the memo?" Gar demanded. She lowered the scarf from her mouth and nose, and Bill gaped. "Did you make copies of it? Did you send them to anyone else?"

In his terror, he forgot to complain and moan.

"Did you make copies?" she asked again, adjusting the angle of her gun.

"I – I didn't send them – I swear to God, I didn't send the copies anywhere –"

She stood up and shot him in the head.

Insha'Allah, the other copies would be lost forever, so long as there was a fatal bullet in Bill's memory.

She had only seconds left. She ripped off her bloodstained *abaya* and *hijab* and threw them into the incinerator under his sink, where they burst into flame and ash. Over her jeans and t-shirt, she threw on her overcoat, filtration scarf, and slouch hat once more, and flung open the door. Around the corner and down the hall, the resident's elevator was on the rise toward the 112th floor. She ran the other way, toward the service elevator, and, with her Comm-Patriot, implanted more false data and video, making the elevator believe it was about to take a contractor back downstairs.

Gar shouted, "No – no, don't shoot! Citizens' Police! Stop!"

As the resident's elevator dinged, Gar shot herself in the torso. The next few seconds were a jumble as she fell, a slave to physics and biology. When the uniformed officers of the Citizens' Police arrived, they found her curled over a burned hole in her coat. One of them jabbed at the service elevator control panel, trying to redirect the contractor who wasn't there.

"She...grabbed my gun," Gar said. "Shot me...my own gun..."

Someone said, "Call the ambulance – are you insured?" She said she wasn't. "Call HQ. Maybe they can authorize a hospital loan."

It took twelve minutes for the ambulance to arrive, on account of Hurricane Yolanda-Najjemba, which had been named after the woman executed for treason in 2037. Dr. Najjemba had spoken out against child marriages in the Hegemony. If Gar had been able to, she would have named her first born Yolanda.

Gar was feeling bored and sorry for herself when Clayton let himself in to her private room. "If it isn't the Citizens' Hero," he said. He set a small black device on the bed tray, and pressed the power button. At first, there was a high-pitched hum, but as the frequency increased, she couldn't hear any sound it made. It would provide enough distortion to prevent any auto-nurse or concierge recording their conversation. Clayton gave a nod. "Nice work. Half the district is out looking for that supposed brown radical that shot you. Forty thousand bounty, too. Maybe I should give 'em a call..."

"Is she all right?" Gar asked.

Clayton sat on the edge of her bed and leaned close. "She's still under suspicion of murder. They found proof of motive."

"Of course they did. The video in Bill's room. Who else wears a *hijab* in Northton District. They're *supposed* to suspect her of murder, so they don't suspect *me*."

Clayton shook his head. "They found evidence at *her* house."

"Stripe me. She recorded his ransom call?"

"No. More like a re-threat, no details. But he did mention the daughter by name, and alluded to all the things he was going to do to her little girl."

"Good God, what kind of a psychopath demands a *child* in exchange for secret documents?" Gar groaned.

"The kind that knows he can get away with it," Clayton said. "No one else in the Hegemony gives a shit about a brown woman and her kid, or if they do, they probably think she needs to be 'taught her place'."

"Are they going to charge her?"

"For murder? No. You can't argue with the alibi. Two dozen Citizens' Police sat and watched her at Bull's Balls all night long. They arrested her around two a.m. on some cockamamie curfew law, but her husband paid her fine and bailed her out." He put his hand on her shoulder. "Doesn't mean they won't stop trying to accuse her of being in two places at once. Good luck to them. It's enough for a shadow of a doubt. I hope. You done good, Djamila."

"There are still copies out there," Gar said.

"Where, do you know?"

She shook her head. "I made him forget where he put them."

"And in doing so, you avenged a lot of mothers and fathers, whether they know it or not," Clayton said. "News'll probably be banned from airing this, seeing as he was Citizens' Police and all, but...looks like our mutual friend wasn't his only victim. His concierge recorded it all.

106

And Qadira's daughter seems to be the only one who escaped unscathed."

"And what about the war?"

Clayton shrugged. "I wouldn't cancel your Bacheloration subscription just yet. A friend of ours talked to certain generals to advise them that they've lost the element of surprise. They'll wait until the Hegemony has been lulled into a new false sense of security – Hey..." Clayton frowned and wiped an angry tear building at the corner of her eye. "What's the matter? We won!"

"I burned my *abaya*," she said. "I had that thing for decades...only wore it twice..."

"Oh, my sweet *hajibi*...I'll buy you a new one," Clayton said.

"No," she snarled. "You'll help me keep fighting for a world where I can buy my own."

Hook, Line and Sinker
Melodie Campbell

"My name is Rod," he yelled. "Can I buy you a drink?
The throbbing beat of the sound system made it hard to hear. It was Monday night at an uptown bar, and nearly time for last call.

I smiled and pointed to the stool opposite. "Still got one. But sit down and keep me company. My date left earlier."

Rod plunked his butt down and had the courtesy to say, "My lucky day. Why?"

I shrugged. "It was one of those E-Harmony first date things. I wasn't his type." It wasn't hard to look sad.

He nodded in sympathy. "It happens."

I had been eyeing him for some time. He was a decent-looking guy, if you don't mind them short. Light brown hair, with a straight nose and regular features. But short. Good thing I'd worn flats.

This was so out of character for me, being here by my-self. But I'd seen others do it. Hooking up at the end of a night was supposed to be easy. This was a Monday, slow day. It hadn't taken much to get his attention.

I looked pretty hot, actually. Short black skirt, red hal-ter top, and plenty of eye makeup. I'm pretty stacked, so that helped. No one from work would ever recognize me.

But it seemed too good to be true. Here he was, the best looking guy still left in the place, chatting me up. And he was actually very charming. I liked how he asked ques-tions about me. So many guys just talk about themselves.

It was getting on two o'clock when he finally got to it. "So do you live around here?"

That gave me my opening.

"Not far," I said, with a shy smile. "We could go to my place. My sister is away until Wednesday. The booze is cheaper there."

He looked a little startled. Maybe I had wrecked his plan? But I could see his mind assessing this new spin.

He had a smile like Rob Lowe. "That would be nice," he said.

I was excited now, ridiculously so. I guess that probably bubbled out. But I'd never done anything like this before. I couldn't stop talking all the way to his car, which he said was parked out back. It was actually a small silver truck, one of those Japanese jobs, with a bench seat.

He held the door open for me, just like a gentleman. I strapped myself in. Before he could start the ignition, I reached into my purse. My hand came out with a small silver flask.

"One for the road?" I said.

Again, I had surprised him. Both eyebrows raised, and a wry smile crossed his face. "What is it?"

"Rum," I said. "The good stuff, high proof. I picked it up in Fort McMurray." I offered it to him.

"What were you doing in Fort McMurray?"

Rod took it from me, unscrewed the top and took a swig.

"My dad used to work for an oil company."

He turned back to me, appraising. Really, he had very nice hazel eyes.

"Cool. I've never been north of Orillia," he said. "This is an awesome flask."

"It was my Dad's. He died recently." Don't think about Dad, I told myself. He wouldn't approve of me tonight.

"I'm sorry. Mine is dead too." Rod put the key in the ignition. Nice hands, but small for a man. "So where are we going?"

"Not far. Oh my God! I forgot my jacket in the bar. Hold on a sec. I'll just run in and get it."

I pushed open the door and hopped out, leaving my purse on the seat. The night was getting colder. I dashed around the side of the building and in by the front entrance.

They were starting to close up. My jacket was there, just where I had left it, hanging on the coat rack. I grabbed it. Then I made a quick trip to the washroom. This night had made me pretty excited, and when I'm excited...well, you know. It wouldn't hurt to kill a minute or two. He wouldn't expect me to do a runner, since I had left my purse back in the truck.

I waved to the bartender on my way out. He looked weary, like he had seen it all before. Another man who wouldn't approve of me tonight.

When I got back to the truck, I went to the driver's side and opened the door. Rod was slumped against the wheel. The flask had fallen from his hand; I picked it up and re-placed the cap. Then I put it in my purse.

I pushed him over to the passenger side. "I'll drive," I said for the benefit of anyone who might be in earshot. "You've had too much to drink."

But there was no one around.

I climbed in and put the vehicle in gear. It seemed a lit-tle jerky but that could be because I had never driven a truck before. Before long, we were leaving the city lights behind us.

It was rather bizarre, but I found myself humming. Rod was out cold beside me. You can pick up that date rape drug easily in Toronto, if you know where to look. Almost as easily as you can pick up a gun.

Luckily, I knew how to get both. But I didn't need to use a gun.

I drove the pickup along the QEW to where it meets the junction, then veered right onto the 403 to Hamilton. I was starting to like this truck. It was nimble and easy to maneuver. The gas tank was nearly full. I'd checked that first, of course. No way did I want to stop for anything now.

The road to Caledonia was lonely at this time of night. I passed one other truck, before driving through Jarvis.

Parts of the Lake Erie shoreline can be pretty deserted. I'd scouted for the right spot the night before. It wasn't hard to find a vacant woodlot atop a small cliff. A small laneway led to the edge. I climbed out of the pickup, taking my jacket and purse with me. I placed them on the ground, out of the way. Then I walked back to the truck, pulled Rod over to the driver's side and positioned him, snapping the seatbelt into place

The garden tool was where I had left it, earlier in the day.

This was the tricky part. The truck was in gear with the driver door open. I stood to the side of the vehicle and reached in with the tool. Once it was positioned over the gas pedal, I shoved hard.

The wheels started to move. I just managed to pull out the tool before the pickup careened over the cliff. Lake Erie is pretty shallow, so it landed with a splash and a thud. I watched it sink into the dark waters below.

When we were kids, Dad used to take us fishing in Lake Erie by Port Dover. This was before Mom died, and he moved out to Fort McMurray. Thing is, I know a lot about catching fish.

The bar was the hook. 'Back to my place' was the line. And this was the sinker.

The Dame Was Trouble

I turned away from the lake, bent over to pick up my jacket and purse, then strode to where Emma and I had left Dad's car this morning.

My little sister Emma lives in a very small condo – one of those 400 square foot jobs in a glass tower downtown. Really, it's just a bedroom with a small efficiency kitchen and a bathroom. It was way past four in the morning, but I knew she would still be up. I used her extra key to unlock the door.

She was huddled in a corner of the overstuffed couch, nursing a mug of herbal tea. The scared-rabbit look was still on her face. I wondered how long it would take for that to fade, along with her distrust of the world in general. The scars would reach long past the nightmare of two nights ago.

"Did it go okay?" she asked. The shake in her voice was something new.

I threw my bag on the floor and nodded. Then I took off the dark brown wig and shook out my blond hair. "Just like I planned. He won't be raping any more women where he's going."

I knew from my training that few rapists ever get convicted. Bad luck for him to use Rohypnol on the sister of a cop.

Hook, line and sinker. Shame about the truck.

Parting Shot
S.G. Wong

A Crescent City Short Story

The usual Monday evening racket. Madeleine shouting for her cigarettes and a fifth of the horrid bourbon she loved so much. Her assistant scurrying away in a tangle of long limbs. Overhead, microphones and fuzzy sponges held aloft at the end of long metal rods by narrow-shouldered men in grubby trousers and stained shirts without collars. Costumers wincing as blithe actors trailed gossamer gowns across grimy plank flooring and kicked off footwear without affection nor ceremony. Makeup people flapping huge cotton pads, holding bowls of rice powder. Lighting jockeys flipping angles and switches, eyes squinting against the trails of grey smoke from pungent cigarettes hanging precariously out the corners of their mouths.

And the jabbering. Oh gods. Everyone, over-tired and twitchy, at maximum volume, desperately bolstering against another week of toil under the tyranny of Wu Studios' best director. Which meant Crescent City's best director.

My head felt like to split.

Madeleine looked around at the chaos. "Mei, get your bony little butt over here and fix this gods-damned camera, will you? It's smoking again. Where the hells are you?" She snatched the bourbon bottle from her assistant.

I walked quietly, coming upon her blind side. "What now, Madeleine?"

She startled, tilting the bottle close to spilling. Alcohol fumes hit my headache, spearing right into the backs of my eyeballs. Madeleine glared, pointing a long red-tipped finger at the expensive piece of European machinery two feet away. "The gods-damned thing is getting sticky. Miz Sam paid a helluva pile a dough for this finicky princess and I ain't gonna be the one to tell the studio's Executive Vice President it's broke." She pointed at me. "You're the supposed camera mechanic, so fix it already. We're burning money here."

I put on a neutral expression. I'd had plenty of practice hiding my anger at the usurper's name and shiny new title. Madeleine never bothered to be subtle about her support for Anna Sam.

The gangly assistant juggled the bottle lid, offered Madeleine a crystal tumbler. She poured as she pivoted toward the filming warehouse door. Private time with her bottle. Again.

"Gods damn it all to the eighteen hells." Madeleine's screech was like fingernails scraped against my brain. "I told you nothing younger than fifteen years, idiot. This is a 1929, for gods' sake. Unless I'm very much mistaken, it's still gods-damned 1938, isn't it? Do you need a bloody abacus for simple sums?" She pushed the tumbler and bottle at him. He trailed after her, fumbling the items awkwardly against his torso, hunched to cradle the heavy glass.

I glanced around, but I knew I wouldn't see Chao. His skill as a cameraman was directly proportional to his ability to disappear when things went awry.

I hefted my toolbox and trod over to the aforementioned princess.

Pulling up on the heavy metal tab, I gently maneuvered the side panel open in the dim light. I clicked on my handheld torch. The camera's innards smelled of warm metal, hot rubber, and something chemical.

"Damn it." I heaved back. Cursing again, I looked around at the milling crew, gestured to a tiny moon-faced girl in an unbleached linen tunic. "You. Yes, you. Get Mrs. Soo and find Chao. Quickly. Tell them it's life or death."

She rolled her eyes. "My ghost says you aren't the boss of us. You're just some camera fixer." She raised her chin, smirking.

I narrowed my eyes. "I don't care who pulled in favours to get you this bit part, but if you wanna grow up to be in any more films, you'd better keep your ghost's opinions to yourself."

119

She scowled, opened her mouth again.

"Now, I said. Otherwise you'll be leaving this studio in tiny, bloodied pieces. And your ghost goes poof. You got me?"

Gasping and wide-eyed, the brat stumbled back, then ran in the direction of Madeleine's office.

I stepped away from the fancy European camera, yelling at everyone to do the same. Not that those few feet would save us, if worse came to worst.

"Here. Everything's better after a cup of tea."

A mug appeared near my elbow. The hand holding it toward me had fine dark hairs and raw, big-knuckled fingers. Rolled up shirtsleeves showed muscled forearms. I gazed up the arm, to a set of broad shoulders, a thick neck, and a smiling visage. His eyes, an intriguing shade of golden brown, were crinkled at the corners, his cheeks and jaw shadowed by the beginnings of stubble. Dark blonde hair parted on the side, natural curls tamed into waves by pomade. My hands twitched. I curled them into fists.

His grin widened. "I—"

Madeleine's flat tones cut in. "You don't look like you're dying, Mei."

I pushed the tea mug into the stranger's hands, turning to face the ill-tempered director. "The wrong film's been put in this camera." She stared at me. I tamped down a sigh. "The Princess here is made to use safety film." I pointed. "This old nitrate stock could catch on fire." I gestured around us. "The whole joint'll go up in flames."

Chao appeared, his clothes immaculate as usual, hands on hips, facing Madeleine. "I loaded it up myself this morning."

"Didn't you replace the reel after lunch?" said Madeleine, eyes beady.

Chao's face reddened. "You know I did. You were all but hunched on my back."

I interrupted their imminent argument. "It could ignite at any moment. As will this entire warehouse and everyone caught inside of it."

They looked at me. I pointed at the camera. Chao turned and fiddled with the reels, pulling on the threaded film gingerly. Any friction could set it alight. I stepped closer to Madeleine.

"That film didn't thread itself," I said. "Make sure someone stays here with the camera and get Chao to get the proper film himself."

She cocked an eyebrow as she looked down at me. I blinked up at her, mild as milk. Taller types didn't faze me. I was used to it.

"I'll stay here myself," she said. I nodded, turned away.

My mystery man stood a few feet away, wearing a small smile, hands still holding the tea mug. I murmured a thank-you as I accepted the tea again.

"Looks like you saved all our necks." His voice was deep, a soft, rumbling counterpoint to the noise of the babbling crew around us.

"Just doing my job." I sipped my tea, stiff.

A single crooked tooth peeked out from behind his full bottom lip. "The famous fix-it girl."

"Just for cameras. I'm no go-fer."

"Ain't no shame in that. I'm one myself."

"Nuts. You're pulling my leg."

He chuckled, an even lower rumble. "A real Abercrombie, are ya?"

"I am *not* a know—it—all." I stopped, cheeks heating. I lowered my voice. "You just don't seem the type." Lame. I just couldn't bring myself to say he was too beautiful to be behind the camera.

"Like they say, fix-it girl, it takes all kinds." He smiled at me, slow and lazy. "Now I feel bad, making you all hot under the collar." His gaze roamed down to my neck and kept on going. He noted my grease-stained shirt, my worn dungarees, my work boots. His eyes rested again on my neck before he smiled again, sweetly this time. "Not that you're wearing a collar, are you?" he murmured.

I shoved the mug at him again, dark tea sloshing over the rim. "Thanks, I gotta be somewhere now." I grabbed my toolbox off the floor.

He grinned, shaking off tea drops from his hand. "See you around, Miz Wu." He paused a beat. "Oh, my apologies. Am I to pretend you're not the big boss's granddaughter today?"

"Nobody's pretending nothing." I tipped my chin upward. "It's just easier if everyone calls me Mei."

"Uh-huh. Well, see you around, *Mei*."

He was right. I would. And it would set my heart thumping in a way I'd never imagined.

I gave the padlock a final tug, setting the chain-link fencing rattling. If anything on this set could be called mine, it was this tiny ten-by-ten cube of storage and work space, tucked into a corner of the warehouse Madeleine had commandeered for her film. Cameras, tripods, reels, reel cases, tools, one long worktable, and a backless stool. These were the things put unequivocally in my charge. I locked them up every night and inventoried properly. Looking over at the nearest piece of machinery, I bade the princess a silent goodnight.

I whirled around at a step behind me, abruptly aware of my isolation and the late hour.

"Er, Mrs. Soo wants to speak with you." Madeleine's assistant bobbed his head, smile apologetic. "In her office."

I took a deep breath, calming my heart rate. "Sure. Lead on."

It was a short walk for a long harangue.

"Get in here, Mei. I've about had it with you and your superior attitude. You don't think I'll get another camera technician in half a heartbeat to replace you? The Wu name is NOT going to net you anything more than snickering around here, let me tell you."

Evidently, it was my fault we were another six hours over budget. My fault the gods-damned fancy pants camera from Europe was a dud. Somehow, my fault Chao ripped through a half-reel of film that was improperly threaded, a horrible end to a disappointing day's shoot.

"Let's just agree it's all my fault and call it a night, all right? I'm tired and I want to see my daughter, Madeleine."

She scowled, mouth agape mid-sentence.

I couldn't resist. "For the record, the princess is not a dud. Treat her with respect and she'll shoot you the most beautiful footage you've ever seen. And you know it."

Madeleine snorted, lit up a cigarette, no holder. Squinting into her empty glass, she sighed.

"What's going on?" I crossed my arms. "Did you enrage yet another union rep?"

She exhaled cigarette smoke in a long plume. "Maybe it's a grudge against Chao. Or you, for that matter. The Wu Studio heiress slumming it with the common labourers."

I stared at her.

She waved a hand at me. "Get out of here. Don't be late tomorrow. We start shooting at the cliffside. You'd better be here to pack up the dud and get it there in one pristine piece."

Typical. Never say a kind word, lest you bring down the wrath of the gods with your arrogance or happiness. She loved the camera, I could tell.

"Good night, Mrs. Director. Don't get too drunk." I nodded to her assistant on my way out, startling him from his hunch against the wall.

I walked through the midnight quiet, crunching over gravel and coarse sand. I knew these backlot paths blind-folded. I craned my head back and stared upward, searching for stars.

A rough hand grabbed my chin, twisting my head brutally to the left. I gasped, then cursed myself for not screaming instead. Too late.

A burning slash across my exposed neck, a hot gush down my skin, and gentle hands lowered me to the beaten gravel path. Mouth agape, I stared at my killer. My mystery man stared back at me, golden eyes now smudged holes in the night.

My heart raced, the engine of its own imminent demise. Soon enough, its beating faltered and I didn't feel anything at all.

I wish I'd said something. Cursed my fate. Screamed for help. Prayed to the gods for my daughter's future. Instead, I stared through a film of useless tears, fading with every heartbeat. My murderer watched me die, his expression unreadable.

Darkness for a while. Then I awoke.

I watch my daughter, crying into her hands.

"Darling, please don't be angry with me."

She glares to her left, unable to see that I'm sitting on the bed on her other side. "But I thought ghosts were a comfort. That's what you said."

"We are. I am. I'm here, darling, by your side."

She's quick, my Amelia. She whips her head around. Damned if she isn't glaring straight at me. "But I can't see you. Or feel you. It's not fair. First *Ba-bah*. Now you."

My eyes burn. It takes me a moment to realize I can't cry anymore. I clench my fists.

I can't manage more than a whisper. "I miss him, too." Widowed two months. Feels like yesterday.

"I know you were murdered," says Amelia, face tight. "*Pau-pau* won't talk about it, but I heard the coppers."

I blink against the searing of my eyes. No tears, but pain evidently remains. "She doesn't talk about it because it's not the business of an eleven-year-old to think on such things."

Amelia splutters, wipes her eyes. "You sound just like her."

My alarm turns to relief. She's giggling.

I discover I can still laugh.

She sighs, wiping at her nose. "It's not how I thought it'd be."

"Darling, I know. Me, neither." I long to hold her. To feel her warm and tight against me. To wrap my arms around her sharp little shoulders, feel the knobs of her spine.

Amelia looks up. "Are you sad, *Ma*?"

126

I'm tempted, damn it, so tempted to tell the truth. I answer a different question. "Only because we can't hug and cuddle anymore."

She looks thoughtful. So much like her father. Those large eyes, high cheekbones. That full lower lip. She abruptly scratches her entire head, perhaps trying to come up with an idea. Her hair, thick and coarse like mine, sticks sideways out from her braids.

"*Pau-pau*'s gonna make you redo those, you know."

She shrugs, my beautiful rebel of a girl. "I'm not afraid of her, *Ma*, not like you."

"Hey!"

Another elegant shrug. How did my baby learn such grace? It's all I can do not to howl and scream and rend things into millions of tiny pieces.

I watch my daughter struggle against the strictures of my mother's love.

"But I don't want to wear white today, *Pau-pau*. It's hard to keep clean."

"Perfect chance for you to practice then," says my mother. "We are still in mourning, young lady." She raises an eyebrow. "I'm sure your mother would tell you the same."

Oh. My cue. "Sorry, darling. Her house, her rules."

Amelia's face darkens and her mouth tightens.

127

"And stop mussing your mourning armband, please." My mother straightens out the offending strip of cloth, then smooths my daughter's hair. "Now. Weren't we talking about your lessons?"

"Yes, *Pau-pau*," says my daughter, tone flat. "You wanted to know if I understand why *Tai-guhng* bought that other little studio a few years ago when it was going bankrupt." She looks at my mother and I can see her diamond of a mind weighing the options of sass versus obedience. I've already been there, I want to tell her. But theirs is a fragile relationship.

Three weeks to the day of my death, my daughter asks me again. "What happened to the man who did this to you, *Ma*?"

"The police are looking for him."

"But someone at the studio must've known him, right? Else how'd he get in? You have to know someone to get on the list. Even *Pau-pau* waits at the gate and she's been going since she was a little girl."

I keep my voice nonchalant. "There are plenty of strangers on the lot at any time, darling. It's impossible to keep track of everyone inside."

She sighs, heavily. "I know that. But how'd he get past the gate guards?"

I silently count to ten. "Darling." I keep my tone gentle. "What's done is done. I'm here now. Let's don't go over this again."

Amelia's cheeks get ruddy. That chin. I recognize the set to it, just like her father's. "Aren't you even a little bit angry?" She screws up her face, her mouth hardening. "That stupid man stole you from me." Her lower lip trembles. She bites down on it. That's my girl. Tears are useless now.

My eyes are stinging again. "I'm a ghost now. I can't touch anything or move anything or make anything happen in the world. I'm barely more than a figment of your imagination."

Damn me, I've made her cry. What the hells am I thinking? I mouth soothing words. Cold comfort, those. Even if I were to put my arms around her, all she'd feel is cold.

Burning with rage is nothing but an expression when you're a ghost.

"Darling, this is a bad idea."

My daughter grins over her shoulder, pinpointing me by ear with effortless grace. "Only if it doesn't work."

She sits on a short wooden pillar, one of a half-dozen meant to mark off the edge of the small visitors' car lot beside the gate. "Besides, *Ma*, Darin's on duty. He likes me. I think he had a soft spot for you." She says this last bit in a lower voice. I search her face for signs of sorrow. All I see is distraction. She's craning her neck, trying to see into the car currently waiting at the gatehouse, a canary yellow roadster.

"Who are those people?" Amelia says.

I purse my lips. "That's Madeleine Soo driving, remember her? In the back is her assistant."

"And the other woman?"

"Mrs. Anna Sam." I pause. "She runs most of the studio now."

"I thought that was *Tai-guhng* and Eloise-*yee-pau* and *Pau-pau*."

I keep an even tone. "*Pau-pau* is raising you now. She was to run the studio with her sister, but Aunt Eloise has…stepped back somewhat these past years. And your great-grandfather is retiring soon." Reluctance stiffens my tongue. "He trusts Mrs. Sam."

Amelia snorted. "I can tell *you* don't."

I can't help a grin. "That's because you're a nosy little monkey." I sober quickly, speak carefully. "It's hard to see the family business in someone else's hands, that's all."

"But *Pau-pau* and *Yee-pau* are his only children and they're smart. It seems pretty natural to me." She kicks the pillar with a heel. "Why not pick you?"

Where would I start? "I suppose you'd have to ask *Tai-guhng*."

"He doesn't like me." Amelia shrugs, makes a face. "Plus, he doesn't know how smart I am."

I force a light tone. "Nobody knows how smart you are, darling. They see how beautiful you are and they stop thinking."

My girl shrugs. I'm hit with vertigo. I can see the woman she'll become, careless about her looks, intent on her

130

goals, not one to suffer fools gladly. I'm so proud my chest feels about to burst.

Or maybe that's sorrow.

"*Pau-pau* says I should pretend to be dumb because it makes others feel bad to feel stupid."

"That's one way to think about it." I don't hide my skepticism. "Does that feel right to you?"

Amelia shakes her head. "I'm just lying then, aren't I?" She straightens. "Oh look, *Ma*. She's sneaking to the commissary now." She gestures with her chin instead of pointing, puts on a bored expression.

When did my baby learn such subterfuge? And from whom?

As we watch, a woman exits the guard booth, glances around, pulls the door shut behind her, and hurries away. As soon as the woman disappears around a warehouse, Amelia boosts up to standing and strolls to the guard-house. She waves to the man inside through the cutout.

"Hi Darin." Innocence and sunshine in her high voice.

"Oh hello, Miss Wu." Darin nods, his round face friendly. "How are you today?"

"Well, thank you. And you?"

"Good, good." Darin searches behind her. "You with your grandmother?"

Amelia shrugs. "She's talking with *Tai-guhng* about something. I have a question for you."

Darin takes off his cap, smoothing his black hair down. "I'll help if I can."

"May I please see the gate log for a month ago, please?"

Darin clears his throat. "Well, I'm not so sure that's a good idea."

"Why not?" She blinks a few times. "You know me. I can be trusted. I've been coming here since I was born, practically."

He shakes his head, voice lowered. "I don't think your grandmother would approve, Miss Wu, not to mention your great-grandfather. And it's his name on the sign up there." He points to the enormous billboard erected next to the gate. "I'm sorry." To his credit, he looks genuinely apologetic.

"It's my name too," says my daughter, cool and collected. "And some day, I'll be the one running things. You oughta be sure to be on my good side."

Darin's face goes blank. "I'll keep that in mind." His face twitches, then a smirk breaks through.

Amelia stares at him. "Where's the other guard? Shouldn't she be back by now? You're not supposed to be alone in here, right? Won't you both get docked pay for that?"

Darin's smirk fades. He assesses my baby for a moment. Stony-faced, he turns away, pulls open a drawer in the filing cabinet behind the desk, and retrieves a thick black ledger. He thrusts it at my daughter.

"Don't worry," Amelia says. "Your secret's safe with me. I'll bring this back, promise."

There are any number of secluded corners on the lot and Amelia scouted them all out years ago, about as soon as she could walk. She wasn't kidding when she said as much to Darin. I returned to work after the obligatory month's confinement after giving birth, proudly carrying her on my back in an embroidered silk sling handed down through four generations of Wu babies.

Amelia sits cross-legged on the ground, back against the side of the commissary. Her pleated skirts are spread over her legs. The thick ledger is open on her lap. She reads through it, undisturbed. People here are accustomed to seeing her in odd places.

She turns the pages carefully.

"*Ma*, I can't read all of these. I don't know some of the characters. What's this name? The one next to *Keith*." She sets a grimy, slender finger against an entry for the correct date, written in haste, smudged but still legible. Her fingernail is caked with brown crud. There's a blade of sere grass on the back of her hand.

"Looks like...Yeung, I think."

She scowls. "So his name's Yeung. Keith Yeung."

I reach for patience. "Darling, there are over a dozen people down for that date. How will you track down every one of them?" I let the silence stretch. "The police have already been through this ledger."

"They musta missed something." The steel in her tone makes me smile, even as I shake my head. "Tell me true, *Ma*, do you recognize the other names?"

I look down at the ledger again, reluctant. "Yes." I rush on. "But this Keith Yeung could be someone's friend, paying a visit." I still, a sudden possibility popping into my mind. Even as I shiver at its chill implications, I keep my mouth shut. The last thing I want is my determined daughter mucking around with other hosts and worse ghosts than me. I tuck away the thought, hastily.

She points down. "Doesn't it say here, *carpentry*? Isn't that the right character?" She lays one hand flat on the crackling paper, taps her chin with a dirty finger. "Was he Chinese, *Ma*?"

I look into her hazel eyes. "Like you," I say softly. "Half and half."

She claps the ledger closed with a puff that sends the grass on her hand flying away. A fleeting expression on her smooth face, ripping my heart out. She says, "Well that's something, right? There aren't that many of us loafing around here." She squints, staring upward. The sky is washed out, flat, so bright it must sting. She says, "Even if he used a false name and lied about being a...a temporary carpenter, we could still describe him, right?"

I feel a sinking sensation in my stomach. "You're too smart for your own good."

"Better too smart than too dumb."

I'm not so sure about that anymore.

I lie to my daughter when I say I'm always at her side.

The tether that binds me is shorter when she's awake. I stretch it to its limits when she's not. In two months, I've made it nearly across the city. I've discovered distances are different in the Ether. I have no need of streets and highways, shaded lanes in the harsh sun, streetlamps at night.

Tonight, I visit Chao again, the fourth night since Amelia squirreled out the name. Chao has no ghost. I know that. He won't know I'm here, can't speak with me without one. But there's always a chance he'll have a guest with a ghost. Everyone knows Chao as the studio's worst gossip, but not everyone knows he's also got an eye for handsome young men. He must've noticed my murderer that day.

Inside the sitting room of his whitewashed brick cottage, Chao's fussing over the fireplace. Knick knacks of his travels to India and Europe stand like misshapen soldiers on top of the mantel. He turns away from the small fire he's started. I stare at the flames, a pale reflection of their heat and colour flickering in the Ether. I place my hand inside of their dancing brightness. Nothing.

"You must be new."

I whirl around. A girl stands five feet away, her black eyes flat and dull. Do my eyes look the same to her?

She cocks her head. "I'm Gloria."

"Mei. I didn't see you."

"I was lurking in the corner."

I glance around. "Your host?"

"My sister, Annabel." Gloria shrugs. "She's in the kitchen."

I nod, polite. I've not met a child ghost before.

Gloria scowls. "He's wooing her."

Despite myself, I smile at her dry tone. "How old are you?" I frown. "Sorry, that was rude."

Gloria smirks. "Definitely new."

A willowy young woman enters the living room, carrying a tray. Annabel, I guess. She wears a pale shirtwaist dress. Colours are odd for me now. I'd guess yellow dress, red belt. Her dark heels tap for a few steps before the sound is swallowed up by the thick rug.

I look from woman to ghost. "You're twins."

Gloria weighs me with her black gaze. "Usually takes longer to figure out."

"How long've you been ghosted?"

"Eleven years." An edged smile. "Just as many years as I lived."

Annabel sets down the tray, looks up. "*Jeh–jeh?*"

Gloria's lips twist. "Just making a new friend, little sister."

"You could change to match her," I say quietly. "Why don't you?"

The girl shrugs. "I did for a few years. I just don't care anymore." She lowers her voice. "She doesn't know any different."

"Something the matter, Bel?" Chao wipes his hands with a handkerchief as he sits down on the sofa. He pulls Annabel down to sit next to him.

She smiles uncertainly, perched on the edge of the soft cushions. "*Jeh–jeh* says there's another ghost here."

Chao raises an eyebrow. "Who is it?" The damned man is calm, I'll give him that.

I assess Gloria for a beat. "I'm Mei Wu and I need his help."

Gloria raises both brows at me. "Tell him Mei Wu needs his help, little sister."

Annabel complies, frowning.

"Mei?" Chao falls back against the sofa, his expression shuttered. "What do you want?"

I use the twins as my relay system. The conversation is short.

"Do you know someone named Keith Yeung?"

Chao shakes his head. "I'm sorry for what happened to you, but I don't know anything about it."

"Yeung was a go-fer on-set for Madeleine's film, or maybe a carpenter." I describe him quickly. "I need to speak with him. Will you help me?"

A long silence.

"For old times' sake. Please?"

Chao frowns slightly. "I'm sorry."

"Why? It's simple enough for you to find out who he is. Or can you not be bothered to care?"

"That's enough." Annabel's face darkens. "Goodbye, Miz Wu." The formal phrase comes next through her stiff lips. "I'm sorry for your bereavement."

Not as sorry as I am.

"What *is* this about?" asks Gloria, her young face shrewd.

"I'm searching for my killer."

She recoils.

My laugh rings bitter in my ears. "I'm not out for revenge, if that's what's scaring you."

"Will it help your host somehow?"

I think of Amelia, her anger and resolve. I shake my head. "Not in the least." I stare at Chao, his arm now wrapped protectively around Annabel's slim shoulders, his face upturned, eyes searching the room. "Tell Chao goodbye from me, would you? I won't be back."

Gloria nods. "What will you do, when you find your killer?"

"I have his name, but not his identity. I know his face, but not his motives." I hesitate. Do I dare trust this strange unnatural ghost when I couldn't trust my own daughter with my hunch? The emptiness in my chest rings. I manage a strained whisper. "I don't know him, never saw him before. There's got to be something, some*one* I'm missing from the picture."

Gloria considers me. "You think this Yeung is a host?"

I bite my lip. "Yes."

She narrows her eyes. "It's the ghost you're truly hunting, isn't it?" She pauses. "Do you want *my* help?"

I nod, calm, belying the anxiety in my belly.

"*Jeh-jeh*, please, don't get mixed up in this, whatever it is." Annabel clenches her fists, shrugging off Chao's arm. "Chao thinks it's a bad idea. We should trust him to know."

Gloria's gaze remains fixed on me. I throw a silent prayer to the gods. She gives a short nod. "I'll find you." A

138

crooked grin. "You'd best hurry along now. You new ghosts never seem to know your limits."

Another month passes. I watch my daughter flourish under my mother's rigid, structured care. Amelia learns the family business. I learn to re-imagine my clothes to whatever I please. I gain profound understanding of the meaning of *bittersweet*.

Amelia finishes her bedtime routine, slips into bed, her expression thoughtful. I wait impatiently for her to sleep, thinking of the night's wanderings ahead of me.

"*Ma*, did they force *Ba-bah* to marry you? Because of me?"

"What?" I stare at her pensive face. "No, darling."

"I've counted, *Ma*. I know how it works. I came three months after you married." She scowls.

"We married for love, darling. That's the truth."

She stares out the window. I can tell she's biting the inside of her cheek.

"Why would *Ba-bah* choose to go to jail? Why did he lie for his friend?"

I feel my insides churn. "He said he owed his friend a debt."

"Was his friend more important than us?" Her face darkens. "His friend whose name he wouldn't even tell us?"

"Darling, let's not do this again. He's gone. The choices he made don't matter anymore."

"They do to me," she mutters. She kicks the bedcovers. "It's not fair."

"That, we agree on wholeheartedly."

She pauses, but I can tell she's still thinking something over. "I'm not giving up. I'm gonna find Keith Yeung and—"

"Stop," I say. "I don't want to hear you talking like this."

"The words are in my heart even if you don't hear them, *Ma*."

"Your father was the same way and look where his choices led him."

"*I'm* not choosing a friend over my family." She slaps her bedcovers. "He was a stupid *gwai*, so stupid he got himself killed in jail." She bursts into noisy tears, curls onto her side.

"Oh darling, it's all right. Shush now, it's going to be all right." Inane mouth noises. I clench my fists. "He *was* stupid...but we loved him all the same. No matter how angry he made us." I stop just short of stroking her hair.

A change in pressure around my head and then an envelope pops into existence in my hand. It's addressed to me in elegant brushstrokes, speaking to an educated hand. Some Conjurer, I guess, paid to write it out and burn it to reach me. Something clicks in my muddled brain. Gloria. She's come through.

I slide out a sheet of paper. *8831 Heaven's Spear Way. Keith Yeung* is crossed out, *Hank Chung* written next to it. I stare at the name until my eyes feel afire.

"*Ma*?" Her voice comes low, sleepy. "You still there?"

"Yes, darling. I'm always here."

My murderer lives in a tidy two-storey house on the way to a monastery.

The moon rides low on the horizon, an enormous sphere of chill silver light. The neighbours' homes are dark. The houses and neatly kept yards, equally unprotected by wards. I detect no other ghosts. I know better.

I glide through Chung's walls that are as nothing in the Ether. I see masculine furniture in sturdy woods and plain fabrics. Spotless kitchen with nary a towel out of place. There are even flowers in a vase on the windowsill. A woman's touch, perhaps.

Upstairs, Chung sleeps alone, surrounded by dark walls, the only movement from a panel of curtain curling gently in the night air blowing in through the single window. I listen to his breathing, steady and quiet. I'm trembling with the desire to kill this man, a stranger made intimate to me against my will.

I hold tight to my rage. "Come out, Sev. I know you're here."

He's too fast for me. His arms are around me, strong, tight. Known. He kisses my cheek. I expect the roughness of his stubble. His skin is smooth as alabaster. He whispers into my ear. "I bet Hank you'd be here within a month. What took you so long?"

"Sev, let me go." I struggle against him. "Severin." His arms are a hot band around my chest and shoulders. "I want to see your face."

"I bet you do," says my husband. He squeezes me, hard, then spins me around in his embrace.

I can see his hazel eyes, large and bright. Lit from within. He grips my upper arms. I look down at his hands. Large knuckles, veins in high relief, silky fine hairs. I pull my gaze upward, trace his strong features. The sharp nose, the high cheekbones, the full lips. It hits me squarely in the stomach. This is the first time another ghost has touched me.

"I missed you, baby." That voice. It's hard to forget why I fell for him. Nights filled with minutes and hours and whispers just like this. The feel of soft sheets, warm skin, of fire in the belly.

Sev nuzzles my temple, sending a tremor down my spine. I find my voice. "What about him? Your host."

Chung's snore catches. He breathes in wetly through his teeth, rolls over, falls silent. The curtain blows inward, snaps as a sudden wind gust unfurls it.

Sev shakes his head. "Don't worry about Hank." He pulls me to him, crushing me against his chest. His fingers run through my hair, kneading my scalp.

I close my eyes, body rigid. He releases me.

I open my eyes to a different space. There is no bedroom, no house, no night breeze. Nothing but we two, inside a private pocket of Ether. Sev's dressed in his favourite fine wool trousers, leather braces, and pale blue linen shirt. He's left his collar off as usual and the sleeves are rolled up to his elbows. If it were sunny here, I know his shoes would be sparkling. What did I expect? Striped prison garb?

My eyes burn. "Why did you hide your ghosting, Sev? Is this what you owed him?"

My dead husband shakes his head, expression sad. "I'm sorry, Mei. Sorry I left you and Amelia. I thought I owed Hank something and I didn't want to be in his debt any longer." He pleads with those beautiful bright eyes. "It was gonna be two years, debt paid in full. I wasn't supposed to die in there." His face contorts. "It was murder, baby, not an accident like they said. Somebody set me up."

I frown. "Have you gone to the coppers?"

He gives a harsh laugh. "Ain't no one gonna listen to poor Hank and his felon of a ghost."

I stare at him, this gorgeous man with eyes full of light. I force myself to dwell on his betrayal.

His smile is wide, warm. "Why're you lookin' at me like that, baby? I'm apologizing, get it? You were right. I should never've chosen him over you."

I clench my fists. "It's a day late and a dollar short, Sev. As ever."

"Don't dwell on the past, Mei. What's done is done."

I flinch, recalling Amelia's face when I said the same to her. "That's convenient for you."

"Is this where you throw my words in my face?" He grins, indulgent. "I don't care. I created a new life for us. A new afterlife. Together. Don't you see?"

I watch him, wary, my mind whirling, gut churning.

The light in his gaze dims. "Don't you want this?"

I force the words past the seeming vise around my throat. "You put Chung up to it, didn't you?"

"Up to what?" His voice is tight now, thrumming, edged.

"Did you have your host *murder* me. That clear enough for you?"

A beat. "Why would I do that, dollface?"

I can see his jaw moving. He's grinding his teeth, eyes narrowed at me. The wheels are spinning, spinning, as he calculates his best move.

"You...*killed* me. You robbed Amelia of *both* her parents. And you expect me to be *happy*?"

He steps in, clasps my shoulders. His gaze is open and loving. "I don't like the way it ended between us, Mei. Before I went away." His voice, velvet again. "I couldn't think of any other way to bring us back together. Make up for our mistakes. I...I went a little mad without you. It was harsh, I see that now, but you're strong. That's one of the things I fell for." He nuzzles my hair. "Say you forgive me, baby."

I put my arms around him, run my hands over his back. He's warm, sleekly muscled. Just as I remember. I slide my hands around to his front, settle them over the middle of his chest. There used to be a heart beneath where my fin-

144

gers lie now. I used to feel its pulse, strong and steady, its beat racing against my skin, until it became my entire world and I shuddered with joy beneath him.

I look up into his eyes, those beautiful, bright hazel eyes I'll see in my daughter's face for the rest of my insubstantial existence. My voice is soft. "Forgive you for betraying your vows and taking up with Anna Sam? Is that what you mean, Sev? Or are you simply talking about murdering me?" I pull away and step back, putting my hands into the large pockets of my old work dungarees, a comfort to me now in an ephemeral world of unfamiliar things.

"Angel." He reaches for me. I move out of range. His arms fall to his side. "Mei. Please. I made a mistake. *She* was a mistake. I'm sorry."

"There were photographs, Sev." I scowl. "It was bad enough I wanted to tinker with cameras. But when I married you, Mother went out on a limb for me. She argued with Grandfather, said you were more than a third-rate *gwai* director. Said you were worthy of our family. Loyal, trustworthy." I push down the sorrow, the regret. "Those photographs. Gods damn it, Sev, don't you understand? They're proof to him. That I truly *can't* be trusted, that Mother was wrong. Grandfather already mistrusts Aunt Eloise. Anna Sam would be his natural choice to take over." I'm trembling, my voice rising. "You almost cost Amelia her legacy."

He hangs his head.

"I'm sorry you died, Sev, truly." I clench my fists, hard, in my pockets. "But it saved us from Anna Sam." I gather myself. "And I'm glad of it."

He jumps toward me, quick as a snake, reaching for my neck. My fingers close around the bundles I've secreted in my pockets for weeks now. I recall the shady little Conjurer's instructions and fling my hands outward, unraveling the cloth. Powder shoots forward, coating Sev in a shower of glittering shards.

"That's for all the months of pain, you cheating bastard."

He dissipates in patches as I watch. I feel a hardening in the cold hollow where my heart no longer beats.

The trickiest part is convincing my mother that the danger is past.

She finds a discreet Conjurer at a hefty price. We wait until Amelia is asleep. Spells are cast and we are left alone to speak, if not to meet.

"The powder dissipated him, temporarily. He's back in jail with his host until they carry out the sentence and the police wards will keep him contained. The coppers are embarrassed enough I found my own killer that they're not asking too many questions." I swallow a bitter laugh. "And Severin's right. No one believes his story."

Mother nods, serene. "So once the host is hanged, Severin will Disperse, gone forever."

"Along with any further threat of his loose lips." I rub at my chest.

"That Starke woman, the private investigator Eloise insisted on, she was thorough. She must've found all the photographs, as she promised, else Anna would have used them by now. And you destroyed them, correct? Before your passing?"

"Yes." I thrust away the memories of those images, long turned to ash, seared into my mind no matter how many times I watch them burn in my memory. Photographs of my husband laughing, embracing Anna Sam, nuzzling her ear, grinning lazily at her kisses along the nape of his neck.

"So we're safe for the time being." Mother pauses. "Mark my words, she'll try again. Her kind always do."

"We'll just have to keep a closer eye on her. There've been too many deaths..." I frown.

"No, of course not. I'm not advocating another killing. You've done enough on that front." Her expression turns pensive. "I know it's cost you dearly." A rare tentative note in her voice.

I push away memories of my marriage. "You needn't worry, Mother. I'm firmly back in the fold. Severin gave me Amelia. I honour that, for her sake." I drag up the damned photographs again, fuelling my resolve. "But he was a mistake. *Guhng-guhng* was right. Sev was worse than third-rate. I'm grateful we kept the family name."

Mother's expression clears. She gives a sage nod. "We're all guilty of youthful indiscretion."

And just like that, I am absolved. This is what I know. This is the Wu family way. If you create a problem, solve it while protecting the family reputation. Lie to everyone else, but family knows the truth. If murder is the solution, make it look an accident—and make damned sure no one can trace it back to you. That goes double if you arrange your husband's death.

Eldorado
Gail Bowen

The night Cole Elliot moved into Precious Memories I was standing in the shadows with my walker, smoking the single cigarette I allow myself each day. From the first I knew that Cole did not belong in an extended care home. Most of our residents hadn't driven in years, but Cole arrived in a sleek, 1959 Cadillac Eldorado with tailfins that glowed in the moonlight.

Cole glowed too. His snowy hair was thick; his tan was deep, and his teeth were improbably white. His step still had the spring of youth and he carried his bags into the reception area unassisted.

The next morning he arrived at breakfast wearing a periwinkle blue shirt that matched his eyes. By the time the dishes were cleared, Cole had explained his presence to everyone's satisfaction but mine.

The Dame Was Trouble

His story was simple. He was a widower who missed his wife's companionship and her cooking, so he moved into Precious Memories. I was not convinced. Intellectually, most of us had long since passed our best before date, and the meals were a succession of grayish-brown casseroles and dishes with names like Hawaiian Surprise.

I watched as Cole attached himself to Angel, the frail blonde across the hall from me. The first time I met Angel, she told me she'd been at Woodstock, then in a sweet voice she sang the Joni Mitchell song about the weekend that changed history. The next time I saw Angel, she repeated her performance note for note. Every afternoon, as Cole helped her into the passenger seat of the Eldorado, Angel was warbling *Woodstock.* Cole was singing a different song. Once as I passed them in the hall, I overheard him urging Angel to give him power of attorney.

Death is a fact of life at Precious Memories and when Angel unexpectedly made her way back to the garden, I felt a pang. Cole did not. At dinner that night, he sat with Rita Dolcetti, an ex-showgirl who had married well. The next day, Rita took Angel's place beside Cole in the Eldorado. Ten days later Rita, like Angel, passed away in her sleep.

That night when I went out for my smoke, I witnessed an odd tableau. Cole approached his Cadillac, stroked her flaring fins, inserted his key into her trunk, removed a lock box and filled it with cash.

Logic suggested that Cole was paving the way to his own city of gold with the assets of the women of Precious Memories, but I needed proof. The next morning when I dithered about needing help with my investments, Cole had me in the passenger seat of his Eldorado headed for my bank within the hour.

My investment portfolio was robust; nonetheless, Cole was concerned. He suspected I was anemic and recommended a vitamin regimen. As a retired pharmacist I immediately recognized Coles' 'vitamins' as depressants that, in combination with other drugs, could kill.

Steeling myself for the task ahead took time, but on a balmy June night, I brought along my BlackBerry to photograph Cole counting his cash. I had him nicely lined up when a cat leapt out of the bushes, straight into my walker. As the cat yowled, Cole looked at me with distaste. "I never trusted you," he said. "Secret smokers have no moral centre."

I moved my walker towards his car. "It's your word against mine," he said, slamming the trunk.

Cigarette between my lips, I removed the cap on the gas tank. Cole was too quick for me. My intention had been to blow up the Cadillac, but just as I threw my lit cigarette towards the gas tank. Cole jumped into the front seat.

The lockbox with the cash was fireproof. Cole was not. His memorial service was held at Precious Memories. We buried Cole with the ashes of his Eldorado.

The Dame Was Trouble

Daphne Disappeared
Darusha Wehm

I was sweaty, my handbag dug into my shoulder and I
wanted a cigarette. A glance at my Swatch told me it was
five after eleven which meant I was five minutes late. I
pushed the button next to the engraved sign that read
"Hanratty," rummaging in my bag for a Kleenex to mop up
my grossness while the tinny speaker crackled out a weak
"Hello."

"It's Marla Phillips," I shouted into the box. "Here for
Mrs. Hanratty." The speaker garbled something unintelli-
gible while I shoved the disgusting tissue into the bottom
of my bag, then the buzzer sounded and I heard the click
of the door unlocking. I stepped into a blast of aircon and
shivered. I looked around the foyer and sucked in my
breath. This place was gorgeous—big overstuffed taupe
sofa along one wall with a vase of fresh gladiola on a side

table that must have cost more than I took home in a month.

I eyeballed the peach wallpaper with adobe accents as I walked to the elevator. How much did a condo in this building cost? I pushed the thought to the back of my mind. The only way I'd ever live in a place like this was if I won the lottery and, since I couldn't afford a ticket, I didn't see that happening anytime soon. It wasn't easy being a sole proprietor at the best of times, and being a "lady de-tective" (lord, I hated that phrase) didn't make it any easi-er. But I was sick of making excuses to bosses who wanted to "talk about the cases" late at night in their bedrooms, so working for myself was the best solution.

Walking through the posh lobby, I wondered if it was worth it. Maybe it was a gilded cage, but I could probably get used to it. I forced myself to stop thinking about it. This was a job and, by the looks of this lobby, Hanratty could afford my fees. So I shoved my envy aside and peered into the mirror of my compact as the elevator doors closed. I wasn't likely to make the best first impression, but I pow-dered my forehead and nose and gave my lips a wipe of frosted pink before the ding and the doors opened.

The woman was trying for a Joan Collins look but hadn't quite hit the mark, facelift and dyed hair aside. Her pale lavender skirt suit with peplum jacket was doing its share of the work, though — shoulder pads nearly filled the doorway. I tried not to feel self-conscious in my best Benetton outlet store finds.

"Ms. Phillips," the woman said, her voice husky. "Come in, please."

I kept my expression neutral as I came face to face with a huge picture window with a gazillion dollar view of the harbor.

"Have a seat," she said and I tore my eyes away from the view. Everything in the room was white, glass or chrome. I felt grubby, like I shouldn't touch anything, but I perched on the white leather love seat. "Would you like anything?" she asked, looking down at me. "Coffee, Perrier?"

"No, thanks," I said. "Why don't we get to the point, Mrs. Hanratty. You called our office and said you have a problem. I think it's best you tell me what that problem is and we'll see if we can help you."

"Very well." She sat on an uncomfortable looking chrome chair only for a second then stood and walked into the spacious kitchen. She opened a drawer and extracted a package of cigarettes and an ashtray. I felt my lungs contract as she lit the cigarette and blew a plume of smoke ceilingward. I managed to keep my silence, but it was a herculean effort.

"Your ad in the yellow pages said you're bonded."

"Yes," I answered. "Do you need to see the paperwork?"

She shook her head dismissively. She drew on her smoke and looked anywhere but at me. "I'm sure this sort of thing is commonplace in your line of work, but it's new to me. I'm having a bit of difficulty knowing where to begin."

"Just start at the beginning," I said.

"The beginning," she echoed and laughed. It was a frightening sound. "And what would that be?" She looked at the half-burned cigarette in her fingers as if she'd never seen it before. "I suppose you're aware that my husband is a very wealthy man."

I nodded, even though I had no idea who her husband was. *Mister* Hanratty, I guess.

"I married young and he has since tired of me, I suppose," she said. "But he won't divorce me. Half of everything he owns is rather a lot more than my current allowance." She trailed off and stubbed the cigarette in the ashtray. The smell of it nearly drove me insane.

"So, you'd like to hire me to find some kind of dirt on him," I guessed. "So you can sue for divorce?"

She laughed again, that crackling sound like nails on a chalkboard. "Hardly," she said. "I understand there is an envelope which, should my husband get a hold of it, would allow him to get rid of me with something rather less than an adequate amount."

"I see," I said, mentally recalculating the fee I'd quote her. "Do you know what's in this envelope?"

She waved the question away with the same gesture she'd used to fan her cigarette smoke. "Papers," she said, then looked away. "Photographs," she said in a quieter voice.

"And you are looking for the return of these photos?"

"Yes," she said. "I'd like to hire you to pay off this...person and return the envelope to me."

"Are you certain the photos really exist?"

A cloud passed over her face. "I was sent an example of the merchandise along with the bill," she said. "It's real."

She believed it well enough and it wasn't my business to tell her how to spend her money. I nodded. "My fee is $250 a day, plus expenses."

"Is cash acceptable?"

"Isn't it always?"

I waited until I was around the corner of the building and out of sight of Hanratty's windows before I pulled the pack of Camel Lights out of my bag and lit one. I dragged a third of it down my lungs making my head swim. In a sec I was good again and took off down the road in my bronze Firebird. It was a warm day so I'd left the top off.

Hanratty exchanged the wad of cash now weighing down my bag for my promise to jump when she called. The whole gig would be over by the end of the week, which was soon enough for me. It'd be easy money, but I didn't really like it. I knew from experience that dealing with extortionists could be dangerous.

The Dame Was Trouble

I drove to my office and opened the tiny safe set into the wall behind the fading picture of Miami Beach. I put most of the cash in the lock box and noticed that it didn't have a lot of company. I took out my Smith & Wesson Model 64 and started cleaning the gun. While I let my body do the work I pondered the job.

Mrs. Hanratty hadn't said much more about her situation and I hadn't pressed. I'd seen it before — bored, aging trophy wife finally decides to have a little fun of her own, but the bit of fun turns around and tries to make a little cash on the deal. Too bad for Mrs. H, but she looked like the kind of lady who knew that everything came with a price. My only question was whether the guy was a pro or not. If he was, the exchange would be a piece of pie. Business was business, after all. If he was just an opportunist, though, that's when things could get tricky, which was why I was cleaning the S&W.

A couple of days later I was settled on the couch in front of the T.V., a rice cake in one hand and a New Coke and bourbon in the other. It was the closest thing to a date I'd had in as long as I could remember, watching Bruce Willis make the googly eyes while I pretended I was Cybill Shepherd, when the phone rang. Mrs. Hanratty's whisky voice trembled when she said, "Blue Lagoon Beach Motel, room 235. Eleven pm."

I switched off the T.V. "I'll be at your condo at ten to get the cash."

She hung up and I sighed. I'd have to catch the end of this episode in reruns. On my way out the door, I checked myself out in the mirror — my blonde hair was getting dark in the roots and was hanging limp in the heat. I couldn't be bothered with a comb and hairspray for a delivery gig, so I just pulled it back into a ponytail. I put my Smith and Wesson into my bag, slid into the inner pocket so it wouldn't get lost at the bottom if I actually needed the thing.

Hanratty was dressed in another power suit. She waved me in to the condo and I couldn't help but gaze out at the lights of the harbour. I turned away and caught a glimpse of a fat envelope on the kitchen's butcher block counter.

"That it?" I asked.

Mrs. Hanratty nodded. "Five thousand dollars in twenties," she said. "I'm expecting a package; photos, documents, negatives."

"Do you want to me to confirm that it's all there before I leave?"

"No," she said quickly, her voice rising. She checked herself and repeated, more quietly, "no, that won't be necessary."

"I can't be responsible if you get stiffed. And I have to tell you, a lot of these guys realize the potential for an ongoing relationship, if you catch my drift."

"Yes," she said, but it didn't sound like she really took me seriously. She picked up the envelope and handed it to me. It was as much a dismissal as if she'd said, "Off you go now, Marla."

"I'll be back around midnight," I said, taking the cash. "If everything goes well." I looked her in the eye. "If you don't hear from me by morning, call the cops."

"I can't go to the police — " she started and I cut her off.

"You don't have to tell them anything about the photos or the money. Just an anonymous tip that something's funny in room 235 at the Blue Lagoon. It's not likely, just a precaution." I gave her a hard look. She looked away but nodded ever so slightly.

"Fine," she said. "See you soon."

There were only a half dozen cars in the lot at the Blue Lagoon, but I parked behind the dumpster anyway. It was a good ways to walk to the stairs up to the second floor, but the dumpster was right under the door to room 235. I wanted a few minutes to check out the scene before anyone in the room knew I was here. I silently climbed out over the car door, a trick I'd perfected after a door slam gave me away on a stakeout back in my days with the D.A.'s office. My Adidas made no sound on the pavement as I stuck to the shadows and kept my eye on room 235.

I wasn't expecting there to be more than one person in the room, and I nearly jumped out of my skin when I heard the voices through the open window. There were at least two different people talking and while I couldn't make out what they were saying, they were loud enough to make it clear that it wasn't a friendly chat. I jumped behind a beat-up old RAM van to hide from whoever was exiting the motel room. I peered out from under the bottom of the van. After the patter of feet on stairs, a pair of sneakers sprinted across the parking lot, skinny dark brown legs coming out of the shoes. Gravel crunched behind me and I wheeled around, when a sharp crack of pain exploded in my head, then the world went completely black.

Your everyday scuzzball thinks twice about hitting a woman, which is usually enough time for me to get in a quick one-two with the old judo. The really bad guys don't give a damn, though, so this wasn't the first time I'd been knocked out. I sure didn't care for it much.

I'd been out for a while and the raging headache and bad feeling in my stomach told me everything else I was going to learn lying on the pavement behind the van. The bad feeling was only partly from the headache and I slowly and carefully picked myself up.

I checked for my bag and was surprised to see it still there — even more surprised to find that everything was still in it. The smart move now was to go home; maybe with a stop at an ER first to check my noggin. I knew that there was not a chance in hell that the meet was going to happen as planned. I knew that I should call on Hanratty, return the blackmail money and be done with this case. I knew all those things, but my feet still walked over to the stairs and climbed up to the second floor of the Blue Lagoon Motel.

Door 235 was ajar and I opened it with my toe. No one home, and it looked like the place had been gone over thoroughly before everyone cleared out. Still, I had to look.

The bathroom had been used since the maid had been last and the bed had been roughly sat on, but that was it. I figured the bed was already messed up, it wouldn't hurt anything by having a bit of a lie down. My head throbbed a disco rhythm that I hoped would go the way of the electric boogaloo soon. I closed my eyes, grateful that whoever conked me on the noodle was more interested in getting away than getting a look at my bag. At least I still had Hanratty's money.

I allowed myself a few minutes luxury lying on the messed up bed, but knew it was time to book it out of there. I grunted as I rolled over, trying to get up without making the throb in my head any worse when a flash of gold caught my eye.

Between the bed and the particleboard nightstand where you'd never be able to see it standing up, was the flash of reflection from the overhead bulb. I reached down, carefully and pulled out a fancy embossed business

card. *Dressler Lyons, Attorneys at Law.* My meeting partner must have dropped it before taking off. I grunted and
slipped the card in my jeans pocket. Maybe I wouldn't give
up on this case quite yet.

I called Hanratty as soon as I got back to my apartment. Well, first I washed a handful of aspirin down with
what was left of my rye and Coke, refilled the glass then
wrapped a bag of frozen peas in a towel and stuck it on
the blossoming goose egg on my head. Then I lay down on
the couch, smoked a cigarette and drank half of my drink.
Then I called Hanratty. It was quarter to one in the morning, but she sounded like I hadn't woken her.

I led off with the fact that I still had her cash, then told
her an abridged account of my night.

"You're sure the papers weren't there?" she asked, her
voice tinged with hysteria. "You searched everywhere?"

"Lady, it's a cheap motel room," I said, "it's a little light
on hiding places. They'd cleaned it out, I'm telling you."

She made a noise that sounded somewhere between
disbelief and disgust and I waited. "They?" she asked, finally.

"Yeah," I said. "There were at least two of them and
they weren't getting along that well. I saw one of them
running off when the other one coshed me in the parking
lot." I'd also slipped the night clerk a twenty to let me
glance at the register and I'd seen that "John Smith" had

163

paid cash for a double, but I wasn't going to bother asking if Hanratty knew any Smiths.

"I don't understand," she said, but she wasn't talking to me. She took a breath and went on as if she'd never said anything. "There's a bonus in it for you if you can track them down."

I probably shouldn't have been surprised when she didn't express any concern for my well-being, but I can't say it didn't piss me off. If it weren't for the business card in my pocket coupled with Hanratty's promise of more cash, I'd have called it quits right then and there. But quitting wouldn't help my headache any, and the rent still wanted paying — at this stage, I would milk this case for all it was worth.

"I've got a couple of ideas," I said, "I'll talk to you again tomorrow." I hung up just in time as the room took a turn to the side. I stumbled to my bed and passed out for several hours.

According to the fancy card, Dressler Lyons had a suite in midtown. The address suggested it could be a nice set of digs in a new office tower or a one-room wonder in a scary walkup. The gold on the card suggested the former, so I guessed it was the latter. It's a lot cheaper to get embossed business cards than it is to get a fancy office with staff.

I pulled up to the address and left the Firebird on the street. I looked around and assessed the neighborhood. I wagered that I'd still have my hubcaps when I got away from Dressler Lyons, but it wasn't a sure bet. I walked into the building, which had seen better days, and eyed the directory. Dressler Lyons was listed along with a publishing company that was probably a porno outfit and some fellow dealing in stamps and rare coins. It was that kind of building.

I took the stairs up to the second floor and walked down the hall to a door marked Dressler Lyons. I knocked and said "hello" a couple of times, but nothing happened except a head poked out from a couple of doors down.

"You got an appointment?" the guy said. He was an ancient geezer; exactly how old I couldn't tell. Maybe a well preserved seventy or a hard-living forty. Old, whichever way.

"Are you with the lawyers?"

He wheezed a laugh. "I ain't no shyster, lady. I'd rather live on cat food than be a lawyer. Crooks, the lot of 'em."

I nodded. "You don't get along with the neighbors, then?"

He leaned up against the jamb. "They's all right," he said. "Family law, you know. Not like they're defending murderers or anything. Just divorces and kids stuff, I guess." He eyed me uncomfortably. "Getting rid of your old man, are you, honey?"

I fought the urge to roll my eyes. "You know when someone will be in?"

The old guy shook his head, a cloud of dandruff forming around his hair. "They's only here when they got an appointment. You gotta call 'em first."

My head hurt again and I wanted out of there and away from this guy. "Thanks," I said and turned toward the stairwell.

"Welcome," he said. "You should get a divorce," he said as I walked away. "Nice looking lady like you ought to be available, you know what I mean?"

I didn't bother turning back.

I sat in the Firebird but didn't start the engine. Family law? What did that have to do with adultery and blackmail? Now that I thought about it, plenty, but not usually from the blackmailer's side of things. Did Hanratty's boytoy need a divorce lawyer? It was possible enough. No reason he couldn't be unhappily married himself.

It didn't feel right, though. There was some part of the story I was missing. Last night's blow to the head might have dislodged something important. I fired up the car and peeled out on to the street. Time to let my fingers do a little walking.

I sat at my desk, the phone lodged between my shoulder and my ear. It wasn't comfortable, but I needed at least two hands to work the pencil and pad, cigarette and coffee cup I had going at the same time.

"Dressler and Lyons, Family Law," a nasal-toned female voice said, sounding as bored as I would be if I were a receptionist at a down-at-heel law office.

"Hi," I said, putting on my dumb broad voice, "uh, I'm not sure if you can help me. I need a lawyer for a, uh, private matter. What kind of work does Dressler Lyons do?"

"Family Law," the nose said.

"I don't know much about this kind of thing. Can you give me an example?"

The nose sighed — an impressive trick. She drawled on as if reading from a promotional brochure. "We have over 25 years of experience with all kinds of domestic legal situations — divorce, pre-nuptial agreements, adoptions, paternity suits, juvenile criminal law, child support and alimony. I'm sure we can meet your needs. Can I set up an appointment with one of our attorneys?"

"Let me think it over." I dropped the phone into its cradle. Time to pay a visit to my favorite piece of eye-candy after Remington Steele.

"Hey, Sam," I half-whispered to the long, cool drink of water behind the reference desk. Sam had been my buddy since my days in the D.A.'s office and he flashed me a toothpaste-commercial quality smile as I leaned over the desk.

"Marla," he said, not whispering even a little. "What brings you down to my dungeon?"

167

"I need to look through the society pages of the Times for a while."

He rolled his big brown eyes and guided me to the door marked *Library Staff Only.* I watched him walk away as long as I could before following.

"I don't know how you can do that job," he said, sashaying toward the stacks of microfiche that held old copies of the local paper. "It's nothing but the most boring research in the world or sitting in a hot car drinking cold coffee and watching windows."

"Don't forget the occasional highlight of getting beaten up by thugs."

"That is not a selling point, Marla."

"It pays the bills, Sam," I said, and slipped into the carrell with a fistful of microfiche.

"Hrph," he grunted but he refrained from maligning my chosen profession any more. "You let me know if you need anything, honey," he said as he walked back to his desk.

"I can think of plenty of things," I said under my breath as I watched his derrière, then fired up the big fiche machine and settled in for a long shift.

It took most of the day, but eventually I got what I needed. Before she was Mrs. Hanratty, she was Daphne Beardsley. A real babe, too, from what I could get from the grainy photos in the paper. Proper society girl, débutante ball and everything, and Hanratty the Mister snapped her up when she was only twenty.

I'd noticed an unusual gap in her appearances in the society pages in the years before her wedding. She'd had her coming out, then there was about seven months of parties, attendance at the horse races, the christening of some rich guy's yacht. Miss Beardsley's photo had appeared along with a half dozen other girls.

Then Daphne disappeared.

The parties still happened in her absence, her girlfriends were all frocked up and smiling, but no Miss Beardsley.

About a year later the engagement was announced with a tastefully expensive color spread. Miss Beardsley became Mrs. Hanratty and lost her chance to drop out, become a hippy and experience the summer of love.

Or did she?

I spent the next day buttering up another old buddy at the Vital Stats office and after an expensive lunch, too much flattery and a cash-filled handshake, I walked away with a couple of barely readable photostats. After that, it was a walk in the park.

Millard Park, to be specific.

It wasn't a bad neighborhood exactly, just one where I stuck out in a way that was somewhat uncomfortable. I was used to being conspicuous, so I just kept my head up and made a beeline for 156 Ryllette Dr. It was a nice enough looking house — freshly painted, the tiny lawn green and short. I walked up the front porch and opened the screen door. I knocked on the sturdy wooden door and waited.

I didn't recognize the man who opened the door but I knew who he was. Two hundred pounds of mostly muscle, a foot taller than me and skin the color of expensive chocolate. I pointed the business end of my Smith and Wesson at his gut. "Sorry about this," I said, indicating my pistol, "but I don't really want to get bopped on the head twice in one week."

"What the — " he began, but I took a step toward him and he involuntarily took one back. Soon we were both in the small vestibule of the house.

"I think we need to have a talk about your brother."

"You don't really know who's blackmailing you, do you?" I asked. This time I had a Camel Light burning between my fingers. I didn't have to impress Mrs. Hanratty anymore.

"I —" Hanratty looked away, then shook her head. "No. The only people who know…" Her voice trailed off again and I fancied I saw a shine in her eyes. It must have just been a trick of the light; she was too much of hard one to choke up this easily.

As it turned out, I'd been wrong about the affair angle. Once in a while, the clients surprise you.

"You find it hard to believe that it's your own son, right?"

Her head flicked back to me, anger writ large on her face.

"What do you know about it?" she said, lighting her own cigarette.

"Quite a lot," I answered. "And you're right, it isn't your son blackmailing you. It's his brother."

She was silent and I couldn't read her face. I pulled a fat envelope out of my bag and dropped it on the table. "Your parents arranged a private adoption into a good home. An *appropriate* home." I watched her eyes, but they didn't betray anything. "You were only eighteen — I'm sure it must have seemed the best idea at the time. What do I know?" I said, stubbing out my cigarette. "It probably was the right thing."

Hanratty made a noise low in her throat, which she covered by taking a swallow from her drink. Neat whisky by the looks of it. I could have used one of my own, but I just kept talking. I wanted to get this over with. It was hard to like anyone in this case, except the poor kid at its heart.

"They had another child, you know," I went on. "Another boy, few years older. Shawn. They never told him that his brother was adopted. He stumbled on the documents while he was cleaning out their mom's house. She's sick, gone into a home. Anyway, he found the birth certificate and adoption papers and thought that you might have money. The home costs a fair bit, apparently."

"But," Hanratty said, dragging deeply off her cigarette, "how did he track me down?" She didn't notice as the cigarette's ash dropped on to her blouse.

"I checked him out," I said. "He did a stint in prison a few years back; got himself a degree while he was inside. He knows how to work the microfiche machines at the library as well as I do."

She nodded but I wasn't sure that she heard. She picked up the papers and rifled through them. "Where is it?" she said, her voice rising with panic. "He sent me a copy of a photo; it's not here."

"Yeah," I said. "That was what was going on at the motel when I got there. Jason — they named your son Jason after the adoption — he figured out what his brother was up to and went to go get the photo back. The one with him in your arms, just a few hours old. I guess it meant something to the kid. Anyway, they argued, there was a bit of a struggle and Jason got away with the picture. He's the one I saw running away. Shawn figured the photo was the lynchpin of the deal and was taking off after the boy when he spotted me. He says he panicked, and that's why he hit me, but I'm not so sure. He got put away for beating on his girlfriend. Anyway, I gave him most of the money and got most of the package."

I dropped a bunch of twenties on top of the documents. "Jason has the photo, Mrs. Hanratty. If you want it back I have a number where he can be reached." I held out a piece of paper torn from my notebook. She caught my eye and then looked away. I don't know what was on her face — shame, regret or plain old anger at not getting her way. I dropped the phone number on the table. "I'll send you a bill," I said.

As I turned my back on that gazillion dollar view and walked out of her condo I couldn't think of a single thing that would make me want to trade places with the woman that used to be Daphne Beardsley.

Rozotica
R.M. Greenaway

Summer of '73

There's a sudden bloom of light in the coffee shop. It's the glass door catching the mixed sun and cloud of a Vancouver midday and pulling it in. The door closes, but the room remains a tad brighter for Heather, and re-tinted in shades of rose, because Jarvis Milestone has arrived. He comes jaunting over to her counter, his dark hair wild and tangled, his words preceding him. *"Heather baby,"* he says. *"What a morning! Dark Side of the Moon, man. It's out!"*

Whatever that means. Heather is already dashing coffee into his cup, saying, "You're taller today."

In some abstract way, she likes his style. He goes for satin and corduroy, vests and bell-bottoms, purple and gold, peace buttons and sunglasses, the lenses so black she can't imagine how he doesn't walk into walls. The shades are off now, and he shows off his clumpy new boots, just scored from the Army & Navy. Being an economist of sorts, he tells her the discount along with the bottom line.

Milestone is Heather's diametric opposite. She's plain, and he's fancy. He thinks the world is a wonderful place. Heather knows it's not. She's a dedicated pot scrubber, while he flits about the city, with no fixed address, and somehow pulls money out of air.

He goes on to tell her of a new device on the horizon, a phone that doesn't need wires, kind of like those two-way radios, but better. He shows her a newspaper clipping of a guy holding a box the size of a toaster. "Someday everyone's going to have one."

"Not me," she tells him. "Wouldn't want to haul that around, would I?"

"They're going to get smaller."

"Still."

Heather knows Milestone could be her antidote, except like all good things, he's bound to stop showing up one day, and then the rose-tint would be gone, and she would be back to square one. Sometimes it's best not to leave square one to start with.

"Heather," he says. "Come here."

She's in the middle of serving a lady toast and tea. When she's done she goes back to Milestone and listens. He beckons for her to lean closer. She leans closer and he says, "Electronics, baby. That's where it's at. I'm going to make us very rich, and we're going to fly away to Puerto Vallarta, or Cuba, or wherever you want, and sit in the sun for the rest of our lives."

His eyes sparkle, like they sparkle every time he comes up with a new scheme -- or even when he doesn't.

"Oh, good," she says. She's trying to imagine sitting in the sun for the rest of her life, and thinking she'd rather be here, in the rain, serving soup.

He reads her mind and says, "That idea bores you, does it?"

"My meaning of life is small enough as it is, Milestone," she tells him.

"It's in your hands to change the meaning of life, Heather," he says. "And when I said sit in the sun, I meant it metaphorically."

"All right. So how will you go about this?"

"We," he corrects. "You're the key. It's your face. It's perfect."

Her face, she knows, is far from perfect. It's roundish, pale, freckly. Her eyes are oddly wideset, her nose and mouth small. Her fawn hair is cut so short the scalp shows. She looks like a baby doll, but not in a good way.

"You're kind of cold and synthetic looking," he says, and he eyes her like an artist eyes an interesting vista. It's only the truth, but she's hurt all the same. "And you don't move much," he goes on, rubbing salt in her wound. "I've watched you, on your breaks. You sit in the corner and look at the wall. It's like you're powered down completely. Zero juice."

"Thanks," she says, with ice.

"No, babe, I mean that in a good way. It's *magical.* You want to hear my idea or not?"

"Not," she says, but only because more customers are cluttering up her section. She goes to take and place orders, clear dishes, expecting Milestone will run out of vim in the meantime and disappear. But he doesn't. Fifteen minutes later he's still there.

Already his insult has lost its sting. One good thing about being a pessimist, she knows, it comes with a high pain threshold. She leans her elbows to gaze at him eye to eye and listen to his idea.

"So that's it," he says, when he's done. "What d'you think?"

Lunch hour has come and gone, and the place is quieter now. Heather begins to buff juice glasses. "That's the weirdest thing I've ever heard, and never in a million years am I going along with it, Milestone. Find someone else."

He's not discouraged. He changes the subject. He talks about Cuba. She only knows Cuba for its conflict with the USA and its cigars and its rum, but Milestone goes on to give it dimension. He paints a whole different world, paints its people, and finally paints her and him within those hot, crooked, colourful streets, walking, talking, exploring. Heather guesses he pulled it all from a travel mag.

"I'm just fine here," she tells him. She doesn't like hope. Hope makes her nervous.

Outside it's begun to rain. People everywhere, looking displaced. Traffic pushes through jaywalkers. The downtown crazies wander and shout about God and doom.

She says again, "I'm fine."

"Bullshit," he says, and she has to admit, he's got a point.

The day arrives. Milestone and Heather look like very different people since their over-the-counter discussion. They've become closer, and she is no longer a virgin. Yesterday they had dress-rehearsed the sting, as he calls it, and today it will be the real thing. They're scrubbed and groomed and fortified with just one swig of vodka each.

Milestone has invested impressive time and money into the scheme. He's rented a room on the fourth floor of a large three-star motor hotel in Burnaby. He's got seven guys signed up, only about half what he had hoped for, but he's not fazed. Heather is inspecting the list, her faith receding, her second thoughts growing exponentially. She refers to the names on the list not as "the attendees", as he does, but "the weirdos".

"They've got to be, to sign up for something like this."

"No," he scolds. "They're not weirdos. They're potential stakeholders. They'll be wanting their own franchises, that's all. Businessmen sussing out an untapped corner of the explosive new electronics market."

He's got the talk down pat, at least. And the setting too. Folding chairs, overhead projector, even a stack of brochures. He's also got a shipping box big enough that a small human could huddle inside. The box is taped up and weighty, and it's here, he's told her, because although the

179

product will be delivered fully assembled and operational, somebody's bound to want to see the parts. The only part in the box is under the taped-down top flap, an eyeless white face shrink-wrapped and nestled in Styrofoam chips. Heather believes it's a manikin head he's either stolen or found. On the exterior of the box he has stuck a bunch of official-looking labels, strings of numbers and some Asian indecipherables, along with the English words: "Assembly required."

"This is going to be a disaster," she tells him, not to be a downer, but because she's got a really bad feeling. "They're going to want to see more. The gears and whatever."

"No, they won't," he tells her. "Trust me." And really, she's got no choice but do just that.

In half an hour the stakeholders will start arriving. She sits in front of the mirror, eyeglasses removed, and puts on the wig. It's platinum, wispy, lovely, and she's an instant stranger in the glass. She knows little about cosmetics, so Milestone helps out. Foundation disappears her freckles. Powder evens out the tones, removes shine, and sets the cream. Lipstick, lip pencil, eyeliner, brow pencil, mascara.

When it's done, Heather admires the girl in the mirror, her dark eyes, her rosebud mouth, her smooth, unfreckled skin.

"Wow," Milestone is saying, reflected at her back. "Even better than yesterday." But there's some sadness in his eyes. "I already miss you."

She misses him too, because she's not the only one in disguise. He's got a square haircut, close shave and cheap suit. He looks like a Bible salesman, or even scarier, like a man about to stand trial. A man in trouble. A man leading himself to the gallows.

She tries to banish the thought as he helps to attach her only other removable parts, the recharge warning light at the nape of her neck -- it's set to a slow blink as a precaution; if anything goes wrong, he can claim her batteries have drained. He also attaches the rubberized wrists over her real skin and bone. They add only a slight bulge to her natural lines. He wants the men to see she has fine, fine seams, and barely visible under the silky skin, like blue gems in a deep river, the faintest evidence of circuitry. He wants them to know she is as real as can be.

"Men *love* gadgets," Milestone tells his audience, as Heather waits behind the screen. "*Almost* as much as men love *girls*. Right?" Finger snap. "What if we offered customers the best of both worlds? One word. *Goldmine*."

She hears a rumble of polite interest. The men haven't warmed up yet, even with all the wine, cheese and crackers they've sucked up in the prelude to the presentation. She can spy them through a crack in the screen. They're watching Milestone, and some are at least pretending to take notes. He has been flattering them for the last half hour. They're sharks, pioneers, empire builders.

181

Heather knows they're not. So does Milestone, and so do they. What they are is a pack of lonely lechers hoping to take home some version of love they can cope with. It's mentioned in his promo material, the chance to obtain at below cost one of the first-off-the-line deluxe models, to test drive, so to speak. Of course the bottom line -- the actual price -- isn't set out, and so they're hooked, not sure what to expect. Just another overpriced blow-up doll, they're thinking. They're waiting, with bated breath, for the demo, which of course is Heather, but that's not till the end of the spiel.

What will they get in the end, if they pay up? Not even a balloon in a box. What they'll get is a long wait, no delivery, and a hole in their bank account, that's what.

"It's cruel," Heather had told Milestone during yesterday's rehearsal.

"It'll teach 'em to grow some brains," was his answer. "These dudes are all made of money, Heather. It's pocket change to them. Don't waste your pity on 'em. The beauty is, they're not going to run to the cops when all is said and done. They'll just duck their heads and pray to God nobody ever finds out how they got duped."

But maybe she's just another dupe. These guys she's watching through the crack don't look like they're made of money. They look middle-class, at best. They look embarrassed, semi-hopeful, semi-desperate. She wishes she could call the whole thing off, but Milestone goes on pitching. "The world is a lonely place these days," he says. "Men have powerful, primal needs that modern women aren't so willing to meet. Am I right? Women have better things to do with their time, God bless them. Well, what's been the solution to date? This."

A picture goes up on the screen, the very thing they're expecting to get for their money. It's an awful photograph of a mail-order inflatable girlfriend, gory red sucker-fish mouth open to accept whatever is put in it. There is a lot of laughter in the room, a bunch of men pretending they're not attracted to the idea of ultimate submission. They're chuckling to fool themselves, to fool Milestone, to fool each other.

Milestone says, "Yet men fall for it all the time. And you've seen the ads, right? Sexy girl wrapped around a happy guy. Hopeful customer sees the ad, sends in his ten bucks, and gets *this* in the mail. I'm here to assure you our product is the opposite end of the spectrum. Our girls are not only good as the real thing, but better. How's that possible? Japan, that's how."

He goes on to introduce his brilliant business partner and good friend, Vincent Latimer, who has spent half his life working and studying in Japan, and Latimer is pictured on the screen now, frizzy haired, wearing a lab coat and smiling at the camera, flanked by Asian gentleman.

Latimer is the fictitious tech department of Milestone's fictitious start-up company. Regrettably he can't be here tonight, as he's back in Tokyo nailing down orders for the many specialized components needed for the product.

Heather notices one man in the back of the room, a hard-nosed looking guy who makes her nervous. She thinks about everything that can go wrong: mob anger, a severe beating, quite possibly a paddy wagon followed by a long indictment.

But Milestone has assured her that all will go tickety-boo. Part of his safeguard is clipped to his belt, a genuine but dysfunctional walkie-talkie he's discovered while dumpster-diving. Not just a great prop to lend credibility to this incredibly high-stakes prototype unveiling, but protection should things go south. If things should, which they won't, he'll simply make the moves of calling up his two fictitious security guys from the bar downstairs. Heather has pointed out that if the stakeholders see through the main act, then the sideshow of walkie-talkies and security guys would have also gone south.

But maybe she worries too much. So far these men seem to have nothing but respect for Milestone as he goes spinning the intricate background of his product. Japan is light years ahead in robotics, technology it guards jealously, but Latimer has brought some of those secrets home. "With Vince's technical genius and my business acumen, we're set to begin production..." Milestone says. "Of...this!"

A picture of Heather in her getup goes up on the screen. She's sitting demurely on a bed, smiling somewhat stiffly at the camera, priming the men for what's to come.

"State-of-the-art *gadget girls,*" Milestone says, with glee. "They don't just lay there and slowly deflate, oh no. They'll walk, talk, hold your hand. They'll respond to voice commands, and even engage in conversation. Take 'em to the bar, show 'em off to your friends. Put these on the market today and they'll be gone before you can finish flipping the open sign on your door. Here's how you can help make these dream girls come true..."

He goes into his pitch. It's all about timing, when it comes to hitting the market with a hot new commodity like this. Supply, demand, infrastructure, all so critical to success. These lucky men have the chance not only to get in on the ground floor, but take home one first-off-the-line product, and at far below cost.

"Why? Because you'll be our testers, so to speak. Any problems, you'll report to us so we can fix them before we go public. Now, as I've mentioned in my material, right now all we have is one prototype, which you're about to see in action, and ten in the box, ready to assemble. What we don't have are the funds to power up the factory. And that's why we're here tonight, guys, to beeline into phase 2."

Heather doubts these men know any more about production lines or stocks than she does, but they're looking half sold. She notices the scary man in the back is sold a hundred percent. He's intense, greedy, single-minded. She knows the type. She gets them at the coffee shop often enough. Dead souls. She's thinking, *here's where it all comes undone.*

Milestone moves from talk of riches to technical flimflam, and then onto fiscal minutia, skimming through the slides to prove he's no liar. There are charts, diagnostics, balance sheets, to pull them all on the same page of self-delusion. And finally, the moment they've all been waiting for.

"So, without further ado," he says, "Here she is, Proto-type Z505, but you can call her *Rozotica!*"

It's Heather's cue. Out she goes in her sexy camisole, her short-shorts, her strappy heels that she's learned to walk in with a slightly jerky grace that only enhances the automaton effect. The men are silent, watching her. A few clap their hands, but most look crestfallen, she notices. She's expecting a mass roar of outrage followed by thrown objects.

Doesn't happen, because Milestone goes about pulling the wool as only he knows how.

Over the next half hour she watches grim silence turn to cheers and enthusiasm. She relaxes, even enjoys her-self. Her job is not hard. Be fairly still, unless spoken to. React to commands in a smoothly oiled way. Serve drinks, make binary code conversation. Let a bunch of strangers touch her wig, feel her hands. They inspect her seams, stare at her circuitry, are wowed. Milestone monitors the activity. *Careful with the merchandise there, dude! No, you can't see under her skirt. This is a prospective shareholders' meeting, not a peep-show.*

He allows one Romeo to sweep Heather around in a bit of a tango-like dance, to show off her mobility. She doesn't do so well, as all she's known since leaving school halfway through grade 10 is waitressing. Milestone explains her awkwardness, saying the technology is still in its infancy. Within this decade we'll see Rozotica tango, cha-cha or whatever you program into her. Not only that, she'll be able to tell you the square root of 276 in the blink of an eye. Even debate politics with you. *May even convert you!*

The men are amused, but their minds are not on politics right now. They're looking at Heather's thighs, mostly, and she's frightened by their focus. She's trapped with wolves, and no way out, except for Milestone's promise that he's got a firearm as a last resort, a little .22, which is no doubt just another lie, like Moe and Johnny downstairs.

But in the end nothing goes wrong. The men are decent. Even the dead soul makes no trouble, standing peacefully in the background, watching. In fact the night becomes a lesson in snake-oil psychology and wishful thinking, for Heather, as Milestone performs the magic of grift. As he had explained in bed one night, "Tell people that this apple is an orange enough times, they'll see an orange. Just watch."

She watches and sees through the skulls of these men as they ogle her. All they want is to get one of these for themselves, back into the privacy of their bedrooms, where they can road-test it to their hearts' content.

There is a brief foofaraw halfway through the demo as one customer decides he's not buying it, and walks out snorting, but not before making a lunge at Heather. To rip off the wig, presumably, to get her in a chokehold and squeeze out a very human shriek. But she swivels out of reach, heart pounding, while Milestone leaps forward shouting a warning at the spoilsport, and then barks commands into his walkie-talkie, and though the skeptic may not believe in robots, he does believe in security guys, and he grabs his coat to go. On his way out he tells Milestone and Heather that they're scammers and whores. He tries to slam the door behind him but it only wheezes shut on pneumatic hinges, and the room becomes a happier place, now that the shadow of doubt is gone.

The faithful remain. Two are ready to dish out on the spot, and three want to think about it overnight. Milestone warns them again that this is a strictly time-limited offer, that he'll be touring across B.C. and Alberta in the following weeks to make his quota. The mild threat squeezes out two more sales. Heather is on standby, watching the men shake hands with the scammer and leave, one by one. She's no longer trying to convince herself that these men are made of money and this is pocket change to them. She sorely believes she has been scammed herself, and that Milestone will end up flying off to Cuba on his own.

She has bought into evil, and for nothing.

What happens next? Later, she tries to sort it out in a blurry playback.

One by one Milestone has collected the cheques, patted guys on the shoulder, said goodnight. All have departed except one, the man who makes her nervous. He's both burly and weedy -- burly body, weedy head. He's got shabby shoes but a real flash trench coat that doesn't fit with his grizzled chin. He hasn't signed a purchase agreement, but wants to hang back with Milestone and chat a bit, make small talk. About the weather, it seems. She sees that Milestone is tired but obliging.

The man's name is Fowler. After some artless talk about rain he says, "This girl of yours, she's real good, real lifelike, almost."

Milestone says, "Yeah." But flatly, because Heather's life-liked-ness is something he's been propounding for the last two hours, and what's the point of saying it again. He's run out of sparkle, not seeing profit in this stranger, Heather believes, and just wants him gone.

"But does she, you know..." Fowler says.

"Does she what?"

Fowler sniffs, looks at Heather, looks at Milestone, and says, "Does she judge?"

"Does she *what*?"

"Judge. Like, judge your performance, or your looks, or whatever. Put you down."

Maybe Milestone sees a potential sale after all. He's got his mantle back on. He also recognizes that this isn't one of those pseudo-franchise types. This one's in it for pure, hedonistic pleasure. Ergo it's time for the lounge-lizard pitch, and he says, "Her only judgment is wow, man." He's gone falsetto and is pumping his thighs a bit. "You're so fucking hard, give me more, boyfriend, ooh, ooh, right there, *yesssssss*."

He stops pumping and smiles broadly to show it's all in good fun.

The man says, "But she won't judge?"

"No," Milestone says, tired again. He's undoing his tie, signalling the night is over. "She won't judge, man. She doesn't have enough RAM for that kind of shit."

"Look, Milestone," Fowler says, finally getting to the point. He's got a greasy old wallet out, cash on display. "I can't put down what you're asking here, but I come into a bit of money last week, and here's what I got. Cash and carry, now, just for the night. It's not for me. It's for a friend. Fifty bucks, and I'll get her back to you first thing in the morning."

Milestone goes even flatter. "Sorry, dude, that's not going to happen."

"Why?" Fowler asks.

"A hundred and one reasons, but it's late, and I'm not going to get into it. Goodnight, sir. Thanks for coming out."

"Two fifty," Fowler says. "Two hundred and fifty bucks, right here, right now, and for collateral you can hold onto my watch."

He shows a watch, and it looks very Rolexy, and Heather fears Milestone will show his true colours and try to rent her out for the night. But he doesn't. He's asking Fowler to kindly leave, or he'll have to call his security guys up, and with those words something runs through Heather like a fine river of gold.

She's got no hard evidence, but just a feeling, as if it's radiating off Milestone's body like an aura. She feels for sure that he *does* like her, and that he would *never* leave for Cuba without her.

"That's your last word, huh?" Fowler asks.

"It is," Milestone says.

Fowler looks disappointed and seems about to turn and leave. Instead he pulls a gun and shoots Milestone point blank in the face.

It's surprisingly quiet, almost a puff, accompanied by a shower of red beads -- or maybe it's the shock that deafens Heather. Milestone, her first and last boyfriend, hits the rug slow-mo, like the time she dropped her grandma's precious china teapot and watched it shatter to a million pieces, delicate 24-karat gold curlicues everywhere, never to be glued back together.

In hindsight she realizes that if she had screamed or leapt back, she too would have been dead on the spot. Instead she freezes. She's looking at Fowler with dumb disbelief, and Fowler is looking down at Milestone, also with disbelief. Then he stares at the gun in his own quaking hand. Heather closes her eyes, certain that the next bullet is for her.

She opens them again when she hears Fowler moan. He's swearing at himself. Then he looks at her again, but blankly, as if she's a table or chair. "I shouldn't a done that," he says. "Oh god."

He turns to go, and Heather knows she's off the hook, that she should just stand quietly like the dummy he thinks she is, wait till he's gone. But she doesn't. Why?

She's been angry most of her life, in a vague, slow-burn way, but the death of Milestone has lit her fuse. She's raw with outrage, and what she does next is damn the torpedoes straight to hell and follow Fowler.

191

She takes Milestone's nice coat and pulls it over her flimsy garments, and she marches after the killer, down the long carpeted hotel hallway, through alternating shadow and wall-sconce light, so quiet, so hushed, so stinking of cleansers, sweat and room service. He sees her there, stops in his tracks and blinks at her. "What the...?"

She's stopped too. She tilts her head and smiles.

"Jesus, you're programmed to follow, aren't you? Come on, then."

He doesn't speak to her again. To him, she is an unfathomable mass of plastic-coated wires.

They descend in the elevator, leave Milestone's body behind, and head out into the cold, wet night.

In Fowler's car, all she's thinking about is how to kill him, and what her last words will be to his ugly, dying face. He drives through the city, to Chinatown, and parks in an alley tow-zone. He walks around to the front, Heather following, and unlocks a narrow glass door between produce shops locked up behind grills for the night. They make their way upstairs. It's an old building, badly lit and creaky, and from behind closed doors come the clicks and conversation of Mah-jongg.

Fowler lets himself into a flat at the end of the hall.

It's a small, bare apartment draped in shadows. A curtain filters out neon and lamplight. There's a central heat roar in the place, and a stale cigarette pong. What at first looks like a heap of dun-coloured pillows nestled in an armchair, to Heather's surprise, turns out to be a man. Her simple plan begins to slip sideways. The man who looks like a heap of pillows seems to be staring at the grill at the base of the wall through which air is blasting, as Heather is ushered further inside. "Hey, Bezel," Fowler greets the man. "Y'okay, buddy?"

Bezel is middle-aged and colourless. He doesn't look around, doesn't answer, only slightly nods. "There's something in there," he whispers. He seems to be referring to the ductwork, and Heather can see he's truly afraid.

"Yeah, something's in there," Fowler says. *"Dust."* It's a conversation they've had before, Heather thinks. Fowler sheds his flashy trench-coat with a sigh. He must have forgotten she's there, for when he spots her he does a double take and swears aloud. He's still clammy and shaking. It's the fallout from murdering Milestone. He's got his reactions backwards. A normal person gets clammy *before* he shoots someone in the face. The term "loose cannon" was invented for assholes like Fowler, and Heather's one meaningful act in this life will be to finish him off before he litters the street with more Milestones.

Not being a killer any more than she's a tango dancer, Heather's plan is loose-knit. Get a hold of the gun, or knife, or something heavy. Bide her time, then soon as he and she are alone together, soon as he starts to manhandle her, she'll spring whatever she's got, knife, gun, or mallet, tell him what she thinks of him, and club, spike or spatter him to death.

She eyes the place, looking for sharp or heavy objects, and all she sees in the gloom is a sloppy hill of cash on the dinette table next to Bezel. Looks like fives, tens, twenties, not neat stacks but crumpled, like used tissues, some roughly sorted into denominations, some fallen to the floor. Wasn't it in the news last week, robbery of a drug-store, two suspects, unsolved?

Fowler crouches down by Bezel and talks to him like he's a child. "Look here, man. I got this lady friend for you. So you can forget about Trudy for a while, pull yourself together."

Heather is startled. Fowler wasn't kidding when he said he wanted her for a friend. Her plan goes sideways another notch.

She's not the only startled one in the room. Bezel turns and sees her for the first time. He gives a hoarse shout. Both men are on their feet, Fowler reassuring his friend, "She ain't real, man. Take it easy. She's -- she's like this life-size fake lady," is how he puts it.

Bezel hides behind Fowler and stares past him at Heather. "Not real? What d'you mean?"

"She's like a robot. But she'll sit and talk with you, the guy I bought her off says, do anything you want."

Again Heather tilts her head and smiles, though her eyes are hot with tears and her mind is whirring. How will she kill Fowler if he offloads her on Bezel?

"She's not like Trudy," Fowler says, still talking to Bezel like he's six. "She won't put you down and call you names. She won't judge. I'm getting a beer. You want a beer?"

"No," Bezel says. He's still cringing and staring at Heather while Fowler disappears into what must be a kitchen nook. Heather wonders what she'll do if Bezel gathers his nerve and decides to take up Fowler's offer. As she watches him across the room the answer comes to her in a flash. She must *be* Rozotica, not the smiling, lash-batting handmaiden, but Bezel's worst nightmare. She winks. He stares harder, and with machinelike precision she cranks mouth and eyes open wide, wider, till they're locked in a silent roar of monster wrath, burning her cheeks with the effort and freezing Bezel's blood.

He screams. Fowler rushes back, beer can in hand, saying, "What?"

Bezel backs his spine against the wall and crawls sideways. "She made a face at me!"

Fowler looks at Heather in the shadows. She stands immobile, shrouded in Milestone's big overcoat. Her face is serene. Fowler turns on Bezel, shouting, "You got to pull yourself together, man. You got to stop seeing things. I need you back. This money won't last forever. We need to pull another job, with or without Trudy and her fucking Impala. I went out specially and got this pretty lady just for you. You know what I went through to get it? You know what I had to do?"

Of course Bezel doesn't know, and doesn't care. He's got his jacket on, stuffs some of the cash in its pockets. He squeezes past Heather like she's radioactive, says he's going for a walk and when he gets back he wants this thing gone. And then he leaves, and she's alone with Fowler.

She's pleased with herself. She's climbed into Rozotica's heart and soul. She watches her prey coldly.

The glory of her disgust is wasted on the man. He rubs at his face for a moment, looking defeated. He tells her to "stay", like she's a dog, then slopes off down the hall. But not before placing his gun on the table with the cash. He's getting naked, dropping clothes as he goes, but she knows that sex is the last thing on his mind. She hears bath water running, and her plan grows wings.

Does she know how to cock a gun? Is this the safety switch? She pushes it down, hoping she's got it right. The bathroom door is ajar. She can hear swing music. She enters barefoot and muzzle first. Fowler is sitting in a miasma of lavender scented bubbles. He looks at her as the music buzzes cheerfully from a radio on the sink counter.

She says, "You killed Milestone. Now you're dead."

The trigger isn't pulling. Fowler rises like a swamp monster and lunges. She swings the gun out of his reach but he grabs her wispy blonde wig and pulls it off. He loses balance, slithers back into his bubbles, grasps her free wrist as he goes down. She's yanked into the tub and is slamming at him with the butt of the gun. Her rubber wrist is ripped off in the struggle. He's focused on grabbing the weapon, and by necessity lets go of her arm. She backpedals to safety, feet sliding helter-skelter, but he's snagged her, got a hold of the gun and won't let go.

She has no choice but surrender the weapon and turn to flee. There's a loud bang, and she skids on the sudsy floor and sprawls against the cluttered sink counter. Beer and toothpaste and clock radio go flying. The radio hits the water with an explosive pop. Heather gains her footing and watches Fowler jitter to death.

She looks at the gun spinning on the tiles at her feet, catches a firecracker whiff. She looks at the radio, and is not sure why she unplugs it and pulls it dripping from the tub. A kneejerk reaction; if you drop something, girl, you pick it up.

There's a numbness in her back, and she's pretty sure she's been hit. She picks up the gun. In the living room, she shakes water off the radio, places it neatly on the window-sill, dries off its prongs and plugs it in. She's always been a tidier of messes. She looks around, decides it's time to go. She stuffs money into Milestone's coat pocket, to fund her flight to Cuba. She keeps the gun, in case the burnt carcass rises from death and comes after her.

She moves funny, as she leaves the apartment. Robot-like. She's on the street. She can't tell what's bathwater and what's blood dripping down her back, but doesn't care. She gets on the first bus that comes along, and she's gone.

VPD detectives figure it out. Two men have rented the apartment, friends named Fowler and Bezel. The messy

197

pile of cash, scattered like autumn leaves, proves these are the drugstore robbers they've been looking for.

Bezel is missing, along with his VW Beetle, and Fowler's dead in the tub, clearly electrocuted. There's no evidence of what did the electrocuting, but they've got that figured out too, through the brochure found folded up in the dead man's trouser pocket. The brochure ties in with a murder scene in Burnaby, where a lot of these same brochures have been found, along with a slide presentation and a whole lot of other stuff, including a loaded .22 calibre revolver, several cheques written out in large amounts, and a signup sheet of some kind. The sheet provides a list of names, guys who will need to be questioned at length.

What matters now is the brochure these detectives are looking at. The brochure is advertising a state-of-the-art female android that can walk, talk, and provide every facet of companionship imaginable.

"Amazing, though, lookit this," VPD detective #1 says, tapping the brochure, a photograph of a very realistic looking young lady sitting cross-legged on the bed and smiling at the camera. He whistles. "Amazing."

VPD detective #2 is more skeptical. "Grow up. It's a scam. What they do is take a picture of a real girl, then the delivered product turns out to be a balloon with two vital openings and a paint-on face."

"And how would you know that?" VPD #1 asks. "Anyway, clearly she was here. Eyewitnesses report him entering building with a strange-looking female."

VPD #2 has forgotten his skepticism. He says, "Clearly Fowler tried to have a bath with her, whereas it clearly says here," -- it's his turn to tap the brochure -- "*Do Not Submerge.*"

They look with some sympathy at the fried individual in the tub. The water looks oily and grey. Along with the smell of death, there's the faintest drift of lavender. There's something in the water that looks like a drowned terrier, but turns out to be a woman's blonde wig. There's also a rubbery bit of flesh-like material clutched in his fist.

"And then Bezel cleared out with what's left of her," VPD #1 says.

"Why didn't he take the loot?" VPD #2 says.

VPD #1 shakes his head at the only mysterious point in the case so far, and lights a cigarette.

Over the radio comes a report of a young female needing medical attention. She's been found in a busy penny arcade downtown, sitting by a bank of pinball machines and bleeding out. Emergency vehicles en route. Later VPD #2 checks for updates on the female, who's described as slim, Caucasian, mid-twenties, no ID, with brush-cut and bullet wound in the small of her back. He learns too that if she's not exactly DOA yet, she will be shortly.

"Shame," he says to VPD #1, who can only nod agreement. *Shame.*

Lights flicker gaily and the music is loud and lively, here in Cuba. There are people everywhere, having fun. Milestone is seated beside Heather, holding her hand. She feels good, under night skies that are dazzlingly strung with multi-coloured lights that blink and flash. No, better than good. She feels ecstatic.

"This was actually a good idea," she says, smiling as a shower of stars course across the heavens. "This was a really good idea, Milestone."

Milestone smiles and squeezes her hand, and she focuses on the stars, watching them extinguish, one by one.

Mona's Last Day
Natalie Vacha

"How does it feel, Mona?" asked Gorski, clapping Mona on the back.

Vee handed Mona a mug with a bow stuck on it, "Mona Horace! Woman of the hour!" The mug said, *I'd rather be golfing.*

Mona, grinned "Great. Feels great. I'm sorry to be leaving you degenerates, of course."

Gorski laughed. "Going to miss keeping us young 'uns in line?"

"For about twelve hours. Then I'll be on the golf course having trouble remembering your names." She punched his arm. "Anyway, you're what, four months younger than me?"

"You'll be having trouble remembering anything about this place soon enough, ya old geezer," said Vee. "But that's not your problem. All your open cases are coming to me and Gorski."

Mona's smile became a little more forced, but she laughed and said, "Well, I better be going, lots to wrap up."

Mona turned down the hall when Gorski's voice floated after her. "Why'd you have to mention her unsolved cases like that?"

Mona paused, tucked away around the corner.

"What do you mean?" she heard Vee ask.

"You know she never solved the Beau Brummell Burglar case. It's been sitting on her desk since I started here. She refuses to close it."

"Oh shit," said Vee. "Well...she could still solve it. She's got one day left till retirement."

"Shhh!" said Gorski. Gorski was notoriously superstitious, and Mona could almost see him crossing his fingers to divert the bad luck. "Don't you watch any movies?"

Mona tiptoed back to her office and shut the door before moving to the closet. Inside were a collection of dusty boxes and out-of-date manuals. A corkboard mounted to the inside of the door held a dense collection of index cards, newspaper clippings, thumbtacks, and string. A photo of a rifled jewelry counter was pinned next to a yellowing headline that read, *Brummel Burglar Eludes Police*. Mona ran her fingers over index cards with dates and times and locations scrawled on them in her own blocky handwriting. She sighed. Time to pack this all up. She unpinned a plastic baggie with a small white business card, turning it over in her hand. Later. She'd take it down later.

Mona sat down at her computer and threw the baggie on the desk. She stared at her email. She was normally the one holding court at the coffee machine. Loud voice, big gestures, taking up a lot of space.

But right now, she couldn't stand to make another golf joke. She didn't even golf. Not that that was the point. The whole day had been golf jokes. And plaques, handshakes, promises of beer calls that would never happen. She pulled a watch out of her pocket. She read the inscription and the dates done in fancy script. It didn't belong to her. It belonged to a whitehaired retiree with bifocals and an RV with a "I'm spending my kid's inheritance!" bumper sticker.

Mona threw the watch into her desk drawer. She frowned, fished it out again, and put it in one of her packing boxes where it ticked at her until she covered it with a stack of manila folders and an unopened box of tea. The overly-solicitous Admin bought her the tea at some hippy store to help her destress and "unbind her bowels." She was tense, true. But no amount of single-source Swiss herbal tea would help, even if it was handpicked by yodeling goatherds, which the box suggested but she doubted.

Mona reached for a pair of reading glasses when she heard a faint voice emanating from somewhere at the front of the station.

"I can still be out by lunch if I hurry."

She stood up and her chair rolled lazily towards the wall. She knew that voice. Manfred. Manfred Winston-Peeks. But it was her last day. She didn't need to continue this farce anymore. Mona sat down and folded her arms. She unfolded her arms. She'd been trying to tie the man to the burglaries for years. She opened, then closed, a few emails, not reading them. The burglaries were a blight on her otherwise impeccable arrest record. She went to cheapskate-vacations.com and searched for flights to Panama. She tapped a pen on her desk. Of course, she'd begged to be assigned to the case all those years ago. *Fuck it.* Old habits die hard. Mona took a deep breath, shoved the baggie in her pocket, and set off after the voice.

Manfred sat at a booking counter at the front of the station, a slight, whitehaired man. With his green suit and milkweed hair Manfred looked like he should be helping a poor tailor turn his luck around, but instead he was chatting up one of the rookie processing officers.

"Is that little French bistro still open? The one down the street? I'm famished." Manfred had to sit at the edge of his chair for his feet to touch the ground.

The rookie didn't answer, keeping his blonde head bent over his desk.

"If it is, and I sincerely hope so – the *escargots* were gorgeous. Would you care to accompany me, Officer...?"

The rookie's face turned to his computer screen with the longsuffering look of a marble saint.

"Manfred." Mona crossed her arms. "Leave the fresh blood alone."

Manfred smiled as if he'd seen an old friend. "At my age, I suppose I should give up the chase – 'I am not as I was in the reign of good Cynara,' eh?" He closed his eyes, reciting, "'I have forgot much, Cynara! Gone with the wind, flung roses, roses riotously with the throng.'" Manfred shot a sidelong glance at the rookie. The rookie's eyes were fixed on the keyboard and the clacking of the keys continued without a pause.

Another officer, dark hair in a knot above her collar, walked over and deposited some files on the desk.

"How about you, my Stygian beauty?" asked Manfred. "If you're free for lunch –"

She walked away.

Manfred sighed. "I should plead with Aphrodite to intercede with Eros." He put a hand over his heart. "Beg her son to play games with some younger man, better able to bear love's exquisite burden...ah, I quite like that." Manfred grabbed a pad and a pencil from the rookie's desk. The rookie's jaw tightened but he must have decided discretion was the better part of valour, and continued typing.

Mona considered snatching the pad from Manfred, but only craned her neck to see the paper.

Love's exquisite burden, wrote Manfred, and then folded the paper neatly in four. Tucking it in a jacket pocket he said, "Now, what can I do for you?"

Mona almost choked. "Do for me? You are in *my* station...let me guess. This is your fiftieth, no, fifty-first shoplifting charge?"

"I have not been detained. Really, Ramona, I'm surprised at you."

"You know your daughter is the only reason you don't have an arrest record as long as my arm." She shook her head. "I don't know why she keeps pulling your ass out of the fire."

"I admit there have been some misunderstandings with the security personnel in the past."

"And these misunderstandings just happen to occur at her department store?"

"The fact that Jessica is the general manager at Baudelaire's is purely coincidental I assure you. I go there because it's the only place in town you can still order a bespoke shirt. Jessica wanted to get rid of James, but I told Jessica, James is a *Master Tailor*. Which is rarer than eunuchs' whiskers these days. The man is a *genius*. To worry about cost under those circumstances would be," he waved his hands in the air, apparently so overcome with emotion he was momentarily at a loss for words. "It would be hopelessly bourgeois!"

"I'm always happy to chat about your tailor, but there's something else I wanted to talk to you about... You stealing-"

"I do not steal."

Mona pushed her breath out through her teeth.

Manfred pressed on. "I do not steal. I liberate."

Mona waved him into silence.

Manfred sniffed and crossed his arms. "Aren't you going to ask why I am here?"

206

"I'll bite."

"I've come to say goodbye to you, of course." He beamed at her.

Mona turned to the rookie. "I'm going to borrow Mr. Peeks for a minute."

"Winston-Peeks" said Manfred.

Mona took Manfred by the elbow and propelled him to one of the debriefing rooms. Vee and Gorski were inside, but cleared out when they saw who was at the door. Vee moved in for another back clap, but Gorski pushed him out the door.

"You've got a lot of nerve," said Mona in a loud voice. She shut the door.

"Ramona, please," said Manfred, giving a chair a few swipes with his handkerchief before sitting on it. "This is a momentous occasion. I wanted to give you my regards, this sort of thing has to be done in person." Manfred straightened his cufflink, smiling down at it the way most people do at babies. "Do you like the cufflinks?"

"Where did you get those?"

"I resent the implication. Do you think any of these *nouveau riche* cretins could appreciate a beautiful object the way I do?"

"Then maybe you can also appreciate that if you keep this up you are in for a lot of trouble—"

"I appreciate many things. Women. Men. Luxury. Life." He ran two fingers lightly along his tie, "and this necktie – Hermes."

"Oh?" Mona kept her face neutral.

"From the second I saw it, I had to have it. A man does crazy things when he is in love."

"With a tie?"

"A hand folded silk twill tie, yes." Manfred made some miniscule adjustments to the knot. "And I have faithfully cared for it and loved it since."

Mona's nose twitched. "You can't really believe your own bullshit."

Manfred leaned back. "I'm merely asking, should I let such a thing to go to someone else who won't appreciate it? Who would shove it in a crowded drawer, or try to pair it, God forbid, with a paisley shirt?"

Mona, who owned several paisley shirts, grunted and said, "If you won't think about Jessica, you might consider that your luck will run out one day."

Manfred shrugged. "Not everyone is made to follow the rules. Life is much more satisfying when you don't."

"You didn't come here to talk about your philosophy of thievery."

"I do not thieve. I liberate. I elevate. I –"

"Jesus. You aren't Thomas Crown, International Mystery Thief. And the Brummell Burglar,"

"Whoever he may be," said Manfred.

Mona looked at the ceiling. "Whoever he may be, he – "

"Or she," said Manfred.

Mona sighed and continued as if Manfred hadn't interrupted "must have a good reason for thinking he'll never

208

be caught, considering he was nice enough to leave literal calling cards at the scene of every crime."

Manfred smiled.

Mona grinned back with all her teeth. "I seem to remember they said, *Beau Brummell, Burglar at Large*. I can't believe the press ran with it."

"I like it, very alliterative," Manfred said.

"But the problem with the cards -"

"Embossed, weren't they?"

"Yes, they were fucking nice. The paper was so heavy you could use it as a paperweight for other paper."

Manfred smiled again.

"Of course," said Mona, with the air of someone making a simple observation. "If we could ever tie those one-of-a-kind cards to someone, we would have them for every single crime the Brummell Burglar ever committed." Mona fished the small bag out of her pocket and threw it on the table with studied nonchalance. The white rectangle inside it glowed in the low light.

Manfred looked down at it and blinked. "Well, that seems unlikely."

The two stared at each other. A siren wailed on the street outside and was gone. Another followed. Then silence.

Mona leaned her elbows on the table. "Our labs do some great work in fiber analysis. The paper was bleached in a very particular way. No store in the country carries them, they would have been ordered from England. It's as unique as a signature."

Manfred examined his cuticles.

"So if we find paper fibers all over your house we'll know you handled the cards."

Manfred peered at the card, still in its little bag.

"If someone gets charged, I have very little leeway. But if you work with me here, maybe I could convince them to go easy on you."

"If you become unpleasant I would have to get a lawyer. Merely a formality, of course," said Manfred. "Just to look out for my interests in light of this nonexistent new evidence." He feigned a yawn. "And that would all take time, wouldn't it? Even if I were arrested, which would be an egregious miscarriage of justice by the way, it would be that common looking, back-slappy detective who would bring me in." Manfred's eyes were bright as he looked straight at Mona. "I'm not sure how much satisfaction one would get from *that*."

Mona sighed. Of course there was no fiber analysis. She made the whole thing up. Given the circumstances, what had she been expecting Manfred to say? She shook her head. Sometimes she got too caught up in her own act. "Thirty years, and nothing ever stuck."

"Why should it?" said Manfred.

"Everyone must be saying that you've got a horseshoe up your ass."

"I wouldn't know about that. Everyone *is* saying that you're the unluckiest SOB that ever lived – I heard that on the way in. Probably also that you're incompetent, thirty years and nothing to show for it."

Mona glared at him. "Look at my record. Nobody has made more arrests than me. Nobody has closed more cases. I've had five commendations -" She pushed her voice louder.

"You are very proud of that, at the end of everything, aren't you?"

"I am. Damn straight I am! Why shouldn't I be?" She banged a fist on the table. "Maybe I wish I'd realized that sooner." Her lip twitched. She shrugged. They were quite again for a moment.

A woman's voice came through the door, muffled but insistent.

"I think I hear your daughter," said Mona as if the words were being pulled out of her. "Time for you to go."

Manfred nodded, then stood and bowed from the waist. "All the best, detective. My dear Jessica doesn't like to be kept waiting. *Au revoir.*"

Mona hesitated, then tucked the calling card back in her pocket. She stuck her head out of the door and signalled to an officer.

Manfred turned as he was being led out the door and said, "Things will be so dull without you."

Mona thought there might have been a sheen in Manfred's eye, but that was unlikely; Manfred's pocket square looked like silk and he'd never get it wet.

Things went well, considering. Mona told herself this several times. She still turned down multiple offers of drinks at Blarney's. They wanted the story. What they imagined was the final, and no doubt epic, confrontation.

211

The Dame Was Trouble

But they already had as much of a show as she was going to give them.

Mona thought it would be better to hole up in the basement and nurse a coffee until things quieted down. She was almost at the elevator when a man rounded the corner, face red. Gorski following close behind him.

"Where are my goddamn keys," said the red-faced man to no one in particular. Mona recognized him as one of the Officer Liaisons…Burton, she thought.

"I'm sure Gorski can help you find them," said Mona, feigning concern as she tried to move past them down the hall.

Gorski, who was still behind the other man, shook his head silently at Mona, miming guzzling a beer.

Burton was a bit of a lush, and his buddies had started pre-emptively hiding his keys after drink number two. It happened reliably at every Karaoke/Pub Quiz/MMA night, and once, memorably, all three.

"It's a goddamn Mercedes, you know how much it will cost to get a new fob for that thing?" asked Burton.

"When I lose something I retrace my steps," said Mona in a mild voice, hoping to get rid of them.

"Bet that happens to you a lot, eh, grandma?" Burton snorted. "Hey, that's the sort of cases you'll get from now on – Mona and the Case of the Missing Keys, Mona and the Curse of the Mystery Ointment." He laughed at the joke until he started wheezing and then moved off down the hall, Gorski shooting her a worried look before trailing after Burton.

Ass.

She slid into the freight elevator and rode down to the dingy police services library-slash-museum. Once curated by some well-meaning non-profit group, now left to the damp and dust.

Mona stopped in front of the *100 Years of Policing* exhibit and looked at the old uniforms and discoloured photos. She was in one of the shots. A much younger woman, one of the officers holding back a crowd outside a building on Main Street. The caption read, *Brummel Burglar Strikes Again.* She remembered that day. Manfred was in the shot too. He was holding the hand of a little girl who must be Jessica. They both had shopping bags. She leaned closer. The picture was blurry but the logo on the bags looked to be that of Baudelaire's.

"The more things change, the more they stay the same, huh?" said Mona to the empty air.

"*Psst.*"

Mona jumped and spun around. It was Gorski. He must have seen something on her face because he said, "Don't worry, I won't tell anyone you're down here."

She gave him a questioning look.

"We can't find Burton's keys," he whispered.

"Isn't that the point?"

"I mean we did hide them, I put them in my drawer, but now they're gone." He rubbed his forehead. "I'm sure I put them in there, they just, poof," he waived his hand, "disappeared."

"Sorry, I haven't seen them," said Mona, "are you sure Vee isn't pranking you?" but Gorski didn't seem to be paying attention. Mona followed his eye, he was looking at the photo.

Mona raised an eyebrow and Gorski gave a friendly smile, "Well, anyway, I thought I'd check, thanks…" he disappeared between the shelves.

Mona frowned, then shrugged and turned away, heading towards the books.

In the tiny library Mona walked down the third row of bookshelves, running the back of her hand along the spines of the books until she found one called *Behind the Badge*. "There you are you little bugger," she said, and slid the book out without bothering to blow the dust off. She stuck her hand into the cavity where the book had been and gave a small smile when her fingers brushed something smooth and cool, her emergency whisky. After dosing her French Roast, Mona took the book and her do-it-yourself Irish coffee – she'd had to substitute the whipped cream with the packets of coffee whitener she found in her pocket and sat reading in the back of the basement.

Mona didn't go back to the main floor until she was sure everyone else was done their shift. Not wanting to pass the front desk, she'd gone up the back stairs to her office. When she got there, she pushed a chair up to the light sconce by her door and fished out a set of keys. They were hot from the bulb and she tossed them from hand to hand, Mercedes fob bouncing as she did.

She would miss old Manfred. Mona dragged the chair back into her office. He had the typical profile of an attention seeker. Probably half-convinced he was the Brummel Burglar. He fit the mould of the gentleman burglar to a "T" with his impeccable suits and his upper crust pretentions. Never missed an opportunity to show off his classical education. It had been a long time since Mona's own school days and she struggled to remember her Latin lessons. *Eram quod es, eris quod sum...* I am what you are, you are what I am...? Or something like that. Mona chuckled. She put the keys in her pocket and picked up the reading glasses. She had no good reason as to why she'd taken them. Or the other three pairs. Or the watches. It was just like...a little snack between meals. She swept them all into one of her drawers, then crawled under her desk to retrieve the briefcase she'd stashed behind the front panel. They would have a coronary when they realized how much cocaine was missing from the evidence locker.

Mona dug a hand in her pocket and grabbed the calling card. She tossed it onto her desk, taking a last look around her office as she did. She was sorry to leave this place. It got her thinking about the changing seasons and the shortness of life and all of that. Someone should say a few words.

"Well," Mona said to no one in particular. "Let's have some fun."

She tossed the *I'd rather be golfing* mug in the trash on her way out.

The Dame Was Trouble

Dinner with Francisco
Susan MacGregor

"Spain is the only nation where death is a natural spec-
tacle. In Spain, the dead are more alive than the dead of
any other country in the world."

Federico Garcia Lorca (Spanish poet & playwright)
(assassinated by fascist rebels, August, 1936.)

April 26, 1937.

I was eleven years old when the bombs fell on Gernika.
It had been a hot afternoon. I wanted to stay with mamá
to help her sell her lace at the market, but she insisted
Gabirel and I go to the southern pasture to bring the cows
home. Our farm was on the town's periphery. Papá was
away, assisting the Republican forces, so it was our duty to
do our bit for democracy and our fellow Basques. I didn't

think herding cattle was a particularly good way to aid the cause, but Mamá had a touch of the fascist about her, so it was useless to argue. After *siesta*, Gabirel and I made our way to the southern pasture to collect the herd.

"Kabroi!" Gabirel swore in our native Euskara as he surveyed the cows. He set his hands on his hips, a thing father did. "That damn bull has wandered off, again!"

I shivered in the heat. I never liked fetching the cows with Gabirel, and the bull scared me. Usually, we left it to do as it liked. As long as we knew where it was, we avoided it – or rather, I did. Gabirel who was fourteen, boasted he would be a *torero* someday, although we both knew that was unlikely. He would be expected to help Papá with the farm and to carry on the family tradition.

"It's probably wandered into the woods." I nodded at the forest edging the field.

"Probably." He made a face and headed for the trees.

"Gabi, don't!" I grabbed him by the elbow so forcefully he swung about. "You can't do it alone, and we'll need help. Besides, Mamá said to bring in the cows...."

He started to call me a coward, when the first plane appeared in the south.

With a roar, it flew over us so fast I felt the heat of its passing. It shot over the red tiled roofs of our village, then banked low, in a wide, deliberate turn, its drone insistent and loud. The air raid siren started to squeal, the two sounds fighting for dominance. The hair on the back of my neck rose. In spite of the heat of the day, I felt queasy and cold. I think I sensed what was coming without really knowing.

"*Madre de Dios!*" Rising from a crouch with a look of shock on his face, Gabirel tore off for the town.

"What are you doing? Where are you going?" I chased after him, not wanting to be left alone.

"Stay there, Jone!" he shouted at me. "It isn't safe! I have to get Mamá and Lide! I promised Papá I'd take care of them!"

If the thought of being alone in a pasture with a bull charging me was frightening, the plane and the siren terrified me even more. "No! I'm coming with you!"

"I said go back!"

Suddenly, the air exploded into fire and flying debris, knocking us from our feet. Behind a hill, more planes appeared in the sky, black wasps flying in formation, followed by a second wave. Gabi screamed, motioning at me to run to the woods, but the bomb had deafened me. With a final panicked wave, he bolted for the town, bent on reaching our mother and little sister.

As I stumbled after him, the plane veered towards us, bullets flying and cutting up the ground. I watched as they punched holes into my brother, making him jerk to and fro like a puppet on a string. Blood bloomed across his shirt and pants. I gave a strangled cry as he toppled, then turned and ran as the earth shuddered behind me, grit spraying my back. All about me, bullets fell like hail, but miraculously, or perhaps because the pilot had already taken my brother, I was spared.

The Dame Was Trouble

More planes swooped overhead. Behind me, the world detonated into chaos as more bombs fell onto Gernika and the sky burned red. Hell was upon me, the earth spewing sulphur and flame, the world now claimed by devils as the Church predicted it would. I clawed my way through the trees, escape and survival the only things on my mind. My limbs had turned to jelly, my throat ached, my mind couldn't grasp anything, except to keep moving. Even this far from the town, the air tasted of ash and smelled of burnt flesh. I blundered on until I could go no further. Terror and exhaustion made me clumsy. I tripped over a root and fell against an oak.

A snort grabbed my attention.

On the far side of the tree, the bull stood, as still as death. I didn't dare move. My tongue filled my throat and the world whirled about me, turning grey. *Breathe*, I told myself. *If I collapse, it will gore me*. As my head cleared, I saw its great chest rise and fall, its flanks heaving in and out, as if that was all the strength it possessed. Occasionally it shuddered, its shoulders flinching and twitching against the bombardment of the noise and the tremors beneath our feet. I'm not sure it was even aware of me. Another casualty, stupefied by the bombing, like myself.

Three hours later, when it finally lumbered off and the bombing appeared to have stopped, I found the courage to move. Afraid the planes might return at any moment to finish me, I made my way back to the town. Like the rest of us who had escaped the carnage, I was too stunned to cry. Gernika was a smoking pit, a precinct of hell. The demons had gone, but they had left their handiwork – a pitted and smouldering desolation. People wandered here and there, some praying at the smoking craters where the church had stood, others staring dumbly at the rubble and timbers. There were bodies, and parts of bodies. I saw a scorched hand sticking out from beneath a burning beam. Black fingers clutched at the sky as if belonging to a beggar pleading for alms. I sat down where I thought our house had been and waited for my mother to collect me.

Three days later, my uncle discovered me lying beside the town's well, sick and half out of my mind. He had borrowed a car from somewhere – perhaps he'd stolen it – and he took me away to Madrid. The roads were dangerous, but we made it to the city. The capital hadn't yet been captured by the fascists. I asked after my father. Uncle shook his head. Like the rest of my family, Papá was gone. Uncle had received word he had fallen in a conflict near Bilbao. We hoped he lay in a mass grave somewhere, lucky enough to be buried by one of our countrymen. There were many corpses along the road. We didn't stop to bury them.

The day Gernika was bombed, I changed, as all of Spain changed. For one thing, I lost my fear of bulls.

I also vowed I would kill all the fascists responsible. Uncle said the planes were German warplanes, Dorniers, Junkers, and Heinkels, with payloads of up to 1,500 kilograms each. Italian pilots were also involved. Both Hitler and Mussolini had been eager to try their new toys, as a prelude to future expansion. Where better than in Spain, where democracy was also being crushed beneath fascist boots?

Years passed. The Republic was a lost cause. Uncle and I eventually moved to Portugal and survived as another great war came and went. Hitler and Mussolini were dead, gone to dust, the world a better place without them. But the fascist pig who had murdered my family still remained, the monster who had tried to stamp out my Basque home-land by bombing our most ancient town. He would learn we Basques were not so easy to kill.

Uncle and I made plans. In Portugal we joined the Spanish underground and bided our time. I took up a new hobby which became my passion: at eighteen, and as a way to honour my brother Gabirel who had wanted to be a *torero*, I stepped into a bull ring. The bulls that once scared me took on a new meaning and focus. I learned the passes, how to dance with the cape and the sword, how to kill. I became a sensation. The first time I killed a bull in Lisbon, the crowd went wild, screaming their support for a mere girl who could move with such grace, yet strike with such force. They threw red carnations at my feet, as vivid as my brother's blood. I was often asked about the secret of my success. I never confessed, but it was simple. When-ever I faced the wild, untamed force of a bull, I never saw it as an angry, crude beast. I saw it as the man who was my enemy, Francisco Franco.

When the time came, I knew I would return to Spain. I would finish him for the animal he was and avenge my people.

April 26, 1951.

It had been some time since I'd been to *Casa Alberto*, a few years in fact, since Uncle and I had been in Madrid, for the city had become too dangerous for us to remain, even for a short while. But it was good to be back, and we were almost certain we wouldn't be questioned by the police. Our years in Portugal had given me a new name and a reputation to match.

Fourteen years had passed since Gernika. I still had the occasional nightmare about it, but today would put those horrors to bed. The meeting today – three years in the making – would balance that debt of blood. I was tense with anticipation, knowing my colour was high. I smiled to myself. Let the *culo* think I was excited to meet him, honoured even. This day would be his last.

With its perpetual façade of red paint, *Casa Alberto* looked the same as ever, but the nationalists had taken it over, making it their place to drink and toast, as if their brutality were the same as the bravery depicted on its walls. *Casa Alberto* was a famous *torero* bar. Many of the best matadors were framed there – all men, of course – no women. Even the bulls had their place of honour. I was here, under the premise I wanted to change all that.

As I expected, two of the general's thugs were standing guard outside the *taberna*. I had chosen a dress of white with pink roses – very feminine which I hoped would ap-

223

peal. I wasn't above using whatever wiles might be necessary to distract him, but I'd also worn my matching magenta *bolero* to make a point. The tunic was heavily embroidered, reminiscent of my *traje de luz*, the traditional costume all *toreros* wear. As a *matadora*, I was a novelty. I could operate in Portugal, but I wasn't allowed the same privileges in Spain. When he had taken over in 1939, the general had banned women from that role. I waited to see if his thugs would pat me down.

"Halt!" the first one commanded.

I lifted my arms and endured his pawing. He let his hands linger beneath my arms a little too long, close to my breasts. He knew of my reputation and must have decided I was the next thing to a *puta*, not content to remain in a subservient, feminine role. The other smoothed his palms along my hips, but no further. It was a tense moment. Uncle and I both knew if they found what I had hidden, it would be all over. Fortunately, they didn't search me too closely. That I could also stare them down might have daunted them. It helped to imagine gutting them like pigs.

All business, the hip *hombre* jerked his head in the direction of the door. I held my head high and passed through the doorway into the *Casa's* dark, wood-panelled interior.

Unlike the boisterous and noisy place I loved and remembered, where I was teased yet included because Uncle had been a *picador*, there was no one inside other than the waiters in their white shirts and black aprons, along with the party in the back – the general and two of his bodyguards. As I passed José and Ramón, fellow Basques, I didn't make eye contact with them, but I breathed a little easier. They were in place and our plan was coming to fruition. I fixed my gaze instead, on the man sitting at the table in the rear.

He was dressed in military garb, tan pants and shirt, as if he had just come from reviewing the troops in Morocco. A glass of *Rioja* sat at his right hand, untouched. He didn't bother to stand as a gentleman would, because he had no pretensions to be a gentleman. On either side of the table, his bodyguards stood frozen at attention. Unlike the general who was small and lean to the point of being delicate, qualities which I suspected pushed him to prove he was bigger and stronger than anyone else, they were big, beefy, and silent. They might have been statues standing along the Gran Via.

I smiled as if his lack of courtesy were a joke. His two thugs, I ignored.

His eyebrows lifted, revealing a spark of renewed interest in his brown, steady gaze. He hadn't expected me to appear as I was – twenty-six years old, petite, with dark coils of hair piled about my head. Perhaps he had never seen my posters. Or perhaps he thought they had been embellished, that they were a lie.

"*Señorita* Cruz." With a sweep of his hand, he invited me to sit.

"General Franco," I replied, taking his palm and letting our fingers linger. "Thank you so much for agreeing to meet me. It's a great honour."

The Dame Was Trouble

We passed along a few pleasantries – the fine April weather, the impressive religious processions he had witnessed during *Semana Santa* – he being a devout Catholic – and other things of little import as we ate our meal. A true *machismo*, instead of asking me what I wanted, he had taken it upon himself to order our food; for himself, *rabo de toro* – oxtail in gravy, a speciality of the house, and for me, *caracoles a la Madrilèna*, or Madrid snails. I wondered if he had chosen my meal to make a point in the same way I had chosen my dress. The ears and tail of the bull are given as trophies to the matador who outperforms against all expectations. I was not to be granted those. Those he kept for himself. Instead, I was to understand my role as the 'snail'. A woman should know her place and crawl.

When he had taken Spain, he had made it clear a woman should never be a *matadora*, or perform the *estocada*, the final act of killing the bull. In his estimation, it wasn't lady-like. Men should not have to compete with women. Women were meant to grace the arm of a powerful man, to be elegant, beautiful, and silent.

I wasn't the silent type.

"You know why I've asked you to meet me today, *Señor*," I said. "It is no secret. I was hoping to convince you to change your mind. To allow women to fight as men do, on foot, in the ring."

"I haven't said you can't fight, *Señorita*, just that you must remain on horseback. It's safer."

"Verónica, please."

"Verónica. Very well. You may call me Francisco."

I smiled, my cheeks dimpling and my lips red with promise. He was happily married and devout, but all men have their peccadilloes. There was too much table between us. I needed to get closer.

"Good." He patted me on the hand, father-like. "Think of me as your uncle. Or as a brother."

Was he reminding himself of which relationships were appropriate? Or was he baiting me? My nostrils flared with disgust. That he should compare himself to Gabirel….

"Has Verónica always been your name? Or is Verónica Cruz your *nom de guerre*?"

I hid my fear. Did he know more than he was letting on? Jone had been my real name. Even Uncle no longer called me that. Jone had died in Gernika, along with her family and innocence. "Does it displease you?" I dimpled at him again.

"I find it amusing."

I cocked my head to one side. "You find me amusing? I don't know whether to be flattered or annoyed."

He burst out laughing, delighted he had vexed me. "Truly, I do want to know you better, *Señorita*." He took a sip of his wine and eyed me speculatively. "You're an intriguing woman."

I pursed my lips, as if deciding whether to forgive him or not.

"Isn't she an intriguing woman?" he added, asking his guards. "Beautiful, as well. A true prize."

One of them coloured and nodded briefly. The other kept his eyes averted and on the wall.

"Lieutenant Gomez agrees with me. As for Sergeant Ramirez...he doesn't care to reply. Which means you bother him more than he's willing to let on."

"General, you're embarrassing the poor man," I protested.

"Oh, the sergeant isn't so sensitive as all that." He paused and something in his mien changed, grew colder. "In fact, that's one of the things I like best about him." He smiled, his mustache spreading across his upper lip in a thin line. "He isn't squeamish in the least."

I could only guess at what he meant by that. It was obvious he saw himself as the master of this *corrida*, the fighter who flirts with the bulls. "You haven't answered my question."

"About?"

"Your name."

"Ah," I replied. "Yes, Verónica is my *nom de guerre*. I thought it appropriate."

"Of course. In the verónica, a matador stands his ground. Or in your case, *her* ground."

"I'm stubborn," I admitted. "I'll do almost anything to get what I want. Which is why I wanted to meet with you today."

"Like all women." He dismissed me with a wave. "Ah, good! Our entertainment has arrived!"

A flamenco dancer and her guitarist appeared from a side hall. The dancer was dressed in a dress of blue with red polka dots, with matching frills about her knees, her partner, attired similarly, except the frills were on his sleeves. I had seen many dancers, particularly in the south, but these two lacked the authenticity of those *gitanos*. I had known Franco loved the bullfight and flamenco, anything that defined the culture as he saw it, but this was a sham, overdone. He preferred flash, display, appearances.

Despite my initial impression, they turned out to be quite good. I wondered if they, too, were forced to become something they weren't. Had José and Ramón, dressed as waiters, known about them? Uncle had told me to wait for their disruption, something the general's bodyguards would investigate, but I didn't think the gypsies were it.

As the dancer executed a series of sharp turns, I slid my hand beneath my skirt and felt the stiletto I had tucked there, along my inner thigh. I slid it free from my stocking, but kept it hidden beneath the tablecloth. It had picked up the warmth of my leg and felt like a living thing, an extension of myself. I shifted closer to Francisco, on the pretense of being better able to see the dancer's feet. His eyes were on her breasts as she performed a final backbreaking *quebrada*. Despite the dimness of the *taberna*, his face was flushed.

"*Olé!*" he shouted, standing abruptly. "*Olé, olé, olé!*"

My heart thudded in my chest. I had been about to strike him. In the same way that a bull will suddenly turn because it has learned the ways of the cape, his lurching to his feet had caught me off guard. I slid the stiletto between my leg and the chair, hoping it wouldn't skewer me.

He sat back down, red faced. "Lieutenant Gomez, see they're taken care of. Pay them well."

The dancer and guitarist bowed at him as they might for royalty and followed the lieutenant to the front of the *taberna*. Sergeant Ramirez remained where he was, as if made from stone.

"Now, that's what I call talent!" Francisco enthused. "A woman who can dance and knows how to be a woman."

Against my better nature, I chilled. "Am I to take it you think *I* don't?"

"Nothing of the sort. But see here, Verónica. You've come here to convince me to let you fight in the ring, on foot as a man does. But it's so obvious. You're not a *man*."

It was time to stand up to him. "Your logic astounds me."

His mouth fell open, dumbfounded that I should criticize him, Franco, the leader of fascist Spain. He burst into amazed laughter a second time. "I'll give you this," he chortled, reaching for his wine and giving me a wink. "You may be a woman but you have *cojones*."

Any talk that hinted of sex or body parts meant I was getting to him.

You don't have to do this, Verónica, Uncle had said a week ago. He turned a bright red. *I know you are a virgin…*

He knew nothing. I had had two lovers, exactly. Both bullfighters. Miguel, my true love, who had died from complications after being gored in the ring, and Tomás, who I had stopped seeing because he wanted me to settle down and bear him *niños*. I left him in Portugal. Had Uncle known, he would have been disappointed in me. It was none of his business, but I was far from being a green girl.

Don't worry, Uncle. I won't let him get too close.

Which was a lie. I would do what I had to. And seduction was always the woman's advantage.

I met Francisco's glance boldly. "The only *cojones* I want are yours."

He stared at me, swallowed, and then set down his Rioja deliberately. I wasn't sure whether I had offended or titillated him. I was betting on the latter. In a moment I would know.

"Don't talk like a *puta*. I'm a married man." Too sternly, I thought. I wondered if this was to protect himself from temptation, or if it were for the benefit of the stuffed gorilla beside us.

I leaned in closer and whispered, my lips barely moving, my breath tickling his ear. "Then I pity your wife, Francisco. Because she trusts you. When we both know she shouldn't."

There is something all Spanish men admire, and that is bravery in a woman. She can be beautiful and clever, but mixed with courage, she becomes an irresistible mix.

He stood, as if affronted. "Ramirez, pay for our meal, then wait outside with Gomez and the others. On behalf of the Church, I will speak with this harlot regarding the error of her ways. Then, we will leave."

His eyes never left mine. I smiled at him knowingly. He meant to take me right there, in the back of that *taberna*, on that table, with the greatest matadors of the past, national heroes like Paquiro, set in their picture frames, looking on as we coupled. In his mind, he was *El Caudillo*, their leader, and greater than them all.

I rose, hiding the stiletto in the folds of my skirt, my *estoque de verdad*, the sword of truth. I turned to him, as if waiting for Ramirez to leave before pressing against Francisco for a kiss. I congratulated myself. I hadn't needed José or Ramón to provide a diversion. I had been distraction, enough.

Francisco waited, hands by his sides for now, his eyes devouring mine. He was breathing heavily. The pulse in his neck jumped. Sometimes, it's like that with the bull. There is an instant when time stops, when you know the defining moment is about to occur. The sword will plunge, blood will spill, a life will end. But it's never for certain who triumphs – the *matadora* or the bull.

Rarely, is it the bull.

I squeezed the stiletto tightly, refusing to relish this moment. Savoring it would cheapen what I was about to do. All those lives lost, my mother, my little sister, Papá, Gabirel. Where were they now? I didn't believe in heaven, having spent too much time in hell.

"General!" Ramirez called out. I couldn't see what the reason was, but I knew I had to act. The moment was upon us.

Francisco turned unexpectedly the same instant I drove the stiletto at his neck. The blade skewered him in the shoulder, missing the jugular which had been my target. Bellowing in outrage, he grabbed my hand as I struggled to pull the knife and strike him again. In the front of the *taberna*, José and Ramon battled it out with his toughs. I could hear the sounds of their struggle, the scuffling of feet, the growls of men. And then Ramirez was on me, pinning me in his simian arms as Francisco swore at me and clutched his shoulder.

"Are they contained in front?" he demanded, his voice a rasp.

"*Sí*, El Caudillo," Ramirez confirmed.

"Take her out back. And the rest, along with her. Obviously, they're in it together. You know what to do."

"Your arm, General...."

"I'll survive. A scratch from a bitch. I've had worse." He turned to me. "It's been a charming evening, *Señorita* Cruz. Or should I say Jone Ibarra? Yes, I know who you are. I saw behind your pretense. Like God, I see everything."

He had played me. I still didn't know how he knew. All I could surmise was his secret police broke one of us – not José or Ramon, for they were to suffer the same fate as me, but someone who had been in our company, someone who had shared our hopes for a free and democratic Spain.

With sick insight, I suddenly knew. It was as if he were standing beside me in spirit, crying and pleading for my forgiveness.

Uncle. They had to have found and tortured him. His suffering must have been great.

They took us out the back of the *taberna* and into a dark, blind alley. It wasn't the bull ring which the firing squads used when it wasn't a *fiesta* day, but it would do. I was sickened to see the flamenco dancer and her guitarist pressed against the wall with us, as if they were part of our plot.

I might have argued their innocence, but there was no point. The fascists wouldn't listen. We were an inconvenience, a waste of bullets, but the job had to be done.

They didn't bother to offer us blindfolds. I would have refused one anyway, preferring to stare down Francisco as he watched me from the *taberna's* back stairs.

There is a saying that the bullet that takes you is painless. You don't feel it or see it coming.

That isn't true.

I felt the bullets rip into my body, spears of fire, then of ice, so immediate and shocking they took my breath away until one tore through my eye and burst through my skull. There was a blast of red, then too many detonations to count, scarlet bloom after scarlet bloom, carnation bombs dropping. Then behind that sensory chaos, a silence that lasted a long, long time.

Finally, after an eon, I heard a voice.

"Jone, Jone! It's finished! Almost!"

I came to. I was no longer dying in a back alley, but standing in a sunny bull ring. I was dressed in a *traje de luz* so blinding in its intensity, I thought I must outshine the sun. The ring was huge, the biggest I had ever seen, with tiers of seats rising to the sky in endless progression. There were people on their feet in the stands. Thousands of them, glowing like candles…except, every one of them was broken. Some were riddled with ruddy holes, others mottled liked cracked porcelain, the light of their pain shining through. When I looked more closely, I recognized my little sister Lide, a shattered but brilliant doll, and my mamá, glowing from a fire that writhed about her in streamers. Papá was there, too, with a gaping hole in his head that shone like a beacon.

"Finish it, Jone," Gabirel insisted, snagging my attention. He was peppered with holes as bright as rubies. "Finish it for all of us, so we can go home."

From across the ring, a familiar figure in tan fatigues appeared, pushed to the centre of the ring by two *rejoneadores* on horseback: Uncle and my one true love, Miguel. My heart swelled as I regarded them. Miguel, especially, was doing me the honour of taking the secondary role.

I studied the puny, furious man in the ring. My gut clenched, stiffening with sudden loathing. "Is that…?"

"Sí. He died moments ago. From cardiac arrest. We've been waiting for him. We've been waiting for you."

I was angry. How dare he pass peacefully in his sleep when so many had suffered by his hand – me, along with them? "He was watching me from the back step. He couldn't have died the same night."

"No. Today is November 20, 1975."

So, I had been in limbo for twenty-four years. Purgatory, except I didn't believe in purgatory. He had had another twenty-four years because I had failed to finish him.

"It doesn't matter, Jone." Gabirel must have sensed my thought. "In the end, we all die. We all come here."

I stared about the sorry, sad bull ring, with its broken and silent spectators. "Where is here, Gabirel? Is this hell?"

"Hell has passed. This is judgement." He handed me my cape and sword.

I frowned. Francisco was already dead. He couldn't die twice, surely. If so, to what end? A continuous succession of deaths? I put the question to my brother.

He considered me gravely. "You know how, in the *tercio de varas*, the first third of the bullfight, they blindfold the horses, so they can't see if the bull charges them?" He nodded at Francisco. "He's blind, too. From arrogance and entitlement. If you slay him, he will see."

I looked down at my *estoque de verdad*, my sword of truth.

"He will relive every life he's taken, see their ends, and know their despair and pain as if they were his own. He will learn remorse, even if it takes millennia."

"How do you know this?"

He shrugged. "Why else would we be here? This is his reckoning."

I glanced at the stands. "And them? You?"

"Perhaps we'll find peace, once you set us free."

I regarded Francisco. The man who had destroyed Gernika, who had ruined Spain and so many lives, including my own. Who hated freedom as all despots do, who believed he knew better than anyone else. A monster, a bull-man, a *minotaur*.

I lifted my cape and my sword and strode purposefully towards him, ready to finish what I had begun. The crowd began to chant, Jone, Jone, Jone! *Viva la Republica!*

Francisco regarded them with contempt and sneered. Then he looked at me and glared, as if through will alone he might defeat me.

But I was a *matadora*, queen of this *corrida*. He no longer ruled here.

After I finished him, his ears and tail were mine.

A Dish to Die for
Alice Bienia

Emma gave the chipped arborite table one last swipe and stood back. Menu…check, salt and pepper…check, raw sugar and Sweet' N Low. Jimmy liked all the tables set just so, and had a fit if everything wasn't exactly like he wanted. Emma flexed backwards, one hand on the small of her back. She was getting old, too old for this shit.

Emma glanced out the window. A worn-out woman, a scrappy juke box and fluorescents dangling over a grill reflected her life against the blackness outside. It wouldn't be long before the place went under, and she with it.

The door swung open, dust and dried leaves blew in across her newly swept floor. Emma startled, and turned. A man stood in the doorway.

"Sorry, we're closed for the night."

"Thought maybe the sign's wrong." The man nodded at the sign Emma had flipped over minutes earlier, dangling against the window. "Saw the lights still on and the door's open."

"Sorry, no, we're closed. I'm just finishing up - aim to be out of here in a minute."

He took a step closer, grinning like some pervert about to steal his junior prom date's virginity. Neither fat nor thin, just solid and not a bad looker. The way he moved told Emma there was muscle under the red plaid shirt, and more testosterone than was good for just one man.

"What's your hurry. Not exactly a nice night out there."

He was right about that. The wind had been howling all day, hurling yard dirt and pebbles against the window, rattling everything that wasn't hammered down tight.

"It's been a long day, mister, the husband and kiddies are waiting." She saw him eyeing her ring free hand. She casually brushed back her hair. Let him look. Lots of people don't wear their wedding bands to work. She had stopped wearing hers the second year she was married, the year before her husband split with her best friend and left her holding the bag on this shitass diner. Then, when she was about to lose the whole damn thing to the bank, Jimmy came along and bought fifty-one percent and made himself her boss.

"I'm outta gas, and I could use a bite to eat. I haven't eaten all day."

Most people would have filled up in town but if they hadn't, hers was the last gas pump for two hundred kilometers. Emma always kept her guard up when she was alone in the diner, and she'd never had trouble. None she couldn't handle. But this one had bad news written all over him.

"I can turn the pump back on for you but you'll have to pay with a credit card. I've already cashed out and shut down the grill for the night. The boss's prone to checkin' up on me. If the place ain't closed like it's supposed to be I'll be in big trouble."

He swaggered toward her. "Darlin' you let me worry about your boss."

Emma was tall but she had to tip her head back to meet his eyes. She saw a coldness there that said *don't mess with me*, despite the *I'm just a good ol' boy* smile. He paused next to her, leaned in and inhaled.

"You sure smell pretty. Now why don't you go lock that door before someone else comes in. Then fix me something to eat. I haven't had a decent meal all day."

Emma stepped back, trying to ignore the sensuality of his mouth, his warm breath on her neck. There was no husband anymore and Emma hadn't spoken to her kid in four years, her daughter's choice not hers. Jimmy wasn't about to check the place either. By this time of night Jimmy would be passed out, his breath reeking of the rot gut whiskey he brewed himself. For one brief second, she considered abandoning it all and running. But her car was parked out back, her keys in her purse, hanging next to her jacket by the back door.

Emma moved toward the door, paused and looked over her shoulder. Behind the cocksure swagger, this one was wound tighter than a diamond back, ready to strike.

He stood watching, a lopsided grin splitting his face, his eyes challenged her to defy him. She turned the dead bolt, the click sounding final in her ears.

"I don't see a car," she said turning back to him.

"Parked 'round the back, right next to a red Chevy. Yours I presume."

Emma noticed his shoulders drop, he was more relaxed now that the door was locked.

"Now, what's your name, darlin'?"

Emma could feel her heart throbbing in her neck, certain he could see it from across the room. Her fingertips pulsed with the adrenaline flooding her body. It was just him and her now. Nothing out there but bald ass prairie, tumbleweeds and a coyote or two.

His eyes narrowed as he took in every inch of Emma's body, still firm under the yellow uniform Jimmy insisted she wear. She watched as his eyes travelled back up her body, a grin parted his lips as his eyes came to rest on the last button of her uniform, too tight to fasten across her chest. She took a deep breath to steady her nerves.

"Emma. What about you? Got a name?"

"You can call me Hunter."

Emma remembered what her mama had always told her when it came to men. *'Best let a man believe whatever they think of themselves is true, even if it ain't. 'Cause a good man will give you what you want, but never his pride'.* Too bad her mama hadn't come across any good men. This one wasn't doing anything to hide the gun tucked into his jeans underneath the open plaid shirt he wore loosely over a black T-shirt. Besides, Emma already made her choice when she locked the front door.

"Okay Hunter. How does steak and eggs sound? And coffee?"

"Steaks and eggs will do just fine. Got anything stronger than coffee?"

"Sorry, we're a country diner not a bar." Jimmy had a half gallon of hooch in the back office but he didn't need to know that.

"You sure are sorry about a lot darlin'. I hate to see a woman sorry. 'Specially a woman as pretty as you. You need to loosen up, live a little."

"Why don't you sit," said Emma, nodding toward the tables as she walked across the room and stepped behind the counter, glad to put some distance between them. "Coffee coming right up," she announced as she filled the carafe with cold water and pressed the on button, the coffee already measured out in the filter, ready for morning.

"So, what do you do for fun around here?" he called out.

"Told you, working and looking after a couple of kids and a husband doesn't leave me much time for fun." Emma turned on the grill and as it heated, she headed for the storage room, then jumped back with a yelp.

He stood in front of her, arm stretched across the door, blocking her way. "Where you going?"

"In there," Emma nodded, giving him a smile she hoped resembled the one she used to snag her husband all those years ago. "It's where we keep the steaks and eggs."

Hunter dropped his arm to let her pass. Emma noticed he had seen her eyes flit to the gun tucked into the waistband of his jeans. He gave her a crooked smile and watched as she walked into the storage room.

He pulled out a pack of cigarettes and lit one as Emma picked up a metal mixing bowl off the shelf, then removed a steak, a tomato and four eggs from the refrigerator. Emma walked back out leaving him to shut the storage door. No point in telling him smoking wasn't allowed. She set the mixing bowl with the tomatoes and eggs down just as a huge gust of wind rattled the building. The lights flickered.

Emma swore under her breath. She poured a mug of coffee and held it out to him. For one flash of a second, she imagined throwing the scalding coffee in his face. Emma smiled as Hunter took the mug, his fingers brushing her hand. He winked at her, reward for job well done.

"Go on sit down – you're making me nervous."

Hunter sipped, winked again and carried his coffee over to a table.

"So where are you heading Hunter?" Emma called out through the pass.

"Nowhere in particular. Maybe the coast. Do a little fishing. Heard it's nice this time of year."

Emma moved to the back counter and suddenly he was there. Emma's hand flew to her chest. "Holy Jesus! You're like a freakin' ninja. Scared the crap out of me."

He dragged on his cigarette and blew a stream of grey smoke over her head. "You want to come? We could drive up the sunshine coast. I could rent us a boat, take it south. Meh-ee-co might be fun."

"Told you, I have a family."

Hunter stubbed out his cigarette on the counter, walked past Emma and grabbed her purse from where it hung, on the back wall. Emma looked up from the bread she was slicing then back to the knife in her hand. Too dull and serrated. What she needed was a nice long sharp one. "Hey leave that alone."

Hunter opened the purse flap and dumped the contents on the counter behind Emma. He picked up her car keys and pocketed them without a word. Grabbing her cell phone, he took it with him back to the table.

"What are you doing? I need that phone. I don't have money for another." Emma watched as he picked up the phone and started scrolling. She grit her teeth and turned back to the grill, picked up the oil and squeezed out a Zed. Smoothing the oil out with the spatula she threw down the steak.

"How do like them? Your steak and eggs."

"Medium rare. Over easy on the eggs."

Emma loaded the bread into the toaster. While the steak sizzled and spat, she added a circle of oil next to it and cracked open the eggs. Emma looked down at the grey granules scattered on the floor under the grill. Rat poison. She didn't dare look at the bottom shelf next to stove, where the box stood. Emma had no idea what affect it would have. Would it make him sick or pass out? Enough of it would probably kill him but it'd be hard to hide that much in his food.

He was back in the kitchen. "Mmmm. That does smell good. Mind if I get a refill." He nodded at the coffee pot.

"Help yourself."

Emma glanced at Hunter's dark hair, thick neck and muscles straining the back of his shirt, as he turned to pour coffee. She knew who he was. Her eyes flit to the darkened TV suspended in the corner of the dining room. It had been on all afternoon, the news ticker scrolling information about yet another robbery, the fifth this month. The M.O. was the same: lone gunman enters jewelry store, quick cash outlet or bank, points a gun, hands over a bag and note. He always wore a mask and gloves. Caught once on a store camera, the video clip showed a dark figure, wearing gloves and a mask, hunched over running for the door. The police description was useless, a Caucasian man, roughly six feet tall, with brown hair and a muscular build. Could be about a million guys out there that fit the description, but Emma knew this was him.

Things always turned out badly for Emma. She'd never even met her father. When she was five, her mama's house burned down and she had been sent to live with her Gram, a withered old woman with no teeth, meaner than sin. Her mama finally came to collect her when she was nine and took her to the place she was living with a man. A big ol' boy who sweated a lot. He never touched her, but he paid her a buck to let him sneak into the bathroom to watch her pee when her mama wasn't around, and keep quiet about it. She'd been kinda sad to see him go, she was still twenty bucks short for the bike she was saving for. After him, there were more guys, each creepier than the one before, most not willing to negotiate the terms of their involvement with her. Then she got pregnant with fuckin' Dougie Lumière's kid. They got married, but she later found out he'd been sleeping with her best friend the whole time. Now she had that disgusting pig Jimmy, bossing her around.

Emma flipped the steak, covered the eggs, took out a plate and retrieved the toast. Her life had been a near perfect run of bad luck. Maybe not this time.

She squared her shoulders and turned. "Butter?" she smiled her coyest smile and flicked her eyelashes at him.

He grinned. "You bet."

"Must be nice to be able to just drive wherever you want, relax, take in some sun somewhere."

He came up behind her and leaned in. She could feel his breath warm against her neck and his deep raspy voice in her ear made her shiver.

"You're a good-looking woman Emma. What are you doing wasting your life here?" He reached down and grabbed her buttock and squeezed. Part of her wanted him to turn her around, slip his hand up below her dress, caress her thigh, her breasts.

Emma looked around her. The place was small, worn. A shithole. No matter how much she scrubbed, nothing would make the chipped faded grey arborite table tops any brighter, or remove the black ground-in grease from the once red carpet underfoot. And Jimmy was a pig, always groping her. At least Hunter was a good-looking man. He had all his teeth and he smelled good too. Maybe she should go with him.

Emma laughed, licked her upper lip and pushed a strand of hair behind her ear. "I bet you say that to all the women you meet. Make yourself useful, hand me a plate there." She nodded at the counter behind her, stacked with glasses and plates.

A second later, he reached around her, his arm brushing her shoulder. The rat poison screamed at her silently from the shelf below but it was too late. Emma took the plate and arranged the steak, eggs and toast.

"Here you go. Dig in."

"Come sit with me."

"I need to clean the grill."

He grabbed her hand and pulled her along. "No, you don't. You gotta stop following the rules. Rules are for losers." He reached the table and pushed Emma into a chair and sat across from her. "This is what following the rules gets you," he nodded at the grill.

Emma's eyes followed his. She pursed her lips and nodded. Sometimes one had to break the rules, just to make oneself feel better.

Hunter dragged the back of his hand across his mouth, wiping away a bit of steak. "Your cell phone says you haven't been calling home much. Didn't find a call to or from your home number in over two months. There's not much there waiting for you, is there?"

Emma stared down at her hands, lying in her lap. Bo would be the first customer to arrive at the diner in the morning. He raised goats and smelled like one. His wife died last year. She cooked and cleaned for that man every day of her life and when her heart finally gave out Bo decided he could afford to eat at the diner every day – breakfast and dinner. What an ass. That's how the men around here still treated their women. They provided a roof over your head and bought a rag or two for your back and in return you cleaned up their vomit, washed their vile clothes, slung hash morning, noon and night, fed whatever little rats you bred and let them slobber and suck all over you.

Emma jumped up. "I need to turn off the grill. As shitty as this place is it's probably best to not let it burn to the ground." Emma met his eyes steadily. When he didn't say anything, she picked up his mug. "Coffee while I'm up?"

He nodded. "Man, this is good."

Emma walked into the kitchen, poured the old coffee out of his mug and reached for the carafe. She watched as he sawed off another bite of steak, put it into his mouth,

249

leaned back, closed his eyes and chewed. Emma reached down picked up the box of rat poison, sprinkled some into her hand and poured it into the cup. She wiped her hand on the back of her dress and ran her thumb over the coffee cup rim, removing the trace of powder that remained there. Heart pounding, she carried it back to the table and set it down in front of him. Her hand trembled and some of the coffee sloshed on the table.

"Sorry."

He stood up and yanked her arm, his face contorted in anger.

"What did I tell you?"

Emma cringed and tried to pull away. She had just blown it.

"On second thought, I don't need to be hauling around some timid-ass little housewife."

"What are you going to do to me?" Emma didn't want to hear the answer. She could see by the look on his face that he hadn't thought this out.

The lights flicked and went out.

"Fuckin hell. Ok doll, we're goin' to move out. He twisted Emma's arm behind her and she felt the gun press into her back. "Don't give me no grief or it's going to end right now."

Emma stuck her hands out in front of her as he shoved from behind. She stumbled toward the cash register and once her hands found the smooth metal, maneuvered through the doorway into the kitchen. Emma felt along the counter as he pushed her roughly through the darkness.

She yelped as her hip crashed into the back counter. Finally, they were at the back door. He pressed up against her and breathed into her neck.

"Open it."

The rasp in his voice, the warmth of his body pressing against her made her shiver. Emma felt a strange energy in the hand that gripped her shoulder, heard the way his breathing had turned ragged. He laughed. His hand slid around her shoulder and he grabbed her breast. Then he tightened his arm around her and pulled her back as she clicked open the lock and swung the door open. Emma felt his hips, pushing, grinding against her buttocks.

"We're gonna go for a little ride. I'm goin' to give you something you've been waiting for all your life. Something you'll never forget."

He pushed Emma through the door, everything beyond it dark and inky. Invisible hungry tongues licked at the spruce trees, their limbs bending and flailing, and whipped up the dirt behind the diner flinging sand in their face.

Emma bent her head and kissed the arm clutching her in his grip. She reached behind her, grabbed the back of his thigh and pulled his hips tighter against her. Emma closed her eyes momentarily. The thought of what was coming next sent tremors down her spine to her belly. She turned toward him as he relaxed his grip, and felt him drop his hand and pull up the back of her dress.

The wind buffered the guttural noise that escaped his lips before his mouth covered hers. She felt him shudder as his hand moved up her back. His fingers caressed the

251

back of her neck before wrapping themselves in her hair. He yanked back her head, his eyes widened, his jaw already slack. The gun dropped from his hand.

Emma scrambled for the gun and screamed. "Hit him again. Come on Carter, hit him again."

Carter brought the bat down on the back of Hunter's neck, one more time, and Hunter dropped to the ground. Emma backed up, the gun pointed at Hunter, ready for whatever came next.

"Shit Carter. I thought you'd never get here."

"Yeah, well I thought I'd give you a minute since you seemed to be enjoying yourself." Carter handed Emma the flashlight he had tucked into the back of his jeans. He grabbed Hunter below the arms and pulled him back inside. "Come on Em, give me a hand."

After dragging Hunter into the front of the diner, Emma made her way into the small office, by the back door. She stepped over Jimmy's body. Took weeks to set this up and she wasn't going to fuck it up now. She unlocked the desk drawer and took out a second flashlight, a bottle of chloroform and the rest of Jimmy's hooch. Jimmy moaned and stirred. She set the bottles next to him and heaved and pulled until he was half sitting up. His skin was grey and clammy, his eyes closed.

"Here Jimmy, drink this. It'll make you feel better." She opened the whiskey and held it up to his lips. He struggled to fight her off but she managed to get some more of it down his throat. She left the bottle next to him, put on latex gloves and a mask, doused a paper napkin in chloroform and held it over his face.

"Come on Emma, bring me the damn flashlight."

She heard Carter knock over a chair and push several tables askew. Jimmy went still. Emma ran out and handed Carter one of the flashlights and the chloroform. While he dragged Hunter over to the cash register and let him breathe in some chloroform, Emma ran back into the kitchen, blew out the pilot light and turned up the gas on the stove.

"Ready? Let's go," called out Carter tersely.

Emma looked at her purse and all its shit scattered on the counter. "Get his car keys. And mine," she called back.

Carter dug through Hunter's pockets. "Got 'em, let's go." He ran into the kitchen and tossed Emma the keys to her Chevy. They ran through the back door and out to the parking lot. The wind tore at Emma's hair as they raced across the broken pavement. Emma got inside Hunter's black Crown Vic, located the release button and popped the trunk. She could hear Carter's yelp of glee above the wind and smiled. Emma got out, raced over to Carter's car and popped his trunk.

"Leave most of that shit," she yelled as Carter lifted out a laptop. "Grab the cash." They searched through the trunk until they found what they were looking for. A DVD box contained bundles of bills. A shoe box held watches, rings, necklaces. Emma scooped out most of the jewelry into a plastic bag, leaving a third behind. They stashed what they had taken in Carter's trunk.

Carter drove the Crown Vic around to the lone gas pump standing in front of the diner. Emma ran back to the diner and into the back office. Jimmy was still laying next to the hooch, the bottle now lying on its side. He must have somehow knocked it over. She ran around to Jimmy's desk, jiggled open the bottom drawer, pulled out the cash box, and extracted a fistful of bills. She could already smell the gas from the stove as she stuffed the bills into her pocket.

She heard Carter yell something as he came in the front door. Emma ran through the kitchen and out to the dining room.

"Shit, for one brief moment I thought I'd blown it." Emma's head snapped back as Carter punched her in the face. Stars exploded in her eyes. She swayed, Carter's concerned face swimming in front of her. Then nothing.

Emma lifted her head. She tried opening her eyes and managed to pry open one of them.

"Sorry, Em. Thought it best to...you know...surprise you."

Carter helped her to her feet.

"Did you have to hit me that damn hard."

"You said we needed to make it look real. Here, I wiped down the bat. Take a grip and make like you're hitting someone with it. I gave him some chloroform and put his

254

gun near his hand. I reset the breaker. The car's full and I spilled some of the gas, like you said."

"Right, the lights, they're back on." She gazed around and then down at Hunter lying on the floor. Emma pulled off her gloves and took the bat. She swung the bat over his head and dropped it. The bat rolled and came to rest against a chair leg. She reached out and gripped Carter's arm, woozy from the effort.

"I think Jimmy might be dead."

"Couldn't happen to a nicer guy,' Carter countered. "Let's go. You okay?" Carter kissed Emma long and hard. "Good luck babe. Sorry about the eye. See you on the other side."

Emma watched Carter leave. It was risky letting him leave with the goods. But she didn't have a choice. He'd followed her every instruction so far. It didn't take a genius to figure out Hunter would be staying off the highway. Emma had watched the crime spree unfolding on TV, and noticed the robberies inching west.

Carter was out of work again, so Emma pried him off her couch and sent him out with a pair of binoculars and a tank full of gas. He spotted Hunter five days later, the Crown Vic parked next to a small cabin near Edgerton. Yesterday, Hunter made his move. If that was even his real name. When it was clear he was heading in the direction of the diner, Carter managed to siphon off most of the gas from his gas tank. They spent the rest of the day putting their plan into motion.

The smell of gas was more noticeable now. With one last look around her, Emma pulled on her latex gloves, grabbed Hunter's cigarette package from his shirt pocket and extracted a cigarette. Taking it with her, she walked out the front of the diner. Using a diner napkin to cover the filter, she lit the cigarette and after a few drags to make sure it was truly lit, dropped it on the spilled gasoline near the gas tank. Watching the embers glow, fade and reignite in the wind, she waited until a few sparks caught the dried grass at the base of the gas pump. Emma ran around to the back of the diner and headed for the far end of the parking lot. With one final look over her shoulder, she stepped into the calm quiet of the trees. Emma felt the explosion before she heard it. Then she heard nothing at all.

"Hey babe, come look at this."

Emma walked out of the bathroom, where she had been doing her nails. Carter was propped-up against the headboard, opening the day's mail.

They had gotten away with it. The local papers had run the story for days. Photos showed Hunter's burnt out Crown Vic parked next to the gas pump, the diner windows black gaping holes, wires dangling in the rubble, the roof caved-in. The sheriff called her a brave little woman for managing to hit Hunter and get herself out the back door, before the cigarette caught on the dry grass and fanned by the wind grew into a roaring fire. No one was surprised to find bits of Jimmy in the rubble. Most folks knew he was passed out, stone-cold, in the diner office by late afternoon.

"Lookee here!" Carter waved a piece of paper in the air. "That little shithole of a diner you owned just paid us three hundred and twenty K. That brings us up to almost a mil."

Emma snatched the check from Carter with two perfectly manicured red nails, the polish labelled Macbeth on the bottle. "How many times have I told you to leave my mail alone."

"You mean our mail. Come on, babe. Lighten up." He picked up a pillow and stuffed it behind his head, along with the other two. "Let's buy a boat. We can take it south, live off fresh fish and beer!"

Emma had been thinking it might be time to head south. The accommodations at the motel were cheap now that it was off season, but the evenings were cool and the wind blowing off the Pacific would soon be downright frigid.

"Can't you just be happy we don't have to go to some dumb ass job every day? I told you, we can't be throwing money around like we just won a lottery. People will get suspicious."

"What people? We can tell them my rich uncle just died. Or you could just tell the truth, that some crazy dude attacked you and burnt down your diner. Besides, since when do I need your permission?"

Carter didn't notice that Emma had grown still, her eyes calculating as she scrutinized every inch of him, and kept prattling. "A million is a lot of pesos. Mucho dinero. We're stinkin' rich. Hey, while you're up, why don't you hustle your sweet buns over to the fridge and get me a beer? Uno cerveza, my little chickeeta."

Best let a man believe whatever they think of themselves is true, even if it ain't. Emma smiled. What a waste. Too bad, Carter didn't get her. Didn't he know the new Emma didn't sling beer or hash for anyone, anymore?

"And what about dinner? I'm starved. What are you making?"

Emma turned and took the pill container out of her sundress pocket and pried the lid off carefully with her freshly manicured fingernails. Lifting the lid off the pot, bubbling quietly on the two-burner cooktop in the tiny kitchenette, she poured in the greyish granules and gave everything a good stir.

"Nothing fancy lover boy, just some Rat-a-touille."

Silk
Meghan Victoria

She taps her umbrella on grimy restaurant tile, the sound drowning against a backdrop of slow jazz. Her cab is late. She leans against the open doorway, watches rain slick the pavement through lowered lashes, as fake as the diamonds she wears at her neck. Grey turns to black, the stench of garbage and urine leaches into the street. Streams are birthed, running over each other, joining until stones are lost to the furious rush. Gulf coast rain, heavy and smothering against a shuttered sky.

She eats for free during rainy season, has convinced the owner that the cut of her dress will lure men with deep pockets. Tonight, he gives her Rohypnol in a plastic bag that she tucks carefully into her bra. She blows him in the back office, on her knees between the mottled filing cabinet and the peeling wall, and they call themselves even.

People shuffle through the door. She refuses to take up less space, drawing lowered eyebrows from a steely-eyed man in a hooded jacket. She blows cigarette smoke from the corner of crimson lips. He pushes past, the back of his hand trailing her thigh, lingering a second past accidental.

Her cab splashes to a stop outside the door. She pulls the last ember from her cigarette and tosses the butt into a stream. Her grip on the umbrella is loose, but the nails of her left hand bite her palm. The concealed bag scratches her skin. She slips into the rain, umbrella closed and dangling at her side as she pulls open the door. Silk against leather seats. The dress was a gift, the smooth fabric a constant reminder of everything she would never have.

"Where you headed, baby?"

She mutters the name of the hotel like a curse, but if her driver notices, he says nothing. She prefers motels. Sheets stained with the night before, furniture scuffed with age and use, and handcuffs. Dirty mirrors made for tarnished reflections. Real and easy to walk away from. Motel clients don't pay her rent. The room that waits across the quarter is plush with high thread counts and gleaming furnishings, where violent tendencies are masked by the shine of money and reputation. Preferences, she's learned, are reserved for the privileged.

The hotel isn't far, blocks that can be counted on one hand. The cab starts and stops as people push into the streets, drunk and loud and heedless of the rain. A girl staggers into the side of the car, laughing, hair plastered to her shoulders, eyes bright and distorted through the rivulets tracking against the window. She knows for certain she's never laughed like that.

The hotel glows grey as the cab pulls up front. She pays the driver and doesn't tip, opening her umbrella with a snap, heels splashing against the puddled sidewalk. She breezes through the door, blinks against the sudden brightness of gilt and marble. The perfume thick air chokes her as she winds towards the elevator. Just her and a man with a briefcase. Off the rack suit, decent tailoring. Tapered sleeves, plastic buttons replaced with genuine horn. The watch is fake, but the cufflinks are real. She wonders if he's stolen them. His gaze hangs off her curves as she exits. She waits until the doors close before moving towards her destination.

She knocks.

"You're late." Her client is taller than she is, even in heels, his face a study in sharp edges – cutting cheekbones, smooth jawline. Once, she thought he might save her. From hotels, from bruises that never seemed to fade, from drowning in back ally gutters like other girls. But he's never been the saving type. She's learned to slay her own dragons. He leans lightly against the doorframe, as much a concession as a stumble or a slur. A flush starts at his temples and bleeds towards his cheeks.

Her smile is forced as she brushes a hand against the jet of his hair. His fingers grip her bicep, pulling her inside with enough force that she knows there will be marks in the morning, and knows just as well that no one will care.

"Drink?" he asks. The scotch bottle sits three quarters empty on a table near the centre of the room.

He takes her coat. It slips from the hanger, his fingers fumbling with the rain slicked material. She palms the bag still hidden in her bra and tucks it beneath the ice bucket. He gives up on the jacket, drops it onto the closet floor beneath his perfectly pressed Saint Laurent.

He's leaning again, this time against the wall, hands in his pockets, eyes never leaving hers. She works the zipper of her dress. Silk pools on the floor. His gaze doesn't change, flat and uninterested.

"You're boring me, darling." He crosses the room and pushes her against the wall. The thud echoes. He strokes a finger down her neck before wrapping his hand around her throat and kissing her. The pressure of his fingers increases until she gags. His lips retreat, but the hand remains, thumb stroking her jawline.

"None of that," he murmurs, spinning her so the textured wallpaper scores her cheek.

One hand holds her against the wall while the other fumbles with his pants. A sharp pop as his belt comes loose, the swish of heavy material hitting the floor. He presses against her.

"Struggle for me." His breath is hot in her ear. He pins her wrists, jamming his thigh between hers.

She jerks down hard against his hold, bucks against him. His grip tightens.

"You're going to have to do better than that." He licks the inside of her ear. A shudder creeps beneath her skin.

Her teeth grind as she pushes the wall away, digging in with her knees, rocking back and forth harder and harder. He slides her wrists up the wall, over her head, and she loses her leverage. She stamps her foot down on top of his. She learned early not to hold back. He grunts. She knows he wants her to scream, wants to make her distress his own, but she can't. She can feel the thud of her heart in her throat, making her breath shallow as she repeats it's just a game, it isn't real – but isn't it? She knows he can feel her building panic, and it doesn't matter that it's induced, that he pays her far more than her asking rate, that she walked in here willingly. The fight or flight response that floods her body might as well be tied directly to his cock. He likes his women powerless and frightened, and she wonders if it matters that he seeks it within the confines of their contract rather than back alleys. If it just makes him a different kind of monster.

The fight leaks from her limbs as he pushes inside. Her world narrows to the slap of skin on skin, the sting of sweat in her eyes. He's erratic tonight, drunk and thrusting hard enough that she has to time her breathing to suck in any air at all. He won't finish, not this far into a bottle. For him, that's never what it's about.

She knows girls who say they tune it out, go somewhere else. She doesn't believe them. There is no tuning out the hot cloud of alcohol against her cheek, the faint chemical smell of condoms. The friction of latex dragging inside her. The clamminess of his hands as they slide down her wrists to her forearms.

Finally, he's done with her. She presses her forehead to the wall, gaze unfocused, golds and beige blending to a murky tan color. His exhales fall heavy in the silence. He pulls off the condom and holds it out.

"Be a love and get me a drink."

She peels herself from the wall, takes the latex between her fingers. The limp rubber drags against polished porcelain and disappears.

When she returns, he is sprawled on the bed, eyes heavy but not yet closed, studying something he holds in his hand. The ice bucket is full. She scoops cubes into his glass. Her fingers brush the plastic bag. She hesitates. Her hand closes around the scotch bottle instead. She pours slowly, shaky. The bag remains hidden and sealed.

The bed dips as she perches beside him. He runs a hand over her shoulder, giving her goose bumps until his blunt nails dig in. "She left me, you know."

She sees the glittering diamond ring clutched between his fingers. Emerald cut, at least five carats. He tips his head back and drains the drink. She places the glass on the nightstand. He tosses the ring beside it. Rainbows trace through the crystal. "She left me."

The accusation in his words drags a shiver down her arms. His fingers tangle in her hair, gripping tight enough that a headache builds behind her temples. He kisses her hard, teeth and stubble and tongue. She pulls back, presses a thumb to his lips. She takes his glass, tips her head towards the scotch bottle. His grip loosens. She runs her tongue over her bottom lip, where she can still feel the cut of his teeth.

She doesn't hesitate, this time, slides a tab from the concealed bag and deftly drops it on the ice. Four fingers of scotch overtop. She mixes the concoction with a clear plastic stir stick. Once, she thought she might save him too. From his unhappy marriage, from his alcoholism, from his violent fetishes. But he's never wanted to be saved.

The drink disappears as quickly as the first, and she wonders that his addictions haven't killed him yet. He smooths a hand around her waist and pulls her into him. Rolls so that she is beneath him. His kiss is gentle. An apology, almost. He brushes a lock of hair from her eyes and draws the pads of his fingers down her cheek. One hand grips her throat, the other pins her curls to the bed. His lips move against hers. She gags, slaps at his shoulders, but he doesn't pull away this time. Doesn't loosen his grip. Her eyes water. She struggles in earnest, jams her elbows into his chest, pushes at his face. He snatches her wrists, crushing them against the bed. Tears blur her vision. He pulls his hand away from her throat and she gulps at air, body shaking with the force of her gasps. He grabs her face so that her cheeks dig into her teeth. Pauses. He rolls onto his back and runs a hand over his forehead. His eyes are unfocused. She scrambles from the bed, into the bathroom, locking the door behind her.

She runs the water for a long time before putting her shaking hands beneath the tap. She uses too much soap, washes slowly and methodically. Her stomach churns and she closes her eyes, forces herself to swallow.

Gagging noises come from beyond the bathroom door. She turns up the water pressure. Loud retching, hard and violent. She turns off the tap, opens the door cautiously. Vomit trails his chin. His breathing is shallow and slow, his chest rising and falling as he tries to suck air through his own puke. He heaves. Brown stains the crisp white linen. She touches her neck.

The ring lays discarded on the bedside table. Her hands are steady as she takes the diamond between her fingers. Such a tiny thing, imbued with so much power. She wonders what it would mean to wear something so fine. No more hotel rooms and thinly veiled lies. No more pretending to be everything that men wanted but couldn't admit to their wives, their friends, their bosses.

His convulsions come quicker now, his body trying to purge and suck air at the same time and failing at both. Vomit dribbles from his lips as his stomach heaves again.

She places the ring back in its place. She doesn't need to be saved. Not by him.

She collects her dress and coat from the floor. She pulls wet wipes from her purse and cleans the faucets, his glass, the bottle of scotch. She checks that the condom flushed properly and wipes down the handle. Stalling. He lies still now, unrecognizable beneath the layer of brown liquid that stains his face, his chest, that pools in the creases of the comforter. He's still breathing, thin breaths that almost don't even count. It's time to be done with this. She plucks a tissue from the bedside table and gently pinches his nose. She expects him to struggle, to thrash, to try to save himself. But he just lies limp, Adam's apple bobbing. And then even that goes still. His skin is clammy and hot as she presses her fingers to his neck. Her heart beats in her throat, pulsing against the bruises she knows will surface in the morning. She takes his wrist, double-checks the result. His chest doesn't rise or fall. His heart is still.

She pulls lipstick from her purse with shaking fingers, draws crimson across her lips. Using the tissue, she keys in the safe number – he never changes his code, hotel after hotel. She takes her due and leaves the rest, plucks her umbrella from the floor and turns up her collar.

She spares him a final glance, committing the scene to memory. She prefers him like this. Silent. Dead. The silk of her dress caresses her thighs as she moves towards the door. Something slithers in the pit of her stomach.

It feels a little like power.

A little like privilege.

The Seeker

M.H. Callway

He came at me out of the night, a white wraith from a dark wood. Instinct saw what my eyes did not. Suddenly my BMW thrashed and fishtailed over the road. I felt the hit rather than heard it.

Awareness came slowly: the shadowy landscape beyond my windows had stopped moving. My hands clutched the steering wheel and my heart churned like a wild thing.

I didn't know what I'd hit and I didn't want to. So I sat there, staring through the windshield into the dark New Mexico night while the chill of cowardice sneaked into my blood.

No witnesses. I could drive off. No one would know.

Except Storr would know. He loved his BMW Gran Tourismo with a passion only those with a Y chromosome could understand. The bastard could spot a micro-scratch, real or imaginary, anywhere on its silver surface. Besides he detested women drivers, especially older women like me, which in fairness The Agency did, too. My boss, Reese, only threw me the job, because his regular guy took sick.

I turned off the engine and slipped the key into the back pocket of my jeans.

The moon was high, shedding a cold white light over the empty road ahead. Pinon pines and cottonwoods cast sharp-edged, silent shadows in the breezeless night. I hadn't seen another car for miles.

I reached for the driver's door. Stopped myself.

Deserted highway, no witnesses.

I dug under the passenger seat for my gun. Hated the damn thing, hated the cold feel of it, its blunt silver muzzle and the tiny black implacable hole at the end. Only bought it because my son insisted. For long, solitary drives through lonely places, he'd said. Looking out for me like always.

The Glock 17 had a complicated three-stage safety mechanism disengaged by pressing the trigger the right way. Nice if I could remember how.

I unlocked the driver's door. Stepped out into the night.

He reared up in front of me, his skin pale as moonlight. My scream echoed over the black pavement. He'd been crouching down next to my front tire.

"Get back!" I rammed the gun in his face. "Get back or I'll shoot."

"Help me! Help me, please!" He lunged for the open driver's door between us. Clung to it with bloodied hands.

I kicked the door, my one chance. Knocked him down. He fell, clutching himself, whimpering.

"Stay the hell away from me," I said. "Or I'll shoot you through the head. I swear to God I will."

"Please, he'll kill me."

"Yeah, right."

"Please!" He rolled onto his knees. I saw now that he was crying. "He's right behind me."

In the distance a powerful engine was cutting through the trees. Could be an ATV.

"Get over there where I can see you."

He stepped into my high-beams, one hand warding off the brightness. He was barefoot, his naked legs streaked with blood and dirt. A rough grey blanket hung over his shoulders, hiding the rest of him.

"Show me your hands," I said. "Both of them."

"Please, he's coming!"

The engine sounded a lot louder, but the kid could have anything hidden under that ratty blanket: a knife strapped to his chest, a shotgun even. "Drop it," I said. "Don't shake your head at me. Do it or I'll run you over when I leave."

He let the blanket fall. He was completely naked under it. Just a boy really.

The roar of the motor loomed ear-shatteringly close now. So I made my decision, a fatal one as it turned out.

"OK, get in," I said.

271

I jumped back into the driver's seat and started the engine.

A black Jeep soared out of the forest and crashed down onto the highway a hundred feet behind us. A rack of blue-white LEDs studded its roll bar.

I rammed the gearshift into drive. The BMW shot forward. The kid was half in, half outside the car, struggling to close the passenger door.

"Shut the goddamn door!" I yelled.

"I can't!" he screamed back.

The open door flapped against the car frame like an over-sized wing, dragging us down like an anchor. I stomped so hard on the brake pedal, the crunch of the ABS system vibrated through my shin bone. He slammed into the dashboard. Cried out.

"For God's sake, close it! Now!"

Somehow he managed it.

I pounded down on the gas. Light flooded the BMW's interior. A roaring force smashed into my back fender. The impact flung us fifty feet down the road.

The BMW pitched and churned like a boat. I clung to the steering wheel, fighting to keep us on the road.

But I'd lost too much time. His lights scorched us again. And he rammed into the rear fender on my side, pitching us sideways.

A deadly vibration as the tires on the kid's side caught the hard edge where the asphalt met the sandy shoulder.

My panic in hyper-drive, I let up on the gas. No choice. I feathered the wheel, coaxing, willing my wheels back on the road.

"He's dropping back," the kid shouted.

Sure. To steer clear of our wreckage.

I felt my tires grip the pavement, run smooth. A damn miracle. No time to think: I slammed down into second gear and the BMW took off like a rocket.

No hanging bodywork to catch the tires, thank God. The transmission shrieked from the strain. The speedometer needle hit sixty. Eighty. We had to outrun the Jeep or die.

I watched the roll bar LEDs grow small in the rear view mirror. And stay small.

"Now you're toast, you bastard," I muttered.

"He's still there." The kid twisted to look behind us. "He won't give up. He'll catch us."

Eighty, one hundred.

"He can't catch us," I said to reassure myself as much as the kid. "The Beemer does zero to sixty in four point four seconds. His Jeep's a pig. It can't do nine."

"He's got a brand new Jeep Wrangler, turbocharged."

"No shit?" Horsepower that matched mine. The tightness in my chest got worse.

The boy looked away, chewing his thumb. In the mirror, the hunter's lights had faded to a single spot like a remote star.

Something slammed into the trunk.

"What's that?" The kid's hands flew out. "You hit something!"

"No, or we'd be flying looking for a place to land." I forced my breath in and out. "Has your buddy got a gun?"

His face was pale marble.

"Come on, the truth. Answer me."

"Yes, yes! Yes, he's got a gun. Lots of them."

"Get down! And stay down!"

He slid off the seat. Huddled under the dashboard, hands over his head.

One ten, one twenty...

The hunter must be using a high-powered rifle with a scope. Easier to shoot us than to run us off the road. Less risk of damaging his Jeep.

"Slow down, slow down please," the kid cried. "The whole car is shaking."

"A sniper rifle has a quarter mile range. Some models have more." I dared not take my eyes off the long black stretch of highway for a microsecond. "What's your buddy's favorite gun?"

"I don't know! I don't know anything about guns."

"Is he a good shot?"

"I guess."

"Guess harder."

"Yes, yes, he said he's a good shot. And he's not my buddy."

I teased the steering wheel a hair. Made the BMW sway back and forth over the road, which ran straight as a line of longitude in these parts.

"What are you doing? You'll crash us and we'll die. Stop, please stop."

"A moving target is harder to hit. If I drive straight, all your buddy has to do is aim and we're done."

"Holy shit, slow down. Slow down, please!"

"I know how to drive." I reached down and killed the BMW's lights. Something I should've thought of before.

"Now what did you do? It's pitch black outside."

"Let's see how well your buddy does firing blind."

"You're crazy!" He clawed his way back onto the passenger seat. "You'll kill us!"

"Shut up!"

I dimmed the dash lights. Stared ahead into the dark, desperately summoning my night vision. These days the rods in my eyes seemed to fire on one cylinder. Even under the full moon, the weathered white centre line was only faintly visible.

Just the same, I eased the BMW over to the middle of the highway, straddling the centre line in a quasi-lethal game of follow the dots.

"Now what are you doing?"

"Slowing down. Happy?" What I was really doing was gambling. Gambling that I'd put enough distance between us and the hunter.

"I don't see his lights."

"Maybe he turned them off, too."

The kid had a point.

We needed help, but I saw nothing but dark, empty woods. No lights anywhere, no oncoming cars. Where the hell was civilization?

"You, OK?" I asked him after a minute.

No answer. I saw that he'd smeared blood from his cuts all over Storr's dove-grey, customized leather seat.

"You got a name?"

"Mike," he said at last. "Mike Green Arrow."

Sure. Why not steal a superhero's cool name? My son called himself Steve Rogers after his favorite hero, Captain America.

"What's your name?" he asked.

"Terry Snow. OK, Mike or whatever, when we hit Espanola, I'm dropping you off at the hospital."

"No! No doctors! I don't have any money."

"Fine, the cops then."

He didn't like that idea any better.

The hell with you, I thought and glanced down at the fuel gauge. Not good. "Where's the nearest gas station?"

"I don't know."

"Think! I'm running on empty here."

He took a long breath. "I think we passed one driving up from Espanola. Closer to town."

"But you're not sure."

"Sorry, I'm not from round here." He rubbed his face with a shaky, bruised hand and leaned his forehead against the passenger window. "We're not going to make Espanola, are we?"

I didn't want to answer that.

"Can you at least turn the headlights back on? Please!"

Truth be told driving blind was scaring me, too. I checked again for the hunter's headlights. Nothing, so I flicked on my running lights.

The narrow, stony edges of the road leaped out of the dark.

"OK, I need those young eyes of yours. Watch the road and watch for him."

I felt those young eyes on me now.

"Just how old *are* you?"

"Old. Just do it, OK?"

We were leaving the hills, I could feel the descent in my ears. At last the road broke free of the trees and struck out over a broad plain: the start of the desert. Under the moon, the sands seemed dimly phosphorescent and in the empty, cactus-dotted wilderness that screamed alien abductions and covert nuclear blasts, I felt even more vulnerable and exposed.

"There, on the left," the kid said.

So he'd remembered right. Half a mile down the road, I spotted the green glow of a solitary service station. Like a hundred others I'd soared past on my 26-hour drive down from Canada stoked up on caffeine and energy bars.

I slowed down and scoped it out: square Adobe building housing a mini-mart set ninety degrees to the road. Large plate glass windows overlooking four gas pumps. The only spot not lit up like centre stage Broadway lay in the shadows by the wall farthest from the road.

The Dame Was Trouble

I doused my lights, geared down and pulled in. Steered clear of the brilliantly lit gas pumps and plunged into the shadows on the far side of the minimart. Pulled up short of an overflowing dumpster. Beyond it lay nothing but sand.

I killed the engine.

"I thought you needed gas," he said.

I held up my hand to silence him and opened the driver's door to listen to the night. No roar of the hunter's Jeep, no squeak of a door opening at the minimart. Nothing but the tick of the BMW's cooling engine and the rumble of ice in the ancient ice machine out front.

"Stay here." I pocketed the car keys, grabbed the Glock from under the driver's seat and climbed out.

"Where are you going with that gun?"

I slammed the door on him. Gun in hand, I braced myself against the rough back wall of the building while the acrid odor of the dumpster settled around me.

The kid scrambled out of the car to join me.

Ignoring him, I peered around the corner at the end of the building and checked out the inside of the mini-mart. A forlorn, dark-haired man sat hunched behind the cash, marooned in an existentialist hell of cellophane-wrapped snack foods, plastic water bottles and dusty racks of remaindered DVD's.

The kid's frantic breath felt hot on my neck. "Don't do this, please. I'm in enough trouble already."

"Do what?" I stuffed the gun inside my leather jacket and zipped it up to the neck. "Mr. Minimart might get antsy. He could come out here with a gun. Watch him."

"He's just sitting there, staring at the ceiling."

"Yeah, well, pray he stays put." Not a second to lose. I went over to the BMW and forced myself to examine the damage to Storr's silver beauty.

Bad news, real bad news. Tail lights and back bumper crushed, rear fender on the driver's side crumpled like paper. The wreckage hadn't interfered with the back wheels thanks to tough German engineering or more likely, dumb luck. I owed the Holy Virgin a load of Hail Mary's.

Add it to my tab, Madonna, I thought and used my keys to pop open the trunk. Leaning in to grab the red plastic container of gas I kept for emergencies, I couldn't miss the neat black bullet hole. Dead center through the rear license plate.

No smell of gas. Dumb luck for sure.

Calling in this disaster to Reese, my boss at The Agency, could wait. Maybe forever. I set the gas container on the ground, cursing the weakness in my wrists as I fought with the screw cap. Women my age complain that they can't open jars and bottles. I can't stand listening to them. Or being one of them.

"Hey you, Mike, come over here. Open this." I nudged the gas can with my foot.

While he bent down and wrestled with the cap, something rippled through the dark of the highway. A car, headlights out, heading south, silent as a fish in a murky pond. The black Jeep, tracking us.

Breathless, I watched it glide past the station. How long before he realized we'd stopped? How long before he pulled a U-turn and spotted us?

"There." The kid lurched back to his feet.

"Your buddy just drove by the station. You're right. He did turn off his lights."

The kid turned the colour of ice. "I'm...I'm gonna be sick."

"Get away from me. Do it over there."

He uttered a cough. Next thing, he was pressed up against the wall, retching. Wonderful.

I grabbed the container and began pouring gas into the BMW's tank. Hopefully the kid would get what was bothering him out of his system fast.

"What are you doing?" Mr. Mini-mart appeared around the corner of the building.

"Holy Mother, you scared the hell out of me!" Gas slopped down the side panel of Storr's baby. Thank God, Mini-mart's hands were empty. No gun.

"Why are you parked back here?" he asked.

We eyeballed each other. He saw a tall, weathered 62 year old woman with a grey braid down her back and I saw a short, chubby, fiftyish man, uncomfortable in his company uniform of baggy brown pants and orange shirt. The badge on his front pocket read "Moe". Short for "Mohammed", I figured.

"We're fine. You got a problem?" I poured more gas into the BMW, desperate to leave.

"No, no problem. What is wrong with him?" Behind me, the kid was still emptying himself. From shock or his injuries or both.

"He ate a bad taco."

"He should use the washroom. He has only to ask."

"The washroom is only for customers, right?"

Moe was taking in the damage to the BMW. "You had some trouble."

"Forget it. You don't want to get involved. We're leaving now."

"Your son..."

"He's not my son."

"Your grandson then. He is ill. He needs help."

The kid had collapsed on all fours, the blanket sliding off him, revealing his nakedness. I swore, rammed the screw cap back on the container, threw it back into the trunk and ran over to check him out.

He looked bad, breathing hard. Dark bloodstains mottled the blanket.

"He needs a doctor." Moe said behind me. I couldn't argue with that. "Why don't you bring him inside the shop? I have medical training. Perhaps I could be of assistance."

The night was deathly quiet except for the crackle of insects drifting into a nearby mosquito light. We should go.

"He's coming back for us," the kid gasped. At the edge of my hearing, the rumble of a motor.

Inside the mini-mart, we'd be safer. Marginally. And there'd be water, painkillers, stuff to help the kid. So I made my second fateful decision that night.

"OK. Help me with him."

Getting the kid inside the minimart was a struggle. Through the plate glass windows, I spotted headlights gliding down the road. Heading toward us: the black jeep.

"Kill the lights!" I shouted.

Thank God, Moe didn't argue. Moving with the swiftness and grace some fat guys possess, he ran behind the cash and yanked a switch, throwing the store and the gas pumps into darkness, leaving us in the dim, violet light cast by the fridge compartments at the back.

Had the hunter spotted the BMW hidden round the side of the building?

"Help me with him," I called to Moe. The kid was sweaty, trembling, barely able to stand.

Moe came running over. "Let us bring him over to the aisle by the coolers. The light is better there."

Together we dragged the kid to the back of the store and stretched him down over the dusty tiles in front of the refrigerators.

"How're you doing, Mike?" I asked. His forehead felt cold under the sweat.

He writhed away from me, restless, out of it. "He'll find us. We're *trapped* in here."

Moe kneeled down next to the kid and tossed aside the grimy blanket. I watched his deft, dark fingers move over the boy's pale body, probing, skirting his many lacerations.

"What's wrong with him?" I asked.

"Obviously he has been in a fight. But without X-rays, medical tests, I cannot say for certain."

"You said you were some kind of doctor."

"I *am* a doctor. Back home, overseas." He stood up, lowered his voice. "Walk with me. Over there." He nodded toward the cash, ten feet away at the end of the aisle.

I didn't want to leave the kid, but I followed him over. "OK, so tell me," I said, hoping he couldn't overhear us.

Moe made a gesture of helplessness. "Your young friend has several broken ribs, internal bleeding, almost certainly. And he has been, well, how best to put it, ill-used."

Male prostitute, a trick gone wrong. Hell, I should have guessed.

"I cannot do much for him here other than water and painkillers," Moe went on. "He needs a blood transfusion. He needs a proper hospital."

The Agency's cell phone went off in my jacket pocket. The Darth Vader ringtone meant Reese, my boss. I pulled it out and killed the sound.

"You are not answering?" Moe asked. I shook my head. "May I ask what this boy means to you?"

"He ran out in front of me. On the highway ten miles north of here. I braked but knocked him down. I could have killed him."

"I see." Moe looked thoughtful. "But why stop to help? Were you not worried? A woman driving alone. It could have been a trap."

"Sure, but I know real fear when I see it. Kids his age make bad decisions, take stupid risks. Like my son…"

"He reminded you of your son."

I wasn't going down that road. Not now and not with Moe. Except for his age, Mike looked nothing like my son.

My son loved danger. That last time danger took the shape of a girl.

My instincts went off the first time I met her. Beautiful, bright and fake friendly as though she were auditioning for a movie role. I brushed off my worries: my son was twenty years old, nearly a man, he could handle himself. But he changed with her. When he hired on at her family's body shop, a name I recognized from my job as a skip tracer for the insurance company, my worries turned to fear.

We had a fight, a bad one. He told me to back off, he loved her. I was over-protective, suffocating him. He moved out that night and I never saw him again.

"Are you all right?" Moe asked.

"Fine." I grabbed a large plastic bottle of water and a dusty package of painkillers off the nearby shelf and dumped everything on the counter. Reached in my jeans and slapped down a twenty.

"That is not necessary." Moe waved my money away.

"Yeah, it is. You got any clothes for sale. Something Mike could wear?"

"Not really, but I will look." He rummaged under the cash and hauled out a cardboard box with "lost and found" scrawled across it in black marker.

I looked over my shoulder into the night beyond the windows. No sign yet of the hunter.

"Terry?" Mike sounded weak.

I left Moe foraging through the junk in the lost and found and went over to the kid. He'd struggled up to a sitting position.

I handed him the plastic bottle of water. He downed half of it in one go. I pried open the container of painkillers and tossed him a few. Waited till he'd swallowed them. "Your buddy did this to you, didn't he?" The kid's look was enough. "You want to tell me his name?" No, he didn't.

"These might fit you." Moe returned with a pair of stained denim shorts. "And this, this corporate goodie you can have for nothing." He tossed the kid a plastic-wrapped gas company T-shirt.

Slowly, painfully, the kid got dressed. Finished, he coughed and slumped back against the glass door of the fridge. "Dujay. His name is Dujay."

Moe stiffened beside me.

"You know this guy," I said.

Moe nodded. "Rancher Grant Dujay. He owns a big spread with an airfield north of here. Planes, trucks, people coming and going all the time. A Canadian like yourself. But not a nice, polite one. No, not at all. All the time, his boys barge in here. Take whatever they want. Money from my cash last time. One thousand dollars."

Add Mr. Dujay to Canada's Scrapbook of Shame, I thought.

My cell phone went off on vibrate. Might as well get this over with, I thought and pressed the Talk button.

"You're late, Terry. Should I be worried?" Reese sounded amiable, his deep voice reflecting the patience and learning of the high school principal he once was. He looked it, too, silver-haired, tall and trim from running marathons. I always found it a weird contrast, Reese in his wire-frame glasses, studying papers in his glassed-in office while his guys splashed grease and sparks in the drive-in bay next to it. At age 40, he'd retired from teaching and taken over his family's body shop, which serviced mostly high-end vehicles. On the surface, at least. He ran a huge operation with drivers and mechanics on the job 24/7. Lots of other businesses, too: some were even legitimate like The Agency where I worked. Not like the chop shop where my son once had a job. I prayed that he'd learned enough never to ask questions about the stuff he saw and heard there.

"Give me the courtesy of a reply." Reese sounded tired.

I needed to keep Reese happy. Only he knew where I could find my son. "Sorry, I was driving. Couldn't pick up. I'm about to hit Espanola."

"You won't make it."

"Who says I won't? Your boys?"

The Agency had me moving cars round Toronto. Reese's boys did the high-paying cross-border runs. Go figure. But then out of the blue, Reese threw me the gig, my first run out of Canada. Reese's buddy, Storr was sunning his ass down at his villa in San Miguel, Mexico and pining for his silver Gran Tourismo.

But why me? And *Mexico*? I'd be dead within minutes of crossing the southern border. So in spite of everything, I told Reese to forget it.

He waved a languid hand. Laughed at me, said he used a special driver for Mexico jobs, a tough Texan. All I had to do was haul ass to the Starbucks in Espanola where I'd hand over the keys to the Texan.

I checked the time. Reese was right. I'd never make Espanola for the handover. "Tell your guy to wait. I'll be there."

"What's happened to the Beemer?"

"Nothing's happened to it."

Reese gave a soft laugh. "You're a bad liar, Terry. I need an answer. Don't waste my time."

Busted! Or was he fishing?

"I thought I saw something move," Mike said behind me.

"Work with me here," Reese said. "You've been stopped for over an hour."

How would he know that unless… Shit! The bastard was tracking me. Through my cell phone, provided by The Agency.

"What's the extent of damage to the Beemer? Is it driveable?"

He knew. I ended the call, cutting him off. Turned off the power, too. Pointless, but I felt better, back in control.

Headlights were gliding past the gas station. Real slow. Too slow.

"Dujay knows we're here," Mike said.

Ice ran down my spine. "Moe, call the cops!"

"Already done." Moe's teeth flashed in the dim light. "After I saw you with the gun."

So he'd been staring at a security camera on the ceiling. Probably had me on tape. Great. "Not smart of you to come outside and confront me empty-handed."

"Well, to be frank, you do not look anything like Dujay's boys." He cleared his throat. "In any case, the police claim it is safer for me not to have a gun. They say that next time the robbers will only use it against me."

"Like now? How long before the cops get here?"

Moe shrugged. "Two, three hours, if they bother to show up at all. Always they are arguing about which county has jurisdiction over the service station, you see. And of course, I am not American."

Enough said. We were on our own.

The Jeep, lights dimmed, turned in to the station.

"Mike, stay down!"

A flash of orange shirt by the coolers. "I hear you."

I slid down behind the cash counter. Felt my gun thump against my ribs. A simple handgun against Dujay's high-powered rifle? We hadn't a prayer.

Moe joined me to shelter behind the cash. He seized the lost and found box and tore it apart. From the detritus of clothes, empty water bottles and junk food wrappers, he dragged out a beaten-up Browning A-bolt shotgun.

So he hadn't listened to the cops after all.

I readied my gun and glanced round the edge of the counter. The black jeep crawled up to the gas pumps. No headlights now, studded roll bar dead. Moonlight silvered its hard squared-off edges, its battered mesh grille.

Behind the windshield, I made out the shadowy shape of the hunter. And next to him, someone in the passenger seat.

"Mike, who's that with Dujay?"

"I don't know. He and I were alone."

"Is there another way out of this place?" I whispered to Moe.

He worked a bullet into the shotgun. "Yes, over there by the washrooms." He pointed to the shadowy corridor that stretched away from the end of the cooler aisle toward the side of the building. "The garbage room at the end has a door that opens to the outside."

I remembered the overflowing dumpster in front of the BMW. "Mike, did you hear? That's your way out."

No answer.

The Jeep's rear passenger doors flew open. Its interior lights flashed on. Two men climbed out: one had shaggy blond hair, the other a shaved head. Both carried serious rifles. Dujay must've circled back to his ranch up north for back-up.

"Bastards!" Moe reared up, aiming his Browning over the counter.

"Get down!" I dragged on his orange shirt. "Don't be stupid. We're outgunned." He wavered. "Surprise them: it's our only chance!"

He sat back down onto the floor, clutching the shotgun to his chest. "I am going to pay them back. On God's name I swear it."

"Then be smart about it."

"You don't know what those two did to me. Green and Whitman, Dujay's dogs. Back home I lost everything, my wife, my children. I came to America with nothing but my honour, so now if I die, I die."

"The hell with that!" I shot back. I needed to live – to live for my son.

Dujay's dogs disappeared, circling the building to make sure we were still inside.

From outside, a whoop of triumph. "The Beemer's over here, chief!" a British voice yelled.

"That is Whitman, the bald one," Moe said.

My heart beat faster. "Can he get in here through the side door?"

Moe stared at me. "God help me, I do not remember if I locked it tonight or not."

"Hey, I'll go lock it," Mike whispered from where he crouched by the coolers.

"No, stay down!"

A metallic boom echoed through the side corridor. "Hey, Moe," the British voice shouted. "It's me, Whitman, your old mate. I know you're in there. " He banged the side door again.

Now Dujay's passenger climbed out. A tall and lean man in a windbreaker and jeans. Moonlight flashed on his wire-rim glasses, turning the lenses silver.

Reese!

"You recognize him," Moe said.

"It's my boss." I let out a long breath. "I thought he was calling me from his body shop up in Canada. But he's been here all along."

"He and Dujay obviously know each other."

"Probably dirty business buddies."

Reese must have flown down to Dujay's ranch the minute I left Toronto. After all, Moe said that planes were flying in and out of there all the time. But what dirty business were Reese and Dujay in on together? Stolen cars?

Perhaps Reese intended that out on that long, lonely highway I'd run into an ambush. Storr's BMW would disappear and me along with it. But why the New Mexico setup? Reese and his boys regularly disappeared luxury cars back home in Canada.

Looked like I owed Mike one. If he hadn't run out in front of me, I'd have ended up dead.

The roar of a V6 engine tore through my ears. The headlights of the jeep flared on. Searing the inside of the shop, burning away my night vision.

And then those lights headed straight for us. I threw myself over Moe.

The plate glass window exploded in a waterfall of shining shards. Flying glass showered over the counter, cutting through my leather jacket, stinging my bare hands like a thousand bees.

Night air flooded in and with it the raw smell of exhaust and burning oil. The Jeep's motor was revving and churning like crazy.

I risked a quick look. The plate glass window had vanished. Twenty feet away from us, Dujay's black Jeep sat wedged halfway through the opening, motor smoking, the ancient ice machine jammed under its front axle. Stopped dead. Good thing or we'd have been crushed to death.

I shook the glass off my shoulders. My gun felt slippery in my bleeding hand. Moe scrambled onto his knees, shotgun ready.

I fumbled with the Glock's trigger.

"*Criste! Tabernacle!*" I recognized the *joual*, the harsh Quebec French dialect. That had to be Rancher Dujay.

"Turn that bloody engine off." Reese's high school principal's voice cut through the din.

The sudden silence left my ears ringing. But the Jeep's fierce headlights still burned through the store.

"Hey Green!" Dujay shouted from outside. "Call the ranch. Get the goddamn tow truck out here."

"Later!" That was Reese. "Terry, I know you're in there. Come out, we need to talk."

"Hell, she's probably dead." That had to be Green, Dujay's blond dog. His Southern drawl turned "dead" into "daid".

292

Glass crunched under heavy boots. One of them, most likely Green, had stepped inside the store through the shattered window.

Not yet, I signalled to Moe whose forehead glistened with sweat.

A faint rustle over by the coolers. I spotted Mike waving from the shadows cast by the shelf in front of him. He held up a bottle of camper fuel: kerosene.

What the hell?

Moe nudged me. With the toe of his worn runner, he poked at a Zippo lighter that had tumbled out of the lost and found.

I got the idea: DYI Molotov cocktail. Risky, we'd probably set ourselves on fire, but why not? I scooped up the lighter with my free hand. Tossed it to Mike.

"Hey, they're in here! Behind the cash," Green yelled.

"Don't fire till I tell you," Reese shouted back.

I readied my gun. Mike wrenched the cap off his container. Dregs of kerosene spotted the tiles.

"I smell gas." Green again, a dog sniffing the air. "Cain I burn them rats now?"

Moe's knuckles showed white on his Browning.

"Control yourself, Mr. Green. Arson is your reward," Reese said. "Upon the successful conclusion of our business."

"*Et mon char?*" Dujay's angry voice cried. "No fucking way are you going to torch my Jeep!"

"Take the Beemer. Tell Whitman to move it out," Reese said.

"Tell him your goddamn self."

Reese didn't react.

"You're an intelligent woman, Terry. Mr. Whitman can't locate my valuables in the Beemer. I know you took them. And we both know you won't live to enjoy them. So let's make things easy, shall we?"

"Drugs?" Moe mouthed silently to me.

I shook my head. Smuggling drugs into Mexico made no sense. But money for drugs sure did. Big time. Where in the BMW had Reese stashed it?

"Fuck it, I'm gonna burn them rats." Green's southern whine sounded way too close. "Especially that fat brown one."

With a roar, Moe lunged over the counter. His shot gun boomed a foot over my head, deafening me.

Green returned fire. Bullets chewed through the cigarette packages behind the cash. Splintered the coolers into spikes of grey and green glass.

No time to think. I leaned round the counter and popped out those damn headlights. One, two, plunging us into darkness. A soft snow covered my shoulders. I smelled tobacco – and blood.

In the distance, a muffled voice was screaming: "He got me! He got me!"

Where was Mike? In the dim light, I spotted a flash of orange heading for the side corridor and the washrooms.

Moe was still upright. He stared transfixed over the counter at Green's bloodied body, crawling through the shattered glass toward us.

"Get down!" I screamed. My voice sounded like I was shouting through a cardboard tube. But Moe resisted, stiff as a statue.

Green lurched to his knees, grimacing through his pain. Oblivious to the rivers of blood pouring from his ruined body, he raised his rifle.

I shoved Moe aside and fired.

"Shoot!" I yelled to him.

I fired again and again. Until Green went down in a spray of blood and bullets. His rifle went off as he fell, shattering the dead fluorescent lights on the ceiling.

Moe lay collapsed over the counter, a dark stain spreading through the back of his orange shirt.

A faint creak of metal on metal. A figure stormed in from the corridor. Light glinted off a polished scalp. Whitman!

I turned and shot him through the chest. He swayed for a heartbeat. Then laughed. Laughed! My bullet meant nothing.

Body armour, the bastard had on body armour. I fired at his head.

And missed.

"Not sporting to shoot an old lady," Whitman grinned and took aim.

And erupted into a pillar of flame.

Mike! He must have hidden in the washroom. Waited for his chance.

"Run, kid!" I shouted. "Get out of here!"

Whitman's terrible, shrill screams tore through my damaged ears. He staggered like a drunk, beating wildly at the flames that ate him. Knocked down the tower of DVD's, scattering pieces of fire and flesh. Reeled out through the gaping remains of the plate glass window and toppled onto his knees.

Where Reese calmly put a bullet through his brain.

"You shot him!" Dujay shrieked over the flames flickering on Whitman's prone form. "*Batarde!* You son of a bitch. You shot Whitman."

"He should have moved the BMW. Not gone ape-shit." The silver Sig Sauer in Reese's hand didn't waver. "I had this."

Dujay, a stocky figure in full Western gear, ran for the back of the Jeep. Light glinted off the silver spurs on his tooled leather boots. He dragged out a complicated-looking black rifle.

"M16 automatic," Moe managed to say in a hoarse whisper from where he'd fallen over the counter.

I grabbed Moe's shirt and heaved, dragging him down with me behind the cash.

The air exploded around us. Snack food containers fragmented in puffs of powder, soda bottles blossomed in fountains, shreds of toilet paper floated in the air like confetti.

Then silence.

Outside raised voices. My hearing returned in waves. I struggled free of Moe's dead weight. The wound in his chest let out an eerie, gasping sound.

I grabbed a handful of loose clothes from the floor and pressed them down over the wound. Forced his limp hand to hold them. "Push down, Moe! Stay with me."

"I needed her alive," Reese was saying. "You idiot – millions – diamonds."

"Two of my guys dead...

"Your problem..."

And then clearly, I heard Dujay say: "I'm gonna kill that kid!"

"He won't get far in the desert."

Mike! He'd escaped through the side door. And he was on the run. Out of their reach - for now.

"He was with *her*. He fucked this up," Dujay said.

"No, because of you and your perverse tastes, you fucked this up." A pause. "What the hell are you doing?"

"Cleaning up."

I risked a quick look. Saw Dujay rip the nozzle off the nearest gas pump. Turn and spray gasoline over the ground, the Jeep and Whitman's still form. "Take your fancy Beemer," he shouted. "Tear it apart, find your ass-hole diamonds."

"Don't be rude." Reese thumped his Sig against his thigh.

"You owe me. One million at least. Don't think you can fuck me over, you *maudite Anglais*." Gas sloshed over Reese's Nikes.

Reese's gun went off in a burst of noise.

Dujay's head vanished in a crimson surge. His Stetson wobbled, tumbled to the ground. But the nozzle in his death grip kept pumping. The choking smell of gasoline flooded in through the ruptured front window.

I watched Reese wipe the Sig off on his jeans.

"Terry, are you still in there?" He leaned in through the cavernous opening, one hand on the hood of the Jeep.

My hands, bleeding from a dozen cuts, nearly lost my gun. How many bullets did I have left? I'd lost count.

I stood up and faced him. He reached the middle of the store, ten feet away from me.

"Stay where you are." I levelled my gun at him. I only needed one bullet. I only had to stay alive long enough to kill him.

"Amazing. You're still alive." Did I hear a faint trace of admiration in his voice?   "Oh, you won't shoot me."

"I killed Green."

"A stranger in the heat of battle. You and I know each other, Terry, we've worked together. It's different."

I fired blindly. Reese was right. I couldn't look him in the eye and pull the trigger.

I walked over to where he had fallen, crunching through the chaos of glass, chips and syrupy drinks.

"Terry..."

He looked as pale as the shreds of paper drifting around us. His dark eyes were luminous with shock, blood loss and surprise. My bullet had blown out his knee.

But he hadn't lost his grip on his gun. A professional - and lethal – to the last.

"Looks like your marathon running days are over," I said. "Drop the gun, Reese. Drop it or I'll shoot out your other knee."

"You old bitch." He laughed out of pain, frustration or indulgence, I couldn't tell which, but he let his gun fall.

"It's time you showed me some respect," I said, keeping my Glock steady. "Your damn diamonds are bogus. They don't exist."

"Is that so?"

"I believe that your plan all along was to clean house down here in New Mexico. Dujay might have been your business buddy, but he'd let his dogs, Green and Whitman, get out of hand. Robbing gas stations, roughing up male hookers, that gets the cops interested."

"Quite the imagination you've got."

"So you told Dujay that I'd stolen your diamonds, that he needed to run me off the highway and get them back. Then kill me."

"Nonsense."

"Dujay never suspected that you planned on wasting him and his dogs. He had some sadistic fun with a hooker. But Mike escaped and Dujay delayed the ambush to chase the kid down."

Reese reached for his knee, his face twisted in pain. "I rather liked you, Terry. I tried to keep you safe, give you jobs in Toronto. I owed you, but then you got greedy."

"Shut up!" I aimed my gun between his eyes. "I never gave a damn about money. Tell me where my son is."

"Oh, for God's sake. I don't know your son."

"He worked for you. He called himself Steve Rogers like Captain America. He was in love with your daughter."

"Steve Rogers was your son?"

"Stop lying. Answer my question. What did you do to him?"

Reese sighed and struggled up to a sitting position. "I'm sorry, Terry. Truly sorry, but we both know the answer to your question."

My last desperate hope that Steve was alive died then. I wanted to destroy Reese, stomp his knee to a jelly, tear him to pieces with my bare hands. "What happened?"

"Why torture yourself with the details? He was sniffing around my daughter. He'd never become part of my family. He wouldn't accept that so he paid the price."

I squeezed the trigger, but my gun clicked on empty.

Quick as a snake, Reese lunged for his gun. Got it in his grip. All I could do was watch.

And then he vanished in a roar of blood and noise.

The smell of gasoline drew me back to reality. My ears were ringing. I saw Mike get up from the wreckage of the shelf he crushed when he fell. Knocked over by the kickback from Moe's shotgun.

I stumbled over to him. Helped him up. "Thanks, kid."

"He was going to kill you." Mike trembled all over. "I came back and hid in the washroom. I heard you two talking. He killed your son. Oh, God..."

I forced him away from the carnage. "Don't look. You saved my life. Go check on Moe."

Reese or what was left of him was still twitching. I stayed to watch him die. But when the life went out of him, I felt no epiphany only a vast sorrow for my son. My only child.

"Moe's still alive," Mike shouted from behind the cash. "He's breathing."

I'd lost blood from my cuts and Mike could barely stand. But between the two of us, we dragged Moe out the side door to the BMW and laid him gently on the back seat. Mike squeezed in beside him.

I started the engine, reversed out past the gas pumps. Dujay's pool of gas was lapping the concrete platform under the pumps. "You still got that lighter, Mike?"

He took the Zippo out of his pocket, flicked it on. We looked at each other.

I gunned the motor. "Let's roast the rats."

He tossed the burning lighter out through the open rear window. In a whoosh of light, the spilled gas turned into a burning sea.

I tore onto the highway, heading south. Behind us, a scarlet surge of destruction erupted into the night sky.

"Moe's breathing funny. He's going, Terry, he's going."

"Talk to him, Mike. Keep him with us. This time we're going to make Espanola. All of us."

Crossing Jordan
Sandra Ruttan

Jordan looked up at the dark beam above her head and concluded she was ready to lose a fight with gravity.

Hanging implement—check.

A length of rope lay in the bottom drawer of the tall, oak dresser that stood between the door and her work bed. The one where she kept all her toys.

Noose—check.

Her father's insistence on curative camping and boating trips ensured that she knew how to tie a solid knot, which had been useful when she'd secured the over-the-door sex swing some of her clients liked.

It was a skill that would come in handy today, too.

Jordan walked through the colorless bathroom to the small room hidden behind the shelves on the far wall and retrieved a measuring tape from the toolbox under her personal bed. She pushed away the feeling of warmth and security she always felt when she stepped inside the golden, sun-filled space that was hers alone. The one the clients never got to see, where she kept her novels and notebooks. A private sanctuary with a comfortable reading chair where she could curl up on her own, with her blue striped quilt wrapped around her on a cold winter's day, and watch the snow drift through the sky.

She returned to the main room and used one of the basic, white chairs to climb up on the round, white table. For a second she remembered how she felt the first time she stepped up on stage to perform. The initial wave of terror had subsided as she found the acceptance and attention she'd longed for.

Jordan wrapped the rope around the beam. Images of her father from one of their hunting trips flashed through her mind. He was scolding her as he made her tie a snare to catch a rabbit. A blur of tears had shielded her from seeing the bunny that eventually ended up in their trap get caught and die, but they had not been enough to block out the sight of father's scowl as he told Jordan the sniveling better stop or he'd give her something real to cry about.

If Father saw the knot she'd tied would he take comfort in knowing he'd taught her something useful after all? A check with the measuring tape confirmed that after taking her height and the length of the noose away she had half a foot to spare.

Six inches of air that would ensure she'd end up six feet under.

Jordan already knew what it was like to want to die, to feel like she was a shadow of her true self. She couldn't live that way again. Jordan would rather be buried with her breasts than face life again without them.

She positioned the chair under the rope, stepped up, slid the noose over her head, took a breath for courage and kicked the chair away.

The rope burned her neck as she fell down. This was it. She closed her eyes. Would Father be happy? Would he consider it karma that the steps she'd taken to become a woman in spirit and body had led to the hormone treatments that had caused her breast cancer? No, not karma. Divine justice. Father was the kind of person who would worship a god that would rather see a person die than embrace their true identity.

She hung there for a few seconds before she heard a crack above her head, felt the whoosh of air as her body pummeled down to the ground and cried out as her ankle twisted beneath her.

Jordan rolled over on her back. The beam, which had looked like a long fence post that someone had stained dark, had snapped into pieces. She should have known. It was a cheap faux studio apartment with laminated particleboard cabinets that sat on wheels and weren't even attached to the walls. They swelled after too many days of rain. She lived and worked in a nondescript space with slanted open white shelves that were dropping away from their wall anchors, crooked stick-on tiles checkering the floor with two shades of cream and nothing but the few items Jordan owned injected color into the otherwise blank space.

Nothing but the beam. The one long, dark block of wood that ran the length of the room had seemed to be the most stable thing that was part of the structure. Now it turned out that the beam wasn't even as strong as her clients' wood.

She sat up, grabbed her ankle and winced. Jordan cautiously got to her feet and tried to put her weight on it. Sore but usable. She'd suffered worse from her father's hands at home on more than one occasion.

Jordan limped her way to her vanity and sank down on the seat cushion, which was stitched from something soft and beautiful. She didn't know much about fabric, other than what felt nice against her skin and what was a pain to wash. Thanks to her father she knew more about carpentry. Although she'd resisted Father's efforts to force her to take on that trade she appreciated the intricate woodwork present in the scrolled legs of the vanity table and chair. The glossy wood surface on top was filled with her makeup and rich cherry wood curved up around the oversized mirror.

The oversized mirror that revealed the dark smudges under her eyes, the dull red line around her neck where the rope had burned into her before her fall. Her hollow cheeks were sunk into her face. Even her thick, dark mane seemed to lack the energy it needed to sustain its natural curl.

Her first suicide attempt was foiled.

She corrected herself. It was her first attempt since Doc's call about the biopsy.

Her actual first attempt had introduced her to Doctor Eaton. Jordan's father had pushed so hard to try to change Jordan that she'd been caught between her failure to measure up to his expectations and the lack of fulfillment she felt every day she spent trying to be something she wasn't.

Father had come home to find Jordan spread out on the front lawn with arms extended, lying on a wooden cross she'd made and painted the colors of the rainbow. Blood poured from her wrists and the places where her crown of roses pierced her head. An intended martyr for her own cause. She'd miscalculated with the timing. He'd finished a job early and come home to find her still breathing and bleeding out.

At first she thought he was going to let her die. He got out of his van and looked down at her, cell phone still buried in a pocket. A voice had called out. Jordan turned her head to see a short, older man with thinning hair, dress pants, a clean shirt and a black case in his hand rushing along the sidewalk toward them, declaring that he was a doctor and that he'd already called 911.

Words proven true by the sound of sirens rising as the ambulance drew closer.

Father had gone into the house, leaving the doctor to wrap her wrists and hold her hands up to stop the bleeding.

"Promise me. No matter how bad it gets, you'll never do this again."

Jordan had looked up into the doctor's eyes and nodded as the emergency lights flashed across the doctor's face and the sound of approaching voices filled the air.

What followed was the inevitable trip to the hospital and a psych hold. Before she'd gone away to a correctional boot camp program specially designed to fix Jordan and anyone like her, Doc had come to visit.

"If you're going to die you should do it on your own terms. Not because of your father. Not like this." He'd told her that living well was the best revenge. "Be yourself. Find happiness. You'll have a life you'll cherish that he can't take away from you. Your life."

That was then. Now she was on the wrong side of a phone call confirming the choice to live wasn't exactly hers anymore. She'd already been through one war with her body and she couldn't face another as the cancer spread through her.

And she was not going to let a surgeon cut her again.

The next morning Jordan had a cup of tea while she considered her options. The wrist thing wasn't very reliable if you didn't know just where to cut and she didn't like the association with her prior attempt a lifetime ago.

Plus, she'd promised Doc, and he was her emergency contact.

Sandra Ruttan   Crossing Jordan

She went out, bought supplies at the hardware store, came home and fixed the beam. It turned out to be nothing more than several strips of particle board glued together and wrapped in laminate. Her repairs would pass inspection as long as nobody tried to swing from it.

That night she worked the street. Different clients. Plenty of competition. More weapons and more violence.

Greater risk.

That was what she expected. Instead, every john was decent and when she finally decided to head home she had $300 in her coat pocket with her keys and her iPhone. Always in her left pocket because pickpockets went for the right side first. Jordan may have felt that she wanted to die but until she pulled the plug she wasn't about to be destitute. If anyone tried to rob her they weren't going to get anything easily.

The hum of traffic, murmur of conversations from smokers shivering together outside the local bars, and footfalls along the sidewalk all blurred together and filled the air as she walked along the streets on her way home. She was about a block away from a string of family eating establishments, including a Tim Horton's and diner, when she ran into some working girls.

"I ain't seen you before," the shorter one said. All curves and booty, with dark curls that framed a heart-shaped face and the poutiest lips Jordan had ever seen.

Her friend was all lines and angles. Tits the size of those cone-shaped Dixie paper cups you got in waiting rooms that held about a mouthful of water. Unbelievably small and just as pointed.

Both wore skin-tight sheer tops and mini skirts that cut off at the cooch and neither seemed worried about frost-bite.

"First time here in a while," Jordan said.

Short-and-Round flicked her wrist and held out a knife. Jordan had to admit it was an impressive move. She didn't even know where the girl could have kept the blade unless it had been stashed up her coozie.

"Here's how it be. We get a cut or you'll get cut... *Aaai-ight*?"

Jordan didn't move. Neither did Triangle Tits.

Short-and-Round stepped closer and pushed the knife against Jordan's side. "You wanna work Kenesha's streets then Kenesha's gonna get paid."

Jordan reached out with her pointer finger and pushed the girl's shoulder. "Kenesha gets paid if she gets her own customers."

Kenesha's chin shot up as she stepped closer, the tip of her blade pressed against Jordan's shirt.

"You steppin' to me, bitch?"

It was predictably easy to press the girl's buttons. "Did you travel to Baltimore to learn the lingo or just pick that accent up watching *The Wire*?"

Kenesha's nostrils flared as she shoved the blade into Jordan's side. The *whoop whoop* of a siren broke through the sound of traffic right behind them as Kenesha cried out. Jordan looked down. The knife had struck the pocket holding Jordan's iPhone.

Result? A smear of blood on Jordan's pocket, a bloody knife on the ground and a bleeding girl running down the street in her three-inch heels dragging Triangle Tits beside her as the police officers approached Jordan.

Jordan looked up to see the cops studying her. She recognized Constable Cruller. He had a reputation for dishing out his own brand of justice and he stood beside an officer with yellow hair who didn't look old enough to shave.

"Let me guess," Constable Cruller said. "You're just out for some donuts."

"No. Pancakes."

Constable Cruller grabbed Jordan's right arm, spun her around, walked her to his double-parked squad car and said, "Spread 'em."

"If that's what makes you happy, Officer," she said.

She winced as a hand pulled her head back and hot breath blew against her ear. "I see you out here again I'll take you for a starlight tour and we'll see how you like it."

Jordan felt a rush of cold fear crawl down her spine. She arched an eyebrow and tried not to betray her thoughts with her tone of voice. "I thought you got your hand slapped for doing that before."

Cruller's nostril's flared. "Nobody's gonna get bent out of shape about me taking a two-bit tranny whore for a ride. Not the way they did over that drunk old man."

She knew who he meant. The Native who happened to be a vet. A decorated war hero. Driven to the edge of town because he was drunk and left to freeze to death in a pile of snow on the side of the road.

Cruller muttered something about civil liberties and the damn minorities as he spun Jordan around. A radio crackled to life behind her and he pointed a brat-sized sausage finger in Jordan's face. "You're lucky we have a call."

With that he pushed her aside and got in the squad car.

Denied her chance to be stabbed on the street because of Kenesha's bad aim and the rock-hard iPhone case she'd bought.

Denied a chance to get arrested, which meant she missed her chance to try to get killed in jail.

Denied the chance to freeze to death on some back road heading out to the Prairies.

If she was going to live to die another day then pancakes weren't such a bad idea, so she walked to the restaurant and splurged on breakfast.

After she ate and paid she stepped outside into the pre-dawn quiet. It was that time just before color starts to seep into the sky. The street was getting ready for it. The sidewalks outside the bars were empty and there was no sign of Kenesha, Triangle Tits or Cruller.

Jordan knew of a place to score that was a block away. It wasn't the way she wanted to go. She'd fought to kick the booze and in all her years on the street one thing she'd never done was self medicate with drugs. It felt like fail-ure, but her options were limited if she wanted to die at home with minimal mess without breaking her promise to Doc.

She walked to the back alley.

"You wanna party?" The kid had a baby face.

"I want to have five parties." After breakfast $280 re-mained in her pocket and she yanked it out.

Pretty Boy looked at the wad of cash and nodded. He slipped through a door and came back with a brown bag that he exchanged for her money.

"This will look after all my friends?" Jordan asked.

Pretty Boy gave her one curt nod. "Takes a bit but it's sweet."

Sweet. Odd description. Targeting junkies with the munchies? When she got home she put the bag on her table and got ready for bed. When she was in her pajamas she went to her kitchenette, put her cutting board on the table, poured the mountain of power onto it, fished a straw out of a cupboard, grabbed a spatula and sat down.

She didn't know why junkies snorted lines or used things like credit cards but she took the flat edge of the spatula and lined up a thick pile of powder anyway. Jordan sucked her stash through the straw, into her nostril. When she was finished she tilted her head back and pinched her nose so she wouldn't sneeze the goods back out.

Pretty Boy said it took a bit. She felt the sting of the powder in her nostrils, which burned, and a pain in her neck from several minutes of leaning back, staring at her fixed fake beam.

Nothing else.

Jordan went to the bathroom, washed her face, entered her private room, climbed into bed and slipped her mask over her eyes. Had Pretty Boy scammed her? She should have felt the drugs kicking in by now, but she wasn't ready to give up. Maybe it really did take a bit.

Jordan went to bed praying for death and woke up the next morning still waiting to die. Peeling the mask off confirmed she wasn't dreaming. The drugs were as fake as the beam she'd failed to hang herself on.

Turning on the news brought a double blow. Survival rates for patients with aggressive triple-negative breast cancer were low without a mastectomy. The latest installment of a weeklong series of reports on transgender health issues she no longer wanted to hear anything about.

She turned the TV off.

That night Jordan tried another round of street gigs. She didn't see any pimps or girls. Just a lot of Johns and Johnsons.

The next morning she went home with $340 and a stomach full of turkey bacon, toast and eggs. She slept past the noon news and decided to work from home that night. It didn't take long to put a notice up on her website and get a few appointments.

The final booking of the night had promise. If she could antagonize any client enough to earn her death it had to be Limp Dick Donny. He'd been banned by a number of working girls for using his fists when he failed to get hard and she slotted him in last, with extra time.

Jordan was a pro but nobody was good enough to overcome ED without medicine. That night was no exception. Rage over his failure to perform—combined with Jordan's choice to laugh at him and call him Limp Dick to his face—gave Donny the strength to lift her off the bed and throw her against the wall.

Jordan found herself curled on the floor having an epiphany about her relationship with pain as Limp Dick Donny's boot hit her side. She didn't enjoy it as much as she used to, which was a realization that gave her a split-second distraction from the spasms coursing through her body.

Was this really how she wanted it to end? It wasn't her first choice. Or her second. She realized now that if she was going to die messy it needed to be on the street, not at home. It wasn't fair for Doc to have to see it or clean it up.

"Filthy whore." Limp Dick Donny tossed in a few expletives as he finished getting dressed.

"I'm not the one who pays for it," Jordan murmured.

Donny spun around with so much pressure in his vine-ripened-tomato face that she wondered if the pimple on the tip of his nose might pop on its own. Jordan chuckled, then groaned as she wrapped her arms around her torso. You know it's bad when it hurts to laugh.

"Oh, you will pay for it, bitch. Like this." Limp Dick Donny stomped across the three-foot gap between them, grabbed her hair and yanked hard. Her roots screamed out as her face rose until her neck couldn't stretch out any further. Limp Dick Donny balled his fingers into a fist.

Jordan raised her arms to fend off his blows, her tall, thin frame curled into the fetal position, her dark hair limp and wet with sweat and blood.

Then it was over. Specks of light flashed in her eyes and her head bounced off the floor with a thud. She wondered if anyone ever listed assault as a reason to favor carpet over hardwoods.

Jordan forced her left eye to open a tiny slit. Limp Dick Donny had his hand on the door.

"You're lucky I like you," he said.

She heard the door slam shut as she closed her eyes. Jordan was tempted to drift off and let the pain slip away while she slept. Instead, she lifted herself up with her arms, stretched out as far as she could and pulled herself forward, wincing as she dragged her body across the floor.

The stars were back after her knees touched her palms the first time. "Just one more time," she told herself. A lie. Shock waves coursed through her body and any split-second notions that she'd been paralyzed faded when her hips shifted as she inched toward the door.

"Just one more," she told herself again. This time, it was true.

As her ribs cried, Jordan reached up and twisted the lock on the knob. She paused long enough to take a few deep breaths. A veil of black flashed over her eyes but she didn't stop. She turned away from the door, inched along the dresser and steadied herself. With one long step to bridge the distance she was able to propel herself onto the bed.

Jordan wasn't sure if she'd actually opened her eye or not. The pain was back with an insistence that rivaled a child beauty pageant's narcissism. The only difference was that Jordan's body had a good reason for expecting to be her top priority at the moment.

It seemed to take all the strength she had just to reach the phone on the nightstand and dial Doc's number. She was lying down and uncomfortably numb when she heard a key in the lock and the creak of the door followed by sharp intake of breath. Doc crossed the room silently, got a chair, and returned to her bedside. He moved with the grace of a gazelle. Jordan had told him that once on another one of those occasions when she'd let her mouth get ahead of her mind.

"Not that I mean to imply you're girly," she'd said.

He'd smiled. "The world could use a little more grace and a little less boorishness, couldn't it?"

Never one to judge people for their shortcomings, he'd helped her. Helped her overcome her suicide attempt. Helped her kick the booze. Helped her become the person she was meant to be.

A cupboard closed and the sound of running water followed. After it stopped she heard nothing until there was a soft thump beside her. The tinkling of water was followed by warm moisture around her eyes.

"Umph." Jordan pulled back.

Doc spoke as softly as he moved.

"You have a golf ball growing out of one eye and a gash along the brow that's still bleeding. I'm going to clean the area so that I can see if you need stitches."

"Head wounds do bleed like a stuck pig."

"I thought that was my line." He pressed the cloth against Jordan's eyes again.

She knew what he was referring to. The last time he'd stitched a cut in her head.

"I only borrow from the best." She grabbed the bed sheet with her fingers and squeezed.

"There we go."

She heard the sploosh of the washcloth being dropped into the water. The slit she'd managed in her one eye earlier was accessible again and seemed to be a little wider.

It may have been reassuring to see the familiar wrinkled face, the kind smile, and the warm eyes with crinkles at the corners if he weren't setting out a tray with suture equipment.

"You'll be back to your beautiful self in no time," he told her.

"With a new scar to add to the collection."

He shook his head. "Whoever did the damage was nice enough to cut along your old wound."

The gash that had made her wait outside his office on a cold winter's night a year after she'd run away. She'd been a different person then. Different clientele. Different equipment.

Dr. Eaton had told her about endorphins. "Your own personal pain management system," he'd explained. Endorphins were a built-in natural high for klutzes and victims alike.

For a while between the time she'd slashed her wrists and the day she'd left home, she'd cut herself on the inside of her thighs. She knew what Doc was saying. It was a euphoria brought on by pain. Her body's endorphins had rushed right in to do her job and the cares of the world faded away. For a brief moment everything was perfect.

Jordan was starting to wonder if your body could run out of endorphins. Were they like any other drug? Eventually they didn't cut it anymore? A tolerance. Wasn't that what they called it? Too bad your body couldn't send them back to its own personal pharmacy and tell your system to up the dosage.

Doc paused mid stitch. "This will be over in a minute and then we'll get some ice on you."

Jordan managed a feeble smile. "Being an alcoholic isn't as much fun today as it was when I was a teenager." The pain made her wish for a drink more than she had in years.

"You got sober. In spite of what you do."

"I never drank because of how I pay my bills, Doc."

He sighed. "Isn't it demeaning to be paid for sex?"

"Doc, I spent so many years longing to be accepted as a woman that every time a man pays to have his way with me it's a compliment."

"Well, with all you've endured you still stopped drinking. You're stronger than ten men combined," he reached above her eye with the scissors, "or women."

Jordan offered a thin smile back.

The pain subsided after a while. Whether that was because her nerves were shot and couldn't scream at her anymore or because of the ice she didn't know. Hell, maybe her body had actually found a way to kick up the dosage of endorphins. Jordan didn't really care why. She felt better and that was all that mattered.

Here she was, glad she was feeling better. Why had she called Doc? Habit? Or was it because deep down she really didn't want to die?

Doc packed his bag and set it by the door before sitting back down by her bed. He reached out and patted her hand but this time there was no smile in his eyes.

"When we talked on the phone you promised to call back and make an appointment."

"You just want to get me naked on a table," Jordan said.

Doc's sober expression remained in place. "Something like that."

He spent a long time talking to her about her options and her odds. Then he helped her walk to her own bed.

She slept for the better part of the next two days. The day she got up she got a call from Doc's office about an appointment that night.

Jordan walked to the main room of her apartment. She could stand upright on her own. A hand on her side was enough to remind her that her skin was tender but it wasn't her physical injuries that brought tears to her eyes.

Her heart hurt. What did they call it? Emotional injury. Psychological suffering. A hot shower and slipping on one of her favorite outfits didn't take years of pain away.

Jordan sat down at her vanity, dulled the facial bruises with concealer and started to apply her eyeliner. Primping in front of her mirror was her one daily indulgence. From the age of eight she'd eyed vanity sets and put them on top of every birthday and Christmas list she produced.

Which meant that the next seven years living under her parent's roof had produced a steady stream of disappointment. For her and for them, apparently, since her father missed no opportunity to talk about how much Jordan had failed them.

Jordan remembered the first time he'd caught her putting on makeup. She'd hidden in a closet with her sister's mirror and a paper bag filled with products from the local drug store. She'd used her reading light to illuminate the space, puckered up, drawn the lipstick around her mouth and mashed her lips together the way her mother did. Just as she thought she'd finished and set the lipstick down the door flung open.

Perfect sister Sophia stood there, with a complexion their mother called peaches and cream, her curly mass of auburn hair tied back in a ponytail, and her bright blue eyes staring out from beneath what seemed to be the world's longest eyelashes.

Sophia didn't blink. Her mouth fell open but otherwise she didn't move at all until their father pounded his way across the room, the floorboards quivering from each heavy step, until he reached the closet and flung the door open even wider.

Her ass couldn't touch a pillow for a week without making her wince.

She got ready and made her way to Doc's office. He talked her through her options again.

"You spend your life wanting boobs and then you have to think about having them cut off," Jordan said.

"That's just one option."

He handed her a stack of pamphlets that she put in her purse and then she put on her coat.

Still faintly smeared with Kenesha's blood.

"You have a couple days to think it through."

"Like how I'm going to pay the rent when I'm getting chemo."

Doc pointed up. "I have an apartment upstairs that's sitting empty. You be my office helper for a few hours each week and you'll have a place to stay and food to eat."

"You aren't trying to make an honest woman out of me, are you?"

"I'm an old man. I don't have anyone. Not——" he swallowed, "not anymore. I didn't understand my daughter. Not until that day I found you on your lawn, but it was too late. She'd been gone six months by then."

Jordan swallowed. She'd never known. Doc had never said, not once, in all these years.

"I can help you," he pointed at the stacks of files covering the desk in his reception area, "and you could help me."

She closed her eyes. "I just don't want to die like that."

Jordan felt his hand on her arm as Doc said, "I promise I won't let it get that far."

A wave of relief washed through her and as she opened her eyes and looked at Doc she knew he meant it. He wouldn't let her suffer.

"Just do me a favor and take this." He walked over to a closet and extracted a long, thick coat that looked like it had never been worn. Jade green. Her color. "Your body temperature is a bit low."

Jordan took off her coat, let him help her put the new one on and slipped her phone into her coat pocket and her keys into her purse.

"I don't know what to say."

"Say you'll start next week."

Jordan smiled and nodded. "Okay. I will."

Jordan left Doc's office on foot. By the time she skirted the edge of the area where she worked she regretted not calling a taxi. Why was it that when you wanted one they were nowhere to be found?

She headed toward a convenience store so that she could get a box of tea and loaf of bread. A cop car rolled up beside her.

Constable Cruller parked the cruiser and got out. "What did I tell you would happen if I saw you out here again?"

"I'm just going to the store for groceries and going home, sir."

The 'sir' must have surprised him.

"You think you can sweet talk your way out of this one?"

Jordan paused and sought out the right words, "I was just at the doctor's office and I'm going home. I haven't done anything."

He grabbed her arm. "Even if you haven't this time, you have before. Hell, you likely stole the coat. No way you could afford it. And it would fit my wife nice."

The back door was open and she was forced inside before she had a chance to wrench free. Cruller pushed her down on the seat, patted her body head to toe, pulled the coat off of her and grabbed her purse. By the time she sat upright she was shut in behind a cage and stuck beside a door that didn't open from the inside. They drove until the number of buildings thinned, all signs of cars and human life faded and there was nothing but fields of white pressed under a black Prairie night sky as far as she could see.

Cruller put the car in park and let her out on an old back road well off the highway. There was nothing to even light her way on the cold, January night.

"Please." She choked on the tears. "I quit the life. I have a new job. In my purse you'll see Dr. Eaton's card. Call him. He'll tell you. He even gave me the coat but you can keep it. I don't care about that. Just don't leave me out here."

Cruller's radio crackled.

"Look's like I've got a call," he said as he grabbed her purse, tossed it on the ground, and got back in his cruiser.

"Please!" Jordan screamed.

She banged her fists against the glass and he turned and gave her that look. The one she'd seen in her father's eyes. The one she'd seen so many times before.

Burning rage.

He clicked off the radio and rolled down the window.

"Fucking tranny whore piece of shit."

Jordan lunged at the car and managed to grab the handle to the passenger door. She saw Cruller glare at her through the side mirror and felt the cruiser lurch forward. It crunched over her right ankle as it zoomed away and left her lying sprawled in the snow.

She crawled back to her purse, careful to keep her right foot raised up off the ground. Jordan's fingers shook as she rifled through the bag and then she patted phantom pockets, no longer there because she'd left her old coat at Doc's and the cop had stolen her new one.

With her iPhone in the pocket.

Cruller was wrong about her. Wrong about what she was doing out that night. Wrong about her being worthless.

None of which changed the fact that she'd been dumped on the side of a road surrounded by fields of snow, several kilometers from home, with a crushed ankle on a winter night when it was at least ten below.

She had thought she would rather die than have chemo. Rather lose her life than lose the breasts she'd fought so long to have.

Thought that if she couldn't live as a woman then she at least wanted to die as one.

Doc offered her hope. If things went bad she could count on him to make arrangements but she'd seen that pain in his eyes. The pain of losing someone you love. She finally realized that she was ready to fight for her breasts for a second time.

Ready to fight for her life.

She reached out with her arms as far as she could and pulled herself along the snow-crusted road, back toward town. Again and again she reached out and dragged herself forward, as her palms turned red and numb. Just one more time. And another. And another...

Jordan blew her breath out and watched the cloud of vapor drift away as her body crumbled down into the snow. She pushed herself back up and resisted the urge to lie down as her muscles protested. Jordan reached out and planted her hands on the road to pull herself forward again.

Just one more stretch. Just one more pull. Just one more time fighting the force of gravity as it coaxed her back down to the ground and promised her rest.

Just one more. Jordan reached out again and whispered to the darkness, "Just one more.

〉

Painted Jade

Jayne Barnard

Even in space, some neighborhoods are better than others.

Working security on the higher levels of a conglomerate-built drift is mostly petting the dogs and smiling at the nice ladies, or, if you're me, trying the reverse. Troubles happen way down in the ear-cracking ore processors and tight-packed workers' quarters. Not my turf. Not, that is, until I was assigned one morning to retrieve an ore-slave's body that was bobbing against a pricey view-plex high up on C7. Bargees aren't permitted higher than the shopping district, so it fell to me to bring down their trash. My day's first java-juice still warming my stomach, I prepped to leave the safe environs of Pyretia for the cold void.

Once the airlock depressurized, I transferred my safety line to the appropriate rail and stepped out. Whether my stomach dipped or my breakfast rose, the effect was the same: a sour burp that tainted every breath I'd take until this helmet came off. Two rails over, three levels up, a long hand-over-hand trek up the curve of C-dome. Plenty of time to peer into the wide plex panes of two- and three-storey habitats I'd never see otherwise. These palatial dwellings housed stock-owning executives, trophy spouses, and a few lucky live-in domestics who got a whole sleeping locker to themselves. Most household staff commuted up a dozen levels from some half-time locker in the drift's underbelly.

As I approached the designated coordinates, there was the escapee bobbing against a massive window. At least in space bodies didn't stink. My free-floating belly wouldn't take nicely to the odor of unwashed ore slave, and if there's a thing worse than burping into your helmet, it's… well. Another good thing about the vacuum of space: it preserves evidence. The bobber could hang there for a month without deteriorating. When pulled in through the airlock, they'd be frozen solid in the same state they'd escaped. The arm patch would tell us which ore barge to call for next-of–kin notification, and then the body would land in the recyclers to become potting soil or whatever.

I took a few photos of the bobber in situ, including a good shot of Mr. Moneybags glaring at me from his high-ceilinged dining room. Let him glare. He's the one who called for this removal instead of letting the eddy from a departing shuttle shunt Bobb out of his outraged sight. I whipped out my grease pencil and ostentatiously scrawled the date, habitat designation, and an outline of Bobb right over Moneybags' multilayer, full transparency plex. My signature alone took up a quarter of the expensive dining room window. Repercussions would come, but those photos of Moneybags' gobbling jowls and fat, fishy mouth would liven up the security room darts tourney. We security jerks might have to kiss their asses and guard their wives in public, but in private we were, well, private. Like any other citizens.

Eventually, nausea wore down my urge to irk the rich. I lassoed Bobb and headed in. With a sealed door between us and the void, I eyed my catch while the airlock repressurized. He was slender, androgynous, smooth-skinned, but the beautiful manicure was the kicker. This was no barge-slave. This was a citizen, which meant a full-on investigation that would seriously impede my chatting up shop-girls. I got my helmet off just in time to belch out more rotten stomach gasses, faintly java-scented.

While I waited for my boss, I took frontal photos of Bobb, now Mister Bobb to us plebs. He wore a trendy leisure suit cut from a single piece of silk, screened with a rare Earth artwork, in this case Monet's water lilies. A hologram in the Galleria wore one just like it, next to a Van Gogh sunflower suit and something white by Georgia O'Keefe. I'd never seen those suits on a man before, but this was a really dainty man. He had accessorized his water lilies with jade jewels at his throat and one ear, and the sort of soft slippers you only see on folks who never set foot on a public promenade. This type rode their personal floating chairs everywhere. All that added up to money, family, friends in high places.

And enemies too, apparently. What I'd first taken for a jade button on his chest was only the head of something sharp that pinned the fabric to the skin beneath. Mr. Bobb had been skewered between the ribs, a finger's width left of center, just where his heart hid. My breakfast lurched. I might have lost it entirely if my boss, Alden, hadn't walked in bellowing.

"Lake! You are in some deep shit now. You lucky if that man don't order you exported, girl. Wanna go back to that ramshackle drift you come from, if it ain't been blowed out by a meteor yet?"

"How'd he know it was me in the suit, Alden? I cleared his window, didn't I?"

"You done wrote you *name* on it first. What you thinking, flashing your souvenir photos all up in his own face? You want us all working the ore processors?" Alden grabbed my camera and flicked over a close-up of Bobb's face. "You seen this mimbo before?"

"A mimbo? Not a stockholder?" Thank the galactic gods. Not that a rent-boy wasn't a worthy individual, but the official heat to nab his killer would be a fading ember before he thawed. "You sure?"

"He got nicer lips than you, girl, and they ain't natural." Alden studied the face. "And stuff on his cheeks. Them dome-toffs up there don't go in for man-makeup. Question is, who rented him?"

"And who threw him out which airlock?"

332

"We'll find out. He mighta been a self-spacer but for that button." Alden flicked a fingertip over the dainty doo-dad on Bobb's chest. "Go get juiced. You look froze. Shoulda come in sooner."

No mention of giving me a real rest. He hadn't been outside in yonks, had long forgotten how Z-Gee work kicked your muscles.

I slouched down to my usual java stop on the Prome-nade, too caked to ogle the fine ladies floating by on their velvet chairs. Whenever I stopped moving, I shivered. I'd been outside for over an hour, crawling over the dome face, breathing my own leavings, my muscles gnawing on the memory of breakfast. Was it really worth the extra space time to annoy old Moneybags? As warm juice slid down to my belly, I decided it was. He likely had a pretty plaything wife, or mistress, or both. Imagine having to kiss that little fish mouth. There wasn't enough dosh on the whole of Pyretia to make me do it. I shuddered and sig-naled for a refill.

As I warmed up, a new floater caught my eye, an am-ber-haired woman with dainty citrine-tipped slippers. She'd never set foot on a public floor. That's when it struck me: if Bobb was a hired companion instead of a dome-topper, he'd walk places. Yet his slippers showed no par-ticular wear. Or did they? I almost went back to check, but soon enough his trappings would be in Security. And any-way, nobody higher up would put gravity on us over Bobb's death.

I resumed normal rounds. After a day or two of sniggering about my graffiti on the rich man's window, I forgot about both Moneybags and the mimbo. There was a new hire in the Galleria, an off-drift girl about my age with that certain look in her eye. I spent a fair few hours of every shift diligently patrolling the front and back of her boutique. Of course I had to chat her up a bit; it was only polite. I arrived after the early rush with a pair of steaming creamies to which I'd added a shot from my hip pouch. Just enough to loosen her tongue.

"How'd a nice girl like you end up behind a counter?"

She licked the foam off her rim. "I was a nanny up on E 6 first. We bought a lot of tot stuff down here, and when they offered me a job, I jumped."

"You traded a private locker upstairs for this?" I gestured around at the sunflower cradles and tagalong kiddie floaters.

"It's private up there but…" she shrugged. "I could never have a friend visit in my boss's habitat, and it got lonely. Now I share a double, one level down from here, and there's always someone to hang with after work. Pals."

That addendum was as clear as a signal flag saying she was single. Security got private lockers too, and some day soon she'd be in mine. It was all there in her look.

I was on my third pass of the day when a salesgirl from the next shoppe popped her head in the back and, after casting a glance for non-existent customers, beckoned desperately to Nuri. After a moment's consultation, Nuri waved me over.

"Can you help her, Lake? There's a young customer bawling in a dressing room over there. Won't come out, and Dina won't get paid for overtime waiting to close up."

For that beseeching gaze, I'd have done almost anything. But. "I'm no good with children."

Nuri smiled. Oh, those lips. "Not baby-young. She's about our age."

Dina nodded. "She's refusing to leave until I find her a suit in her size and print."

Some stockholder's tot all grown up, facing her first-ever thwarting. I wasn't sure what I could do, but with Nuri's hand on my arm and her face smiling earnestly up at me, I said I'd try. I followed Dina along the service corridor to her own rear entrance.

Dina pointed at a door. "We only brought one suit in each size and they're all sold, so there's simply no way I can give her another without special-ordering one."

I tapped. "Miss, I'm with Station Security. May I come in?" And not to snitch a look at your high-class undies, either. Well, not only.

A sniff. "Why?"

"You seem to be in distress. Perhaps I can help."

"All right."

The dainty person within was bundled up in a flowing three-quarter tunic in gold over loose ochre trousers, with a matching ochre scarf looped around her neck. Her citrine-tipped slippers matched the gold-and-amber hair that

335

flowed to her waist. No undies to be ogled, no cleavage to covet, no graceful neck to dream of nibbling. Her artisan nose with its scattering of pale freckles had turned primrose at the tip from sniveling. She huddled on an upholstered bench, dabbing at her eyes with a lace hanky that cost my week's wages all by its lonesome, and stared up at me hopelessly.

I sat down beside her, within a sphere of delicate scent that was nicely judged to skim under the drift's official olfactory intensity limit. "What seems to be the trouble?"

With a few hiccups and backtracks, the story came out. She was not a stockholder's darling daughter but his darling bit on the side. Toto - the only name she gave – lived in a cozy little unit on C4, a few convenient levels below her sugar daddy's much larger pad near the crest. Sugar, whose real name she was careful not to mention, had recently bought her an expensive leisure suit, a going-away present when he went off-drift for a bit. Toto didn't like the suit – watery blues and greens did nothing for her red hair and freckles – and had promptly loaned it to a friend.

"Now Sugar's on his way home," she sniffled, "expecting to see me in the water-lilies. But my friend never brought it back and I'm almost out of time." Her breath caught again, and she leaned into my shoulder. "I thought I could buy a replacement but they have none my size and Sugar will be furious. What if he throws me out? Where would I live?" She gazed up at me, her face smeared with gold and ochre makeup. A homeless puppy couldn't look more forlorn.

After drowning in her gold-flecked despair for a while, I had a brainwave. "I know where there's a suit that might fit you. It has a small hole in front. Would that be a problem?"

"Oh, no! I could accessorize over that." She tilted her face, bringing her lips to easy kissing distance. "You're wonderful to help me this way."

With difficulty I resisted the innocent invitation and sat up straighter. "I'll bring the suit up to your place in a couple of hours, if that's all right?"

"Oh, yes. I'm in C4-15. And I insist you stay for supper. I have a generous catering allowance and I don't use much when I'm on my own." Possibly misinterpreting my silence, she added, "I have real dirt-grown wine. Or liquor. Three solar systems to choose from."

"That sounds fine. I've got to get back to my rounds. See you soon." I bailed out of there as she started wielding her makeup brushes. A quick thumbs-up to Dina and I was on my way to Security for the Monet leisure suit. Robbing a corpse was a small price for dinner with an old man's darling and a thoroughly stocked liquor cabinet. How drunk would she have to be to model that suit for me? I wouldn't tell her where it came from. No point spoiling any mood that might develop.

There wasn't the blood I feared on the suit, only a paler spot around the tiny slice in the fabric. Swabbed off for ID sampling, no doubt. As I refolded the cloth, I realized I'd crawled almost past Toto's plex to reel in Bobb. Could she ID him? I almost hoped she couldn't. It would never do to have a new friend mixed up, however peripherally, in a murder inquiry.

An hour later, washed and brushed and wearing my best silkies under my most touchable suit, I chimed the door on C4. Toto answered, her over-tunic abandoned for a wispier drape that displayed golden shoulders and a delicate trail of coppery sparkles disappearing into her cleavage. I'd have promised her the moon for a chance to follow that trail. Instead, I handed her the parcel.

"Oh," she cried sweetly. "You're a dear. Come in, do. Can I get you a drink before I try this on? Not that I doubt you, but if it needs tailoring I'll have to send it out tonight."

I sent her on her way and spent the next few minutes soaking up the details of a fourth level domicile: a contoured couch and a real dining area, with a separate media console whose sidebar showed not the light entertainments I'd anticipated, but study modules in disciplines as varied as human biochem and space station subsystem controls. Beautiful, and brainy too. She was using this gig to prep for independence.

Art panels decorated the walls and she even had a window, not large but not a porthole, either. The plex wasn't green. If all this luxury was bought by a willingness to sweeten an older man, who could fault her? It was five levels beyond shop-girl lockers, and four more from the ore-processing habitats.

"Lake, could you come in here, please?"

Hurrah. She wanted a second opinion. I passed the sliding panel and stopped dead, my lustful designs temporarily sideswiped. She had a bed. An honest-to-asteroids freestanding bed, wider than any two people I knew, with walking room on three sides. Nobody I knew had a bed.

It took me a moment to realize she was jiggling a hand below her breasts for a reason. "Should I wear this brooch or this flower over the hole? Or something else?" She waved her free hand at a drawer filled with feminine bric-a-brac: ribbons and bows, fabric flowers, baubles large and showy, jewels small and exquisite. By the time we'd narrowed the selection, the backs of my hands burned from repeatedly pressing against the undersides of her breasts to hold up the various pieces.

"Thanks," she said breathily. "You're so helpful."

"You look fantastic," I said as I made a totally unnecessary adjustment to the chosen knot of ribbon. "But this suit looks complicated to get out of."

She slid a finger down a shoulder seam and the cloth parted, giving a glimpse of golden skin. "Microfasteners. Why don't you try one?"

Who could refuse a challenge like that?

By the time I got the hang of the exact pressure necessary to open a seam from top to bottom in one go, I'd lost most of my own suit. The bedcovers were more off than on, as was my lip liner from exploring each freckle and fleck of glitter revealed along the way. Eventually, the only thing left on me was Toto's bare leg, lying heavy across my hips. Her breath coasted over my neck.

"If Sugar could see this he'd have six kinds of heart failure. He's always trying to talk me into having another woman so he can watch."

"This was a dry run for indulging his fantasies?"

Her tongue touched my earlobe. "Oh, no. I want you all to myself."

Over a late supper, I finally got around to asking about her friend who'd borrowed the suit.

"Milo Renc," she said. "He hasn't been home in days. I thought he lucked into a shack-up with some high-roller, but he usually answers his messages eventually."

"Do you often swap clothing with him?"

"We all do it." She looked down at her hands. "Keeping men attracted is a job like any other. There are… investments. If we switch clothing and accessories around between us, we don't all have to buy new and can put aside some savings for when the work runs out."

"And then you'll switch to station maintenance?" I nodded at the console. "You've been taking instructional courses, preparing for later."

Her lovely eyes flicked that way. "Just looking for options. I haven't taken any accreditation tests."

"You'd make an inspiring medic." I stroked her fingers. "I could test your bedside manner right now."

What with one thing and another, I was late to work the next morning. Alden frowned but made no objection when I asked for a look at Bobb's file.

"No ID from the blood swab?" I asked.

He grunted. "Still stuck in a test tube, where it will be for the next six months."

"I might have a lead. A classy rent-boy isn't answering his messages. He had access to that kind of suit. Name's Milo Renc."

"Milo Renc?" Alden flexed his fingers over his console and tapped a few icons. "Not listed in Departures. Nothing in Medical. Gimme a sec." While he chatted up somebody in Central Credit, I skimmed the file.

My photos had turned out well. I was admiring Mr. Moneybags' mottled rage when something behind him caught my eye. One of the elegant oddments in his deluxe dining room was a squat jar with a bunch of stalks sticking out. Topping each one was a carved button, creamy ivory or jade green. I fished Bobb's jade doodad from the evidence bin, keeping my hips in the way so Alden wouldn't notice the missing suit, and laid the stick beside the photo. It was close enough to warrant further inquiry.

Alden spun in my direction. "Good work, Lake. Milo Renc hasn't accessed his account since the day before we pulled in the stiff. I'll send a patrol past his pad on a welfare check. If he's at home recovering from a bad date, no harm done."

"Meanwhile," I said, shoving the photo and skewer at him, "Look at this. What if old Moneybags was his bad date? Can I go up there and see if this rod matches the others?"

"First off, old Moneybags is not how we talk about a major player on this drift. Second, after the doodles you left on his window, he won't let you past the door camera."

I smirked. "Check his location first. If he's not there, I can go up right away on a stolen-items check, be in and out with no trouble at all."

Moneybags was out at his office, and I was in with no more trouble than flashing my ID. Mrs. Moneybags looked barely older than I, with cool skin and aqua eyes. Her flowing hair was streaked in watery hues from silver through blues and greens, to the odd hint of lavender. She'd look fab in the Monet suit. What she wore was Van Gogh sunflowers, whose turquoise background made only a token nod to her personal palette. Did it have those fascinating microfasteners? Would she slap me if I stroked her arm to find out?

She was bored, and a bit cross, but she came through like a lady when I showed her the jade stick pin. "Yes, it's from here, but no, they're not stolen. And it's missing a part." She led the way to the dining room and pulled a similar one from the jar of mingled jade and ivory. "See? There should be another jade button, same size, twisted onto the bottom."

"What are they?"

"Raleurian hairpins. It was the fashion for a while to have a yard or more of hair, all wound up in a chignon that was held in place by sticking one or more of these through and screwing the buttons back on. All you'd see were the decorated bits at the ends. Not that anyone has a yard of hair these days."

Toto's came close. How would she look with it twisted up? Jade would nestle wonderfully in her amber-and-gold curls, especially if some tendrils flowed down her long, graceful neck. Or maybe ivory suited better. Like it, she was soft and easily scratched, and her skin took on a pearly sheen when rubbed the right way.

Ahem. "You said they weren't stolen. Is more than one gone?"

"Yes. One jade and one ivory. I gave them to a friend."

Aha. "A male friend by any chance?"

Her eyes iced over. "Did my husband send you up here to ask me that?"

"No, ma'am. I've never spoken to your husband." Making faces at him from inside my helmet didn't count. "This hairpin turned up in suspicious circumstances with a young man."

"Suspicious circumstances, hmm?" She thawed slightly. "If you can assure me my husband doesn't need to know about this, I'll tell you why I gave them to him." I nodded. That seemed sufficient to reassure her. "He was sent here by, well, by my husband's current sex kitten. To seduce me and show some evidence of infidelity to my husband. Kitty is rather ambitious." She smiled, warm as water trickling off a glacier. "The problem with using prostitutes is that they're always open to a better offer. I gave him all my cash, and it was enough to get that much truth."

"But the pins?"

"They were a down payment. To inform my dear husband what Kitty was up to in his absence. Once she was

343

history, I'd pay Milo with another set of pins. My husband doesn't count his possessions. After he has them, he rarely looks at them."

I was betting that statement applied to wives as much as hairpins. Maybe my sex life would be livelier if I eyed the trophy women.

"Has the young man fulfilled his share of the bargain?"

"I haven't heard from him. I wondered if the kitty had made him a better offer, but wouldn't you expect him to try a bidding war?"

He couldn't if he was already dead. "What was he wearing, this young man?"

"A Monet one-piece suit. I'd have killed to own it, frankly." I mostly believed her, at least about not killing him for the suit. Some other reason, maybe. She was a jade hairpin herself: cool, hard surface with a sharp, dangerous edge.

When I reported back, Alden agreed about the suit. If she wanted one that bad, she could afford to order it special. He pointed out, though, that if she had done the deed, she wouldn't leave a weapon that could be traced back to her.

"You got a name for the scheming mistress?" he asked.

"Kitty was all she said. I figured it would betray too much interest to ask outright."

He grunted and cued up his console. "Kitty. Could be a home world diminutive of Catherine, or some weird variant from the asteroid belt. I'll run all the kept girls and match up any likely names with addresses. They mainly live on levels 3 and 4 in the same dome as their keepers. Convenient to stop by on the way home from work. Like the rent-boys in the evac bays."

"Huh?" Evac bays were the life support areas on every level. Small rooms lined with prepped suits and barely enough aisle space to don one in an emergency. Not enough suits for every resident, but something big enough to blow a whole dome wouldn't leave many alive to need suits.

"Didn't you know? Rent-boys pick up a nice living in the upper bays during commuter hours. Keep the lights off so the cameras can't spy and any old guy can slip inside for a quickie. Cash in hand is a blow job, cash and a condom means a fuck. No words needed. And here I thought you were a fly girl, knew everything about this place."

"Not that, I didn't. Eww. And they go home to supper like nothing's wrong?"

"From their angle, child, nothing is. But now you put me in mind of it, that's a likely place to look for Milo. Lights may be off inside the bays, but the corridor cameras still do their thing. Now we know he was in that dome that day, won't take long to find his trail."

I left him to it, returning to my belated rounds of the Galleria. Nuri was ready to banter but my heart wasn't in it. My night with Toto was top of my mind, but best not to let on if I wanted to keep that sparkle in Nuri's eye.

"Want to hear something creepy?" I asked instead. "A lot of the powerful men on this drift, who keep both gorgeous wives and delectable mistresses for their amusement, still stop off in the evac bays for a fast spin with a rent-boy on their way home. Lights off, no words, fast in and out."

Nuri wrinkled her nose. "Ick. Anonymous and uncomfortable. No sensuality at all. Sounds like every male back on my mining drift." Her slim fingers walked up my forearm. "I prefer mine slow and comfy."

Yesterday I'd have captured those dainty digits and given her a sample of my sensuality. Today, with Toto's perfume lingering in my taste-buds, I slid my arm away.

"I don't get how any woman could stay married knowing about the mistresses. Do they value luxury over dignity? Mistresses scheme to become wives of the same men who cheated with them, knowing they'll be cheated on in turn." Lovely, soft Toto was not scheming. She was saving her money and studying for her future. Suddenly, I'd had enough work and was ready to skive off to see her.

Over the next couple of days we developed a code for visits. When I could get away, I'd send a message up the public net, purporting to schedule a maintenance call. If she was clear of a potential visit from Sugar, she'd hit the affirmative. If I shouldn't come up right away, she'd key a later hour and I'd slip away then for a taste of her lips, her skin, her tantalizing array of lingerie. Thanks to her earlier investigation of station maintenance processes, we had a good variety of possible repairs to choose from.

During one of those illicit afternoon visits, with my back to Toto's wall art, my uniform jacket on the floor, and her pouty mouth all over my left nipple, I got buzzed by

Alden. It could be anything from a shoplifter to another bobber, but I had to take it.

"Lake? The hell you up to, girl? I don't see you on the Galleria."

We'd been careful about Sugar catching on, but obviously I'd been off my patrol once too often if Alden was scanning for me down there. I had seconds to make up a good answer, one that would stand up to his fingers on the camera console. "Up on C4. I got a lead to a girl who might know what that rent-boy was up to."

"That so?" Alden sounded slightly thoughtful. "Well, since you're in the neighbourhood, take a look around evac bay 2 on C7. That's where Renc went after he left that stockholder's digs."

"And he never came out alive?"

"You want I should ask every guy who left with his hand on his belt whether he stuck little Milo with a hairpin on the way out?"

I removed Toto's beautiful lips with a finger that her talented tongue immediately greeted like the intimate friend it was. "When did the body go out? And which air-lock? That must be recorded somewhere."

"I'm scanning the airlock logs for that level. When you finish up with the girlie, get on up to the evac bay. Likely too late to pick up any traces after days of the supper trade, but seal it off and turn up the full-spect lights. If there's anything there, I want it. Hear me, Lake?"

I looked down at Toto, who was daintily brushing one of her darker auburn curls over my exposed breast. He'd said, "when you finish up with the girlie." I heard that plain as day.

A scant few minutes later I stood in her miniscule bathroom swapping the rest of my uniform for a set of her silkiest under-things while she did the same in the bedroom. I took an extra minute to fluff my hair and rub some of her reddest stuff into my lips. My hand was on the door panel when I heard the voices. One voice. Male. Loud.

"You had a dozen maintenance calls this week alone. And now this jacket? You've got a man in here, you lying little tramp."

It had to be Sugar, and he had been monitoring her messages. Shit. If he saw me in here, in lingerie, he'd think Toto was finally giving in to his fantasy. Double shit. There wasn't enough dosh on this drift to make me share her with a fat old stockholder. And what if he wanted to touch me, too? Gross beyond words. Not even for love of her would I let that happen.

To the dubious music of his ranting next door, I skinned the uniform on over the lingerie and dropped my own undies into the sanitizer before palming the door.

"Thanks, miss," I said, half over my shoulder as I double checked for traces Sugar might find suspicious. When I turned, the red face goggling at me sucked all further words from my tongue. Sugar was old Moneybags himself. How had I not made that connection?

"A woman? A security patrol? What are you doing here?"

On autopilot, I gave him my neutral professional smile and summoned my flat work voice. "Miss reported a lag in her message web when she passed our office earlier. Technical flagged it as possible interference, so I came up to do the onsite analysis."

His fish lips pursed while he thought that through. "It was probably my monitoring program. Supposed to be undetectable."

"They all are, sir. I hope you didn't pay too much for it." I looked at Toto, her amber eyeliner streaked down her soft cheeks. "There's your answer, miss. If there's nothing else?"

Her eyes met mine, grateful and pleading all at the same time. "No. Thank you. It was...good of you to come all the way up here."

"All part of the service. Don't hesitate to call if you have any other concerns." I lifted my jacket from Money-bags' limp hand and headed for the corridor with stone-hard, jade-green envy tinting my vision as surely as any cheap plex visor. Toto would be having make-up sex with that disgusting old man any minute now.

As the door slid shut behind me I wanted nothing more to collapse against the wall, but Alden might be monitoring this corridor while he waited for a report. I hid my shaking hands by thrusting each arm in turn through the jacket sleeves and set a fast pace to the nearest elevator.

I was keying the door seals on the evac bay before images of Toto with that greedy old stockholder stopped recycling at high speed. Then it dawned on me: Milo Renc had last been seen alive after leaving that man's palatial habitat, and first been seen dead on the space side of that man's expensive transparent plex, stabbed with a jade hairpin from that dining room. I might have left my beloved alone with a murderer. I touched my ear.

"Alden?"

"You find anything?"

"Not yet. I was taking the girl through some stuff when her keeper walked in. He's the same guy who reported the body outside his window. The one who owns the jade hairpin. Did he go into that evac bay the day Milo didn't come out?"

Keys clicked on Alden's end. "He's got a personal airlock and a private shuttle. I've queued a search of both their logs. If he used them that afternoon, he could have dumped the body." More clicking. "Face rec will take a bit to ID all the customers that afternoon. You go through that bay and find me traces of everybody who was in there any time."

I gritted my teeth against the image of Toto and Moneybags in the bed I'd so enjoyed. If he was among Milo's clients, we had a solid overlap. Not solid enough to charge a stockholder with murder, though. Palming the full-spec lighting, I flooded the evac bay with its glare. Somewhere in this narrow room could be a skin cell, a blood droplet, even – yuck — semen connecting Milo with Moneybags. It might be on, in, or behind any of the two dozen evac suits, or down the half-million identical holes in the synthesized flooring. Good thing nobody was waiting supper for me.

As I ran my spec enhancer over the first floor tile, I wondered why Moneybags would bother to kill Milo. Because he was wearing Toto's suit? Because he had the hairpins? Because he added Moneybags to the bidding war between Mrs. Moneybags, and Toto? If the last, it went down as one of the shortest negotiations in Pyretia's fifty year history. Nobody got a second bid.

Every time I shifted position, faint drifts of scent from Toto's lingerie slithered out the neck of my uniform, conjuring her soft, warm sweetness only to torture me with visions of her being crushed beneath that capitalist codfish for his selfish pleasure. Given a handy hairpin, I'd almost stab him myself for making her streak her makeup with tears.

Speaking of streaks, the human traces in the floor were too many to quantify, and too disgusting to think about. We'd have to take up all the tiles for proper analysis. How could a man who appreciated Toto's delicate femininity and all his other luxuries also choose to dump his seed anonymously in these industrial surroundings? As my light swept over the organic leavings from a hundred cheating men, it bounced off the protruding leg of an evac suit. No tech put that suit back that badly. I shone the light behind, then into the neck, but nothing glowed. When my foot nudged the attached bootie, something rattled. It might be Milo's earnings. We hadn't found any on the body. I dangled the suit upside down and shook. The something tinged and pinged its way down the leg, dropped through the torso, and ricocheted off the neck-ring. I dropped the suit and made a grab, snatching the noisy pebble before it could vanish into a tile.

The jade button lay, green and serene, on my palm, a perfect match for the one I'd found on Milo Renc's androgynous chest.

I dropped the button into an evidence bag. The little folding freight lift was aslant on its hooks, too. It could have moved the body across the corridor to the airlock. I called Alden to request a crew and a cargo lift to take the lift and the suit both for scanning.

"Good work, Lake," he said. "I got news too: somebody been messing with our corridor cameras, taking copies of time-stamped photos of Milo Renc's movements. They cut the feed from the evac bay terminals for twenty minutes, ending an hour before the first commuter arrived."

"So, Milo was dead before the daily trade started?" Twenty minutes dark. Barely time enough to get into a suit and drag dead Milo across to the nearest airlock, shove him out, re-pressurize the airlock, and get back to the bay to remove the suit. Even if the killer suited up before Milo died, the cameras would come up right on his heels. A delayed elevator would doom him.

Unless he lived two doors along, like Moneybags.

He must have assumed Milo would drift away into the void. Instead, the minimal seepage of artificial gravity held the body close to the dome. Backwash from the residents' personal shuttles shoved it around until, in the morning, there was Milo, staring in the dining-room window at his murderer.

"You there, Lake?" Alden sounded uncharacteristically alert.

"Yeah, until the salvage crew shows up. Why?"

"You see that stockholder around today?"

"In his girlfriend's pad, C4-15."

"Until we know for sure if he's our killer, I'm putting a camera on him. Who knows what will happen to the next person to piss him off?"

Or the latest. I had left him with Toto, but I couldn't just dash away. There was chain of evidence to maintain. Five long minutes to hang around watching the crew plod along the corridor, guiding their temperamental cargo lift between the expensively finished walls. Ten precious minutes showing them what all had to be collected out of the evac bay and supervising their bag-and-tag. Finally I was free to run.

And run I did, with only a stop by the closest security locker for a duralene-lined jacket that I swapped for my own in the elevator. If old Moneybags tried to stab me with a hairpin, he'd be in for a big surprise. As I stepped out onto C4, I was ready for anything.

"Lake?" Alden again. "He done left the girlie's pad. You get yourself down there and go straight in. Hear me?"

"On it, chief." If he'd hurt Toto, I would take him down.

I stood outside her door with fear crowding out my usual anticipation. Was beautiful Toto beaten, injured, even dead? Only one way to find out. I keyed my code and, as the door slid open, called out, "Security. Official welfare check. Show yourself or make a noise if you can."

A door hummed further in. As I stepped into the living area, Toto stepped out of the bedroom. She was in my arms as a blur, her scent weaving around me.

"Oh, Lake. You came back. I thought you'd left me for good."

I held her and stroked her as her heart thudded against me, relief making wobbles in my chest. She was alive. She might have cried on me, I wasn't sure; I near as nothing cried on her. After a moment, I pushed her back enough to lift her face. It was unmarked and freshly made up.

"You're not hurt?"

"Sugar would never. Did you rush back to protect me?" She pulled me toward the lounge, giving just enough distance for me to appreciate that she was wearing a leisure suit. Not the Monet this time, but the Van Gogh sunflowers.

"New suit?"

"Sugar brought it. It was supposed to be mine all along, but the packages got mixed up in delivery." She raised my hand and twirled under it, showing off all her attributes. "Suits me better, don't you think?"

It could have been painted onto her perfect body by the long-dead master artist's own hand. Her hair was up, showing a seam not quite closed at her neck. I licked the skin before running my finger up the microfasteners to seal away the distraction.

"Toto, we have to talk about Sugar."

"Yes, we do. It's so exciting, Lake. I'm going to be moving up to C7 at last. I could ask for personal security and have you live with me. Would you do that for me? Give up your job to—" she giggled "—guard my body round the clock?"

"He's ditching his wife for you?"

She turned her shoulder to me. "You don't need to sound surprised. Aren't I wife material? Especially with my hair up. Looks dignified, don't you think?"

It looked...like an ivory-tipped Raleurian hairpin held her chignon in place. "Did Sugar give you the hairpin, too?"

"No. I had that already. It goes with the look, doesn't it?"

I eased back a step, cold foreboding displacing the relief of moments before. "Why is he divorcing his wife all of a sudden?"

"I showed him pix of Milo going into their place. You saw how he was with me over a male visitor. If you hadn't saved me with the security check story, I'd have been the one out on my ass. Now she is." She closed the gap between us. "He won't be back tonight. We could...celebrate."

Toto had the still photos of Milo Renc entering old Moneybags' front door? I stepped away from her.

She knew where Milo would be visiting that day. She was wearing the ivory hairpin he had acquired only an hour before he died. She had been looking up station maintenance, and could have learned how to hack the cameras. She could have been hidden in the evac suit the whole time he was dealing with Mrs. Moneybags.

355

"Don't you like my hair up?" She lifted her arms, setting the sunflowers dancing as she twisted the hairpin out. Locks of auburn, ochre, and gold whirled around her shoulders and mingled with the petals. She leaned in close against my chest, nudging me back against the wall. "Make love to me, Lake."

"No." My voice came out sharper than the ivory hairpin.

Her eyes flattened, colder and harder than the frozen asteroids outside. Now I could believe that lovely face hid the grasping spirit that skewered Milo. She had tossed him to the void the instant he left Sugar's wife. Did she intend that all along, or did he say he'd sold her out? Did it matter now? Did any of it?

For three heartbeats we stood, just looking.

I caught her wrist as the ivory hairpin's sharp tip scraped across the duralene below my ribcage. Didn't matter that it never reached my skin. She'd already cut me to the core.

Liner Notes

Sarah L. Johnson, Senior Editor

Diversity is the name of the Dame.

I love a classic trope. Red lips, dark eyes, a black net veil slanting across one crystal cut cheekbone. This is the iconic Dame. Or is she? With respect to the classics, what I love even more is possibility. Discovery. Diversity.

My co-editors and I put out the call, from Labrador to Vancouver, to our Canadian crime writing sisters. Guidelines were intentionally unrestrictive in terms of what constitutes a Dame. Basically, we asked for female driven crime fiction and hoped to get a few stories that tickled our trigger fingers. Show us your Dames, we said. And god damn, did they ever…

We got subversive femme fatales, fresh ingénues, old Dames, teen Dames, queer and trans Dames, Dames with disabilities, and Dames of colour. Smart, wounded, greedy, resilient, kind, sinister, and sweet. These women are no mere plot device. They've got skin in the game and they play rough.

All we wanted was to give the Dame a voice, and this kick ass collection of authors gave her a whole life. Sixteen of them. Enough to convince anyone that while the Dame may be trouble, you want her on your side.

Halli Lilburne, Editor

French for black, the term *Noir* describes a bleak and foreboding environment. Cynical characters, engulfed in crime and fatalism, reflect our own struggles, rarely overcome. Coined in the 1930s, the realistic, perpetual failures of human kind makes Noir a bitterly unique genre. This anthology sets the tragic female protagonist in diverse and speculative worlds. Its purpose is to show the usual femme fatal breaking out of her shell. Turning from sidekick, love interest and damsel in destress, she becomes hero, heartbreaker and misfit. She fights her own battles, she plots her own course and seeks her own revenge, just like the best of us. And like us she may slip and fall. She might lose. Sometimes she gets caught. Sometimes she dies. Karma is a bitch.

The Dame was Trouble is Coffin Hop Press' tribute to The Year of Publishing Women, 2018. We need to publish more women. Give awards to more women. Purchase and stock your libraries with more women. (Whatever your definition of women may be.) Our words are important. Let us be heard. Read us. Share us. Support us.

I'd like to say thank you to our families, and to all the wonderful dames for their strong messages.

Cat McDonald, Editor:

The props department is full of people who've come to represent more and exist less. The steely-eyed sheriff, the peaceful alien perplexed by human barbarity, the final girl to survive the slasher, and there on the shelf next to them, the Dame, in her candy-apple red lipstick and insincere mourning veil. She is a wisp of cigarette smoke winding past a mostly-empty whiskey bottle, in a world that seems to be perpetually lit in horizontal stripes through venetian blinds. She is the sound of typewriter keys while police sirens scream in the distance.

Some excellent scholars have written deeper pieces than this one on the femme fatale as an embodiment of suspicion toward female sexuality. Like every other stock character, her societal and symbolic roots are deeper than she is. She is an intertwining of the revolutionary and the reactionary, the anima of an era unsure of its sexual politics and the poster child for the new woman, cool and capable and free.

Some excellent authors have expressed her in this book. Not as a prop, but as a human being. They have imagined someone daring, someone terrified, someone cold, someone wounded. We see femmes here who are more than fatal; they are real. The lipstick is not entirely gone, nor is the veil, nor is the smoke; they exist here as part of a deeper image. Sometimes the lipstick is a rubber prosthetic meant to look like a robot's seam. Sometimes the veil is a hijab. The woman beneath, however, is a person with a beating heart. Her heroism and her villainy are rooted in her own nature and her own choices.

Some of the Dames in this anthology fight to preserve what matters to them. Some of them are willing to burn everything down around them. Some struggle for their own survival, some scheme for their own gain, and some could give a damn about either.

I never wanted to discard the Dame; I wanted to get to know her better.

This anthology is everything I wanted it to be

About the Authors

Kelley Armstrong *(Indispensable)*

#1 *New York Times* bestselling author Kelley Armstrong is the author of the *Cainsville* modern gothic series and the Rockton crime thrillers. Past works include *Otherworld* urban fantasy series, the *Darkest Powers* and *Darkness Rising* teen paranormal trilogies, the *Age of Legends* fantasy YA series and the *Nadia Stafford* crime trilogy. Armstrong lives in Ontario, Canada with her family.

Elle Wild *(Playing Dead)*

Elle Wild's debut novel, *Strange Things Done*, won the Unhanged Arthur Award for Best Unpublished Manuscript in 2015 and then went on to win the Arthur Ellis Award for Best First Novel in 2017, both from the Crime Writers of Canada, as well as winning the Women in Film's "From Our Dark Side" Genre Competition 2017. Wild's short fiction has been published in *Ellery Queen Mystery Magazine* and in the Canadian Authors Association's anthology of short literary fiction, and won second place in the National Capital Writing Competition. She has been on several longlists in 2018 for short fiction, including PRISM International's Jacob Zilber Prize

Hermine Robinson *(A Cure for the Common Girl)*
Hermine Robinson loves all things short fiction and refuses to be the place where perfectly good stories go to die. In 2012, she went from scribbling to submitting and since then her work has appeared in numerous print and on-line publications, including: *Free Fall Magazine, Fabula Argentea, Vine Leaves Literary Journal* and Exile Edition's *Anthology of New Canadian Noir*. She also blogs intermittently at **www.wordflights.wordpress.com.** Hermine is married with two children and most people know her by the nickname Minkee.

Pat Flewwelling *(A Premium on Murder)*
Pat Flewwelling is a novelist and short-story author from Oshawa, Ontario. By day, she is a senior business analyst at a major telecommunications company; on her weekends and evenings, she runs Myth Hawker Travelling Bookstore, and is a co-editor at ID Press. Please send more coffee to **www.mythhawker.com** or **www.patflewwelling.com**.

Melodie Campbell *(Hook, Line and Sinker)*
The Toronto Sun called her Canada's "Queen of Comedy." Library Journal compared her to Janet Evanovich. Melodie Campbell has won the Derringer Award, the Arthur Ellis Award, and eight more awards for crime fiction. In 2015,

she made the Amazon Top 50 bestseller list, sandwiched between Tom Clancy and Nora Roberts.

S.G. Wong *(Parting Shot)*

Arthur Ellis Awards finalist and Whistler Independent Book Awards nominee, S.G. Wong writes the *Lola Starke* novels and *Crescent City* stories: hard-boiled detective tales set in an alternate-history 1930s-era "Chinese L.A." replete with ghosts and magic. She is a member of the Writers' Guild of Alberta and Past President of Sisters in Crime—Canada West. As an acclaimed moderator and creator, she presents in venues ranging from ChiSeries Winnipeg to Bouchercon 2017 to Ignite Change Global Gathering for Human Rights. She is based in Edmonton where she's often found staring out the window in between frenzied bouts of typing. **www.sgwong.com**

Gail Bowen *(Eldorado)*

Canada's "Queen of Crime", Gail Bowen's first Joanne Kilbourn mystery, *Deadly Appearances* (1990), was nominated for the W.H. Smith/*Books in Canada* Best First Novel Award, and *A Colder Kind of Death* (1995) won the Arthur Ellis Award for best crime novel. *The Winners' Circle*, (2017) has been named a finalist for the Arthur Ellis Award for best crime novel as of this book's first printing. In 2008, *Reader's Digest* named Bowen "Canada's Best Mystery Novelist"; in 2009 she received the Derrick Murdoch Award; and in 2018 she was recognized with the Crime Writers of Canada's Grand Master Award. In

2018, she was invested with the Saskatchewan Order of Merit, the province's highest honour. Now retired from teaching at the First Nations University, Gail Bowen lives in Regina, Saskatchewan.

Darusha Wehm *(Daphne Disappeared)*
Darusha writes science fiction and speculative poetry as M. Darusha Wehm and mainstream poetry and fiction as Darusha Wehm. Their science fiction books include: *Beautiful Red*, *Children of Arkadia* and the *Andersson Dexter* cyberpunk detective series. Mainstream books include the *Devi Jones' Locker* Young Adult series and, most recently, *The Home for Wayward Parrots* from NeWest Press. Darusha's short fiction and poetry have appeared in many venues, including *Terraform, Nature, Escape Pod*, as well as several anthologies. Originally from Canada, Darusha currently lives in Wellington, New Zealand after spending several years sailing the Pacific. For more information, visit **www.darusha.ca**.

R.M. Greenaway *(Rozotica)*
Her first novel *Cold Girl* won the 2014 Unhanged Arthur Award, was then published in March 2016 and subsequently shortlisted for the Arthur Ellis Award for Best First Novel. Her second in the series, *Undertow*, was released March 2017, followed by *Creep* in 2018. R.M. is a member of the Crime Writers of Canada, Sisters in Crime International, and not the new local chapter, Sisters in Crime Canada West.

About the Authors

Natalie Vacha *(Mona"s Last Day)*
Natalie's work has appeared in *In Places Between*, and she was a finalist in CBC Radio Calgary's Cowboy Poetry contest. She still maintains she might have won, if only she'd been able to convince her parents to vote for her (she was not). She lives in Calgary. You can follow her on Twitter **@natalievacha1**

Susan MacGregor *(Dinner with Francisco)*
Susan MacGregor is the author of *The Tattooed Witch* trilogy (Five Rivers Publishing), the first book of which was short-listed for an Aurora Award in 2014. Her short fiction has appeared in various magazines and anthologies. A past editor with *On Spec Magazine*, she has also edited two anthologies, *Tesseracts Fifteen: A Case of Quite Curious Tales* (Edge Books) and *Divine Realms* (Ravenstone Books). Currently working on a new historical fantasy set in Edwardian England, Susan lives and works in Edmonton.

Alice Bienia *(A Dish to Die for)*
A trailblazer for Canadian women conducting field exploration, Alice Bienia's former work as a geologist fuelled her passion for adventure, reading, storytelling, coffee, and all things absurd and sublime. She now writes full time. Her first novel, *Knight Blind*, was a 2016 Arthur Ellis finalist for Best Unpublished Crime Novel.

The Dame Was Trouble

Meghan Victoria *(Silk)*

Meghan grew up in the frozen wilds of Labrador, listening to too much symphonic metal and writing really bad poetry. Lured across the country by the promise of true love, she now lives in Calgary with her husband and their five cats. (Kidding. About the cats. Not the husband.) Meghan has been published by Morning Rain Publishing and in the *Antigonish Review*, and is slogging through the final draft of her first novel. When not crying over the editing process, you can find Meghan hiking across far-flung continents, practicing the art of flying yoga, and still writing questionable poetry.

M.H. Callway *(The Seeker)*

Madeleine took a detour through science and business before turning to dark crime fiction. Her thriller, *Windigo Fire*, was a finalist for the Debut Dagger, Unhanged Arthur and Arthur Ellis Best First Novel awards. Her short stories and novellas have also won or been short-listed for the Arthur Ellis, Derringer and Bony Pete awards. She loves to explore weird and wonderful experiences and shares them on her website: **www.mhcallway.com.** In 2013, she co-founded the "Mesdames of Mayhem" whose three anthologies are: *Thirteen, 13 O'clock* and *13 Claws.* Find them at **www.mesdamesofmayhem.com**

Sandra Ruttan *(Crossing Jordan*

Sandra Ruttan is a walking disaster. She has been hit by a car, had a foot partially severed, fell down a waterfall and survived a car crash in the Sahara Desert. There is absolutely no explanation for how she's managed to stay alive as long as she has. Ruttan has five published mystery novels, including *Harvest of Ruins, What Burns Within* and *Suspicious Circumstances*. Her next book, *The Spying Moon,* is due out September 2018 from Down & Out Books. Get the latest news from her author Facebook page @sandraruttanauthor or her website **www.sruttan.wordpress.com**.

Jayne Barnard *(Painted Jade)*
Jayne Barnard's award-winning short fiction has appeared in numerous Canadian magazines and anthologies. Her Steampunk adventure, *Maddie Hatter and the Deadly Diamond* is a Prix Aurora and BPAA Award finalist. Her mystery work has won the Unhanged Arthur and been shortlisted for the Debut Dagger. Her novel *When the Flood Falls* will be released in 2018 by Dundurn Press

Sarah L. Johnson *(Senior Editor)*
Sarah L. Johnson lives in Calgary where she's mastered the art of the writerly side-hustle, as a literary events coordinator, freelance editor, and creative writing teacher. She runs ultramarathons, does daily battle with curly hair, has a filthy mouth, and is the author of the short story collection *Suicide Stitch: Eleven Tales* (EMP Publishing) and *Infractus* (Coffin Hop Press). Her short fiction has appeared in numerous publications and anthologies.

Halli Lilburn (Editor) is a speculative fiction and horror author with works published with Leap Books, Edge Science Fiction and Fantasy, Carte Blanche, Renaissance Press among others. She teaches workshops on poetry, art restoration, creative writing and opens discussions on feminism, diversity, mental health. She is an artist, librarian and mother of three.

Cat McDonald (Editor) can see just about all of Edmonton from here. She loves solitude and hates silence. Her fiction has appeared in Tesseracts 15, Here Be Monsters, and Sirens, and her non-fiction has appeared in On Spec magazine, where she has worked as an editor and designer. She often struggles with her own glibness when trying to be sincere.

COFFIN HOP PRESS

New Crime. New Weird. New Pulp.

Visit us online at
www.coffinhop.com